Choosing Grace

About the Author

Regina Jamison is a writer who lives in Brooklyn, New York. Her poetry has appeared in *Sinister Wisdom: Black Lesbians—We Are the Revolution!*, *Mom Egg Review*, *Five Two One Magazine*, *Magma Literary Journal: The Deaf Issue*, *The Americas Poetry Festival of New York Anthology 2016*, *Promethean Literary Journal*, *Off the Rocks: An Anthology of GLBT Writing Vols. 14 & 15*, and *Poetry in Performance Journal Vol. 43*. Online, her poetry has appeared in *The Lake*, *Indolent Press HIV Here & Now Series*, *Silver Birch Press—Me as a Child Series*, and *Promethean eZine*, and is forthcoming in the *Switch Grass Review*. Her short stories have appeared in *Zane's Purple Panties: African American Lesbian Anthology*, and *Girls Who Bite—Vampire Lesbian Anthology*. She received her MFA in Creative Writing at City College in New York.

Choosing Grace

REGINA JAMISON

BELLA
BOOKS
2021

Bella Books, Inc.
P.O. Box 10543
Tallahassee, FL 32302

First Bella Books Edition 2021

Editor: Kenrya Rankin
Cover Designer: Kayla Mancuso

ISBN: 978-1-64247-226-4

Acknowledgments

Thank you Lambda Literary for choosing me to be a Lambda Literary 2014 Fellow. I made a lot of great friends while I worked on this manuscript.

Thank you Woodstock Byrdcliffe Guild where my month-long writing residency allowed me to write many things, this manuscript included.

Dedication

To my children, PJ and LJ. Never give up on your dreams.

To LP—
"Now I know for certain/that you were always right/because if a breeze could blow you/out of my life/it was only smoke and ashes baby."
                                        —*Smoke and Ashes* by Tracy Chapman

To the Bronx—the borough with the most!

A GLIMPSE

Prologue

I promised myself that 1986 would be my year. My year to spread my wings, be my authentic self, live *my life*.

After having watched the Space Shuttle Challenger blow up after launching at the beginning of the year, I was shaken, and it hit me square in the face—tomorrow may never come.

I was just twenty-five, but thirty wasn't as far off as it once was, and I knew I needed to stop living my life for everyone else. I needed to own who I was no matter the consequences. But I also realized that I needed to grow some balls because things were always easier said than done.

—Sky Valentine

CHAPTER ONE

The table creaked loudly, but I could still hear the reverend's deep baritone voice through the old wooden door. He had said something that sounded like "matrimony" and "man and wife," but I wasn't sure. The sound of his voice, more so than his words, was so robust, so full, so hypnotic, that even in my discomfort it soothed me.

With my eyes shut tight against the pounding, I fell into his voice, and her face slowly appeared before me. Her tiny, square teeth and big brown eyes, so delightful, so intense. I saw her hair as it bounced against her narrow shoulders; saw the sway of her silky shorts when she walked up the block to greet me. I remembered the rich brown color of her skin against the glare of the sand that day at Sachuest Beach and the outline of her full guitar-shaped hips pressed into our rainbow-striped beach towel. She was my first love, but I was afraid to call her that, afraid to name what we shared. To do so would have been a declaration and, at the time, I wasn't ready to declare anything. Even in the dark, behind locked doors buried under sheets and comforters that pressed into us, I had been afraid. I had closed my eyes so as not to witness the love we were making. Buried there, I could hold her hand, touch her breasts, and kiss her lips. Locked in and tucked away, I could do these things, and I had. But it was a love I could not rejoice in, couldn't flaunt nor nourish. It was my first love and I had destroyed it.

Delbert, my husband-to-be, moaned and the memory I held of her vanished. The table shuddered with his climax and a piece of me fell away. The reverend knocked twice and said, "We are about to begin." Delbert didn't bother to wipe, just shoved it down into his pants and straightened out his shirt and jacket.

"Tell them I'll be right there," I said.

Delbert turned to leave. I watched as he strode toward the door, his ego so big there was no room for a shadow. The gray and black hairs of his goatee no longer made him appear distinguished. Now they reminded me of a skunk. His smile was that of a dirty old man. The twenty-year age difference between us was now a monolith. He grabbed the doorknob then turned back toward me. I saw the smirk on his face before he closed the door. The scent of his Brut cologne lingered like Delbert's own personal enforcer.

I stood there like an angel all fluffed up in white, semen glistening atop the tissues that I held in my hand. At this point, it was as if he were a client, nothing more. His sneer, a visual reminder that the deal had been sealed. And thanks to my conniving mother and malleable father, it had been.

I found some more paper towels and wiped myself down. There was no time for soap and water. I bent over and picked up the small bottle of perfume that had fallen from the squeaky table Delbert had laid me upon. Poison by Dior was on the label. If only it was so, I thought. There was another knock at the door, then a large purple hat bobbed through.

"Everyone's waiting on you, Sky."

It was Odeta, my childhood friend. She was what we called "big boned," and she always looked sharp in a suit. Today was no exception. However, her big, purple hat looked ridiculous. It sat like an uncooked eggplant nestled safely inside the fluffed-up coil of curls Odeta had atop her head. The black veil attached to the front of the hat fell over her eyes and made her look old. On any other day I would have laughed at how ludicrous her hat was, but, today, I loved her for it because it was so indicative of who she was—an old soul. It was as if she was playing dress-up and had raided her grandmother's closet. Odeta wasn't a fly girl or hip to the latest fashions or ideas, but she was always there for me.

"I'm coming."

"What are you doing in here anyway? Is that my perfume I smell? Decided to use it, huh?"

I walked toward the door and handed Odeta the perfume bottle. I didn't bother answering any of her questions. It was the reverend's forthcoming question that lay heavy on my mind: "Do you take this man?" Besides, Odeta liked to ask a lot of rhetorical questions before she got to the question she really wanted answered. The first few questions were like pre-ejaculate. I let her talk as I waited for the climax.

"You're not getting cold feet now, are you?"

"My feet are fine," I said.

I tried to smile, but I couldn't. That was not the question I wanted Odeta to ask. I wanted her to ask, "Are you sure? Are you doing the right thing? Do you love this man?" But Odeta wasn't that type of person. She dealt with surface things so, for her, wedding equaled love. I couldn't and never did tell her about my first love—a woman—and how those feelings still lingered. She would not understand, couldn't comprehend, so I kept my doubts to myself.

"Everybody gets nervous on their wedding day," Odeta said.

"How do you know?"

"Well, that's what everybody says."

"Oh."

I wanted something more. Statistics. Testimonials. Video footage. All she had was hearsay. Hearsay and a big purple hat. Now she seemed even more ridiculous. I considered telling her that it was inappropriate to wear such an outlandish hat to a funeral, but then I remembered, this wasn't a funeral, I was getting married. In my mind, that long walk toward the altar was me on a plank, heading toward my doom. Suddenly, I realized that that plank was the only way out. I needed to stand at the edge. I needed to be ready to jump. I needed to face it. Perhaps, just perhaps, there would be a net underneath.

"Let's go," I said. "I'm ready."

CHAPTER TWO

The church was packed. Cardboard fans swayed and rocked images of a white, blue-eyed Jesus back and forth against ample brown breasts. The pipes, when the organ was played, reminded me of thunder. I knew from rehearsal that Delbert's family and friends took up most of the shiny wooden pews. On my side of the church there was my mother, my brother, my aunt, and a few friends; the rest of the pews saved for my family would be empty. But I was sure that Delbert's family and guests would spread out into the remaining pews. They would surround and colonize my guests in order to watch him in his greatest performance as loving husband. Sadly, I couldn't complain. He paid for the wedding. He paid for the photographer. He paid for the band. He paid for the gown. He even paid for the bride, gifting my parents with an all-expenses paid vacation to Barbados. He'd told me that gifting the parents of the bride for her hand in marriage was how it used to be done, and being a man of tradition, he wanted to keep with the old ways. I was sure brides in the old days felt as I did—like goods bought and sold.

I stood at the threshold, my life as it was. I was one step away from my life as it was to be. Just a slight nudge and I would be there. The band played *Here Comes the Bride*, but I didn't want to go any further. Sweat gathered in the palms of my hands, and the white roses I carried, now strangled, sucked up the moisture. All eyes were on me. I heard the wedding march stop then start once again, but I couldn't move. My father stood beside me, hand at my elbow, ready. But I held back. Why would he want to give me away? Who, in their right mind, would agree to give away their child? I saw my mother sitting upright, a worried look on her face. She turned, looked at Delbert, then looked to me again, her small hand waving me forward. Again, another chorus of *Here Comes the Bride* had started. The organ pipes shook, heavily emphasizing the chords that shouted "bride" and sent B sharps and flattened F chords into a black cloud above my head. I noticed that all eyes were still on me. I looked down at my white satin shoes. Drops of sweat ran past my ear. A neglected thorn jabbed at my palm and a tiny cut formed. More sweat. My foot lifted and came down on the other side of the line. I had stepped into the new me. With each step I thought about Delbert: left foot, Delbert's goofy smile. Right foot, his "I made the sale" swagger. Left foot, his ability to always get a conversation to be about him. Right foot, his total disregard for me. Left foot, my acquiescence. I didn't know this new me. This momma's girl. This soon-to-be wife, partner, plaything. Who was this woman, who smiled, bent over, and bared her ass on her wedding day? Who was she? And what did she do with the real me?

CHAPTER THREE

The music stopped as I stepped up to the altar. Delbert looked at me briefly and then turned his attention to the reverend. His face was cloudy and kaleidoscopic through the multi-layered veil, but I could see that his shoulders were back, his head was high, and his chin was squared. The bright white of his tuxedo made the flecks of gray in his hair and goatee sparkle. He was like bits of stained glass through my veil. To me, he was just that, stained.

My dress seemed to grow heavier as it absorbed the streams of sweat my body produced. The reverend recited the usual words, but I was not listening. The table that Delbert fucked me on only moments before flashed in my mind all bent and broken, but still standing. I reminded myself that it, too, was once whole. There was a time before this when it, *I*, was strong. I heard Delbert say, "I do." Then the reverend turned to me. I looked at him and suddenly realized that I didn't even know his name. I had simply been calling him "reverend." But this was Delbert's church. I didn't belong to one.

"Do you, Sky Valentine, take Delbert Sample to be your lawfully wedded husband?"

I watched the reverend's lips. My name sounded pretty in his mouth. But I couldn't speak. Delbert looked at me. I looked at him. There was a smile on his face. My throat was parched and cracked. The spit seemed to bypass my mouth and, instead, head straight to my hands. They were beyond damp. My arms, shoulders, neck, breasts, muscles were sweating. My gown clung to me like a wet towel. My underwear felt drenched. My feet hurt. I tried wiggling my toes, but that only brought more pain.

"Do you, Sky Valentine, take Delbert Sample to be your lawfully wedded husband?"

I felt numb, tongue-tied and when I didn't respond the reverend repeated himself yet again. But he said it louder and slower this time, like people did when they spoke to foreigners who didn't speak the language.

"Answer the man, baby," Delbert said in a low, slow drawl.

And for a moment, my head was filled with the lyrics of an old Roberta Flack song my mother used to play on our old record player when I was a child: *Strumming my pain with his fingers/Killing me softly with his words.* I didn't know what the lyrics meant at the time, but I'd felt Roberta's pain and anguish then and I felt it still. Only now, it was my own. I thought about who I'd become when I was with Delbert and I couldn't recall the last time I had smiled or acted silly or lost my breath due to laughter. This saddened me. A tight knot began to form at the base of my throat, round and lumpy and hard. I forcefully blinked back tears as I gazed at Delbert and the reverend. I turned and saw the congregation, all eyes upturned. I saw Odeta with her eggplant hat bulging atop her head and I smiled then I giggled and both the reverend and Delbert looked at me. The confusion on their faces was the push I needed. I covered my mouth, one hand on my veil. I tried to stop the laughter; but it was no use. The ground beneath me moved, my body shook, and the lava overflowed. I threw my head back, held on to my stomach, and I laughed for the years that I hadn't. There was movement and whispering behind me, but I did not care. I was being tickled by a ghost from my past. It was the old me trying to get the new me to remember. Remember your smile. Remember your wisdom. Remember your strength. Remember your laughter, she said. Remember to get out when you can. I thought about the broken table. I didn't want to live the rest of my life barely standing.

"Baby, what's wrong? Are you okay?"

I let go of my belly and collected my breath. I kicked off my shoes and handed them to Delbert.

"I am now, Delbert. I'm not your 'baby' and I am not marrying you."

The people behind me gasped. My gown wavered. The reverend looked at Delbert. Delbert looked at me.

"You can't be serious. Do you know how much I paid for all this shit?"

I smiled as I grabbed and lifted the hem of my gown into my hands.

"Do you hear me talking to you, Sky? Do you know how much I paid for all of this?"

I looked at him. His skin was smooth; he had gotten a facial earlier in the day. His eyebrows banged into each other. Remember your strength, said the old me. I turned away from Delbert and I stepped down from the altar.

"Sky, where the hell are you going?" my mother yelled. She was on her feet, white-gloved hands pressed sternly into her sides. She was in punishment mode.

Another smile crossed my face as I ignored my mother, Delbert, the heated whispers. Instead, I stepped forward and announced to the stunned, sweaty congregation, "Gotta bounce!"

I quaked with laughter and bunched the bottom of my gown into a manageable ball.

Then I was gone.

CHAPTER FOUR

It was the Fourth of July and it was hot. The stray booms and scattered pops of illegal fireworks could be heard all around Lincoln Street, reminding me of my childhood. But growing up in North Carolina and having spent twenty-five years here had been enough for me. I was tired of the squishy sweetness of sweet potatoes. Tired of the dead animal taste of pork barbeque and the red clay grit of homegrown collards. Tired of being labeled a Tar Heel and having to live in a place that touted Krispy Kreme as its new claim to fame. I was tired of it all. I had put in my time and now, it was time to go.

I gathered several boxes of sparklers that I planned to set fire to later on. I, like the rest of the country, planned to celebrate my independence. I had emancipated myself... again. Attending Roger Williams University in Rhode Island when I graduated high school at seventeen was my first taste of freedom. Life was different, freer somehow, up north. I'd absorbed everything northern, everything Yankee in an attempt to erase small town Durham from my bones. I had changed the way I dressed, changed my hair and my attitude, and worked hard on eliminating my "cute" Southern drawl. Now, I was free again and, like before, I was headed north, but this time, it was for good.

Delbert had called several times. He'd left messages of hate and love on my answering machine. He had threatened revenge and total forgiveness. He'd said I was beguiling, a coquette, a saint. He didn't know what to do with his freedom. He was like a master without a slave: lost. I deleted his messages and unplugged the phone. I had packing to attend to.

"Girl, why these boxes so heavy? What made you wanna move to the Bronx of all places? Don't they have gangs up there?" Odeta was helping me move.

"Where you want these boxes?"

She was doing a whole lot of sweating accompanied by a whole lot of talking which resulted in minimal boxes being moved.

"Put those two on the floor behind our seats. I have some glasses in them that my grandmother gave me."

Odeta took the box from me and walked to the van. I heard, what sounded like fireworks exploding from behind the seats where Odeta had just dumped the boxes. She was that bull in the china shop.

"Odeta, I just told you that box was filled with glasses and did you not see that big sticker that said "fragile" on the box? Come on now, you are big and strong enough to lower those boxes without breaking stuff."

"Look, don't start. It's hot as hell. I'm sweaty. I'm tired and I need a drink. And it's the Fourth of July! I should be at a barbeque somewhere shakin' my groove thang and munchin' on a pulled pork sandwich. But I'm not. I'm here moving 'fragile' boxes with you."

"You said you didn't mind helping me."

"That was before I knew you was fixin' to move on July fourth."

"Well, go on home then, Odeta. Or go to your barbeque or whatever. I can handle this alone."

She was beginning to annoy me. We had been friends for decades, but she was like a robot, always going along and doing what was expected, never straying from the status quo. On the Fourth of July go to a barbeque. For Christmas, go buy presents and decorate a tree. Easter, dye smelly eggs and put them in a stupid basket. The same thing every year. She missed one barbeque and her world crumbled. It was why I had never told her about my relationship with my roommate in college. She just wouldn't understand and that, to me, was sad.

"No. No. No. I will not be dismissed. Odeta always keeps her word. I said I would help so, I'm helping. It's just the heat is all and the thought of havin' to drive, what, eight to ten hours up to New York?"

"We're splitting the driving."

"I know, I know, but why can't you just stay here in Durham? Why you need to go live all a way up in New York? Delbert's not threatening you is he?"

She turned around fast and faced me when she asked about Delbert. The redness under her brown skin was highlighted by the sweat that had collected on her forehead.

"No." I didn't want to talk about Delbert. I wanted to remain focused on my task. I wanted to get what was salvageable from my past into the van and drive toward my future. But Odeta is no Harriet Tubman. To her, the North Star is only one of the many lights in the sky. For her, freedom could be found in the arms of the right man.

"Oh, good. Now tell me, how you gon' leave that fine man at the altar? I think you should stay and give Delbert a second chance."

I almost dropped the box I was carrying. I turned and put it down easy, but a loud booming sound exploded in my head. I couldn't believe what she had said to me. I was shocked and angry. I wrapped my hands around the dirty edges of the box, which helped to steady me. I knew I couldn't face her without lunging so I talked to the box.

"Why would you say that?"

"'Cause Delbert is a good man. What you should a done was sent him over to me. I would've taken care of him like he needs to be taken care of."

I spun around so fast I dropped the box and almost fell over it. I could not believe this was Odeta, my friend. I looked at her. There was need and wanting in her eyes. She would hurt me and anyone else who got in the way of her "white knight" dream. But I was angry too.

"I cannot believe you just said that to me."

I brushed past her and grabbed another box.

"Why not? Everybody feels the same way."

I threw a box of plates into the back of the van. Then I threw a small box of bowls on top. All of it cracked, along with my relationship with Odeta. I should have dropped the bomb about my attraction to other women in her face. Let the details of having made love to a female be the M80 that would blow her away. Instead, I turned to face her and said, "Everybody feels that way, huh? My best friend too, I'm finding out. Aren't you supposed to be on *my* side?"

"Hey, a *real* friend would tell you the truth and that's what I'm doing. Delbert is a handsome, respectable, hard working, progressive black man and every black woman needs one."

I looked at Odeta. She was only twenty-eight, but it seemed like she was forty-eight and had gone through three divorces with the desperation she was displaying.

"One?" I asked.

"Yes, one decent black male in her life who makes her feel like a queen."

"I have one. I call him Daddy."

I knew that her father wasn't around while she was growing up. I also knew my words would sting.

"Well, there are women out here who are just itching to call Delbert...*Daddy*."

"Then go fuck him, Odeta, and get it over with!"

My calm was splitting into threads.

"Me?"

"Yes, you. Don't worry, I won't hold it against you. You can go hold his hand right now, or whatever else he may want you to hold. Go. I can take care of this stuff."

"I didn't say that I was interested in Delbert. I'm just tellin' you that you let go of a good man."

"Good or bad, whatever he was or is, I let him go. Delbert, of all people, doesn't warrant a pedestal. Swing your arms, Odeta. Feel what it's like to be free. Make your *own* decision about what *you* want."

"I'll tell you what I want, Sky. I want the option to leave someone at the altar, but no one's ever asked for *my* hand in marriage. I wanna be called 'Mrs.,' but it don't look like that'll be happening any time soon. I want someone who is hardworking, respectful, and ambitious. I want someone to love me, but no one ever has."

"So, you want me to stay here, in Durham, and give Delbert a second chance in order to fulfill your dreams?"

"That's not what I'm sayin'."

"Yes it is, Odeta. That's what *everyone* is saying. And because everyone is saying it, you think it's the right thing to do. It's not. I can't and I won't live my life for them, you, or Delbert anymore. Now, I'm focusing on me, on what I want and need. And right now, I want to get the hell out of dodge. The more distance between me and this place, the better."

I turned, saw another box near the van, and walked toward it.

"Why? You think things are gonna be different up there in the Bronx? Why? 'Cause it's New York? Men are men, Sky, north or south. It'll be the same thing no matter where you go."

I turned to face her.

"Okay, Odeta, hear me now. Listen closely. I am not moving to get away from a man. I am not moving to find a man. I'm moving because there is more to life than Lincoln Street. More than Durham. There's a whole world out there that I know nothing about, but I'm really interested in finding out. *That's* why I'm moving."

I walked past Odeta, put a box in the back of the van, and then headed toward the house. I wanted to explain the longing that I felt to her, but I couldn't. Her world was so much simpler than mine.

A cube of boxes swelled out toward the steps. The smell of newly lit charcoal from the neighbor's backyard smudged the air. I coughed and grabbed the top box and walked toward the van. Odeta stood there, silent. I, too, was silent. Maybe she sort of understood what I was seeking. Or maybe she didn't— not everyone was searching. Some people had their Eden right outside their door. For them there was no need to look further.

I heard Odeta sigh and I faced her. She looked at me.

"What is it *you* want, Odeta?"

I posed the question to her one more time, but gently. I prayed she would dig deeper.

"Right now, I want some sweet tea," she said. "We need to cool things down a bit. Do you have any tea in the house? Do you still need help with those boxes? You're not mad at me, are you?"

Her words softened me. The anger rolled down my arms and rested on top of the heavy box I'd put down near the van's dusty black rear wheel.

"Come on," I said. "Let's go get some sweet tea."

I put my arm around her waist. She put hers around my shoulder. As we walked toward the house, I knew that our friendship was cracked, but not completely shattered.

CHAPTER FIVE

Getting to the Bronx was a journey, but we'd made it. I tipped my beer and watered the grass to pay homage to this place, my new home. Odeta took a few boxes into my new place and looked around for a bit, but when she looked out the kitchen window and was able to see right into the neighbor's small triangle of a yard to see them looking right back at her, she mumbled something about feeling closed-in and high-tailed it back to Durham. But I was heady with excitement. The Bronx, at midnight, was still buzzing with life! Cars zoomed back and forth, kids on bikes and skateboards yelled to one another as they raced down the narrow sidewalks. Others enjoyed a fast-paced game of double-dutch as they jumped and simultaneously recited jump rope rhymes while keeping time to the rhythm of the ropes. Young guys with thick chains around their necks and large, rectangular boom boxes in their arms walked around the neighborhood surrounded by other guys and girls as they blasted rap hits like "South Bronx," "My Adidas," and "Chick on the Side." The girls sang all the words, their large, gold earrings swaying back and forth while their heads and necks kept time with the music. Streetlights, high up on their metal poles, floated across the backdrop of night like fireflies while the scent of charred meat, still on the grill, rose lazily upward into the night air and hitched itself to a dense breeze that reached my bedroom window where I was perched, smiling, and soaking up my surroundings. The people who lived two yards over laughed and talked loudly above lively, French-speaking music with an integration of heavy drums at its base, and just like in Durham, fireworks popped here and boomed there, accentuating the night.

The apartment, a condo really, that I was renting at a terrific price from Stephanie, the cousin of my college friend, Daisy, was perfect. It was why I had chosen the Bronx. When I saw the pictures of this place and did some research on the area, I knew I could call it home.

The condo had two levels with two medium-sized bedrooms—which might come in handy if I needed a roommate should times get hard—one and a half baths, a small kitchen with a window that saved the space from feeling too cramped, a backyard about the size of a sheet of poster board, and a decent-sized living room that I basically fell into as soon as I stepped foot inside the place. I could see into the kitchen from the living room due to three-quarters of the living room wall having been knocked out to allow for a pass through between the two rooms below the kitchen cabinets. There was also a dining room with sliding doors that allowed entrance to the backyard. All of this within a gated community that bordered on the East River and the Long Island Sound. A home with a view. I had definitely hit the jackpot!

I stared out my bedroom window into a blank night sky—not a star in sight. The tops of the multitude of trees that populated the neighborhood swayed just a little. Whenever the music died down, I heard the click-click-click of a few crickets that sought to communicate in the night coming from the dense darkness across the courtyard where the remains of a cluster of damaged lockers still lingered. The lockers once belonged to the bathhouse that used to mark the spot. From my little window I surveyed the area and thought about how lucky I was to have a place to live, a job waiting—another hookup from Daisy—and a new life to begin, and I felt tremendous gratitude. I held two thank-you cards in my hands that I planned to fill out in the morning and mail to Daisy and Stephanie, but they felt like such small tokens. I could never fill it with enough words to express my thankfulness for what they had given me, but I vowed to try.

Every day, for two weeks, I headed out into my new neighborhood to discover new things. Stephanie warned me not to venture too far. She said things would get a bit rough the further up I went along Lafayette Avenue or if I got off course and ended up near one of the projects where the effects of crack still lingered. Revitalization was occurring, she said, but not as fast in some neighborhoods as in others. To be on the safe side, I took her advice for a while, but ultimately I had to make the Bronx my home. I also wanted to take a picture of myself standing in front of 1520 Sedgwick Avenue—the birthplace of hip-hop, the place where DJ Kool Herc changed the game. But, for now, I was still excited by "closer to home" things that I discovered on my outings.

Harding Park, which was close to where I lived, welcomed me with a large rock painted sky blue with "Welcome to Harding Park" painted across the top of it in big red block letters. A painting of a Taino native stood guard on one side of the rock and a huge painted sunflower occupied the other side. Next to the sunflower was a drawing of the Puerto Rican flag and beside the Taino native someone had painted the American flag. In the center of the painting was either a huge eagle or a hawk. The New York City skyline and a painting of a bridge were displayed in the foreground.

The park was small, but there were mothers with strollers occupying worn wooden benches while their children ran around half-naked beneath the bountiful spray from several sprinklers in an attempt to ward off the heat and humidity of the sticky July afternoon. I soon learned that Harding Park was not just a park, but a community. It was known as "Little Puerto Rico" and the residents lived in cute, tiny bungalows situated in the area directly behind the park. Many of the homes sat along an inlet of the East River. Some of the homes had docks that made boating possible. The low roofs, small squat structures, richly painted shutters, and white picket fences that surrounded many of the homes made the place look like a tiny fishing village. I assumed that the homes, like the lingering remnants of the dilapidated locker room across the courtyard from my apartment, once belonged to the Shorehaven Bath Club that had previously occupied the area. I imagined that the bungalows in Harding Park were once used to house the well-to-do who came to the club for a weekend stay. In my origin story, the houses remained after the club closed and a change in ownership ensued. It seemed likely, but I was just trying to make connections.

I came across a lot of abandoned lots on my journeys too. Some of them were fenced, as if there was a need to protect the grass that grew within, while other lots were open and the grass grew wild and tall and was decorated with soda cans, shiny potato chips bags, and intact as well as ripped apart old black tires.

I was especially excited when I discovered a nature trail on one of my neighborhood walks. Here, it was called a "greenway," which was basically a paved trail surrounded by grass and plants I didn't know the names of that grew as high as my shoulders. On the trail I saw rabbits that scurried in and out of the high grass and once I saw a big, wild bird stick its head out, flap its wings, and then run back to its hiding place. I liked sitting and thinking on the boulders that bordered the river. I was glad I had stumbled upon the trail. It was nice to be able to spend time in nature.

I could see Manhattan from Clason Point Park, which was down the block from where I lived. It was just swatches of grass and trees really, with some paved strips in between, but it was right on the water, which made it a great place to sit and relax. Men with fishing poles lined up along the rockface, big white buckets perched beside them to store their catch. Salsa and merengue beats often serenaded parkgoers. An old rusty ship sat in the middle of the water; it was full of holes, but it was still afloat and anchored. I wondered how long it had been out there. I was also able to see Manhattan from the park inside the gated community. It seemed like a hop, skip, and a jump away across the Long Island Sound. Its skyline was pointy and jagged and the buildings were packed together tight. But here in the Bronx, there was room. I could breathe.

It was Monday afternoon and I had nothing to do. I looked in the bathroom mirror at my face and my hair. My dreadlocks had grown longer. They swept past my eyes and covered my shoulders. I gathered them into a ponytail, then decided to just wear them down as usual. I was glad I'd decided during my last year in college to put my hair in locs. The style allowed me the luxury of not having to fuss with my hair every day.

I turned my face from side to side and checked out my skin, which had become a gleaming reddish-brown from my days of strolling in the sun, and I felt pretty. I wondered what lesbian women thought when they saw me. Did I look like a viable option or just another straight girl? I didn't know.

It was one o'clock and I hadn't eaten lunch, but I decided to skip it and walk to the local library. But before I got to the front door, the phone rang.

"Hello."

"Sky, it's your mother."

"Oh, hi, Mom. How are you?" I replied with limited enthusiasm.

I was still angry with my mother for her role in that sham of a wedding she'd conjured up with Delbert, but I wanted to forgive her, wanted to let it all go.

"I'm good dear. Your father and I miss you."

"I miss both of you too."

"Are you eating?"

"Yes, Mom."

"Did you start teaching yet?"

"No, Mom. It's still summer vacation."

"Well, what are you doing for money?"

"I have enough saved. I'll manage until September."

"Delbert called me yesterday."

I rolled my eyes. "And?"

"And he would like to get in touch with you."

"You didn't give him my number did you?"

"Well…he made it sound urgent that he speak to you."

"Mom, how could you?"

I threw the orange bag I was carrying at my second hand couch, which was also orange. It missed, dropped to the floor, and everything inside spilled out.

"First Odeta and now you. I just changed my phone number so Delbert couldn't call me. That's another meal, Mom. Changing my number again will cost me another meal."

"For heaven's sake, don't change your phone number again. It's confusing me, all of those numbers. Why won't you give Delbert another chance? He's a good man, Sky."

"Mom, I liked Delbert. Hanging out with him, going to fancy restaurants, buying expensive clothes that he paid for was fun and all, but I *never* wanted to marry him. That was *your* idea so, of course, you think he's a good man and you only think that because he has a lot of money. You think if I marry him I'll never want for anything, don't you?"

"Well, all of that is true dear. It would do you good to be more settled."

"Mom, if I would've married Delbert or if I were to give him another chance, I would always be searching for something."

"Searching for what, dear?"

"Self-respect!"

I slammed the phone down. Of course, I'd have to call back later and apologize, but, for now, I needed to let my anger simmer.

I decided to walk to the library to take my mind off my mother and her betrayal. The walk was virtually quiet until I got to the corner of Randall and Taylor. There was an unusually shaped building, about two stories tall, all reddish brick with stairs that led to a miniscule park on the roof. On the building was a plaque that was partially covered with graffiti. Under the graffiti the name "Seven Corners" was displayed. I looked around to see if I was at an intersection that consisted of seven corners or if the building itself had seven corners. I was about to count when a young guy in a red Kangol hat who sat with his feet dangling off one of the building's corner ledges turned his boom box on high. Rap music blasted from the speakers and the four young guys who were standing around a large, flattened, square of cardboard began break dancing and spinning around on their heads. I stopped and watched them for a few minutes. Their dexterity and grace was awesome. Break dancing was just creeping into Durham when I left, so the moves these guys were executing were almost otherworldly to me.

"Hey beautiful! Put some money in the cup!" The young guy in the red Kangol hat yelled down at me. Then a black and white Adidas sneaker jutted into the air as a different guy writhed and shook and took his place on the buffered cardboard box.

I searched in my purse for two one-dollar bills and placed them in the small, blue and white coffee cup that was propped up against the building.

"Thank you!" The red hat guy yelled.

I waved and continued on my way.

Soundview Library was a long, low, white and brown building that sat right beside a liquor store. Up the block was Holy Cross church and across the street from Holy Cross was Ortiz Funeral Home. It was like passersby had two choices: fill their lives with books or religion, or end up at the funeral home.

Inside the library, it was quiet and, thankfully, air-conditioned. I sat on a slick brown chair at a rough brown table near a window. A delivery truck and two old, broken-down cars looked at me from the empty lot directly behind the library. The sweet, sticky smell of candy and children drifted toward me, but it was beaten back by the pungent smell of a large bouquet of marigolds that sat in a clear vase on the library's information desk.

I had *The Yellow Wallpaper* by Charlotte Perkins Gilman open in front of me. I imagined that Delbert was a piece of wallpaper that I ripped and ripped with gusto in an effort to eliminate him. I scattered the tiny pieces on the ground, and I stepped on them. I saw his head squashed beneath my shoe and, oh, the satisfaction! Then he pulled a Jesus on me.

I read a few more lines of Gilman's story, then I looked up and to my left. A woman with large eyes and a 1960s Angela Davis Afro was seated at a table across from me. She's cute, was my first thought and then she stared at me. I smiled quickly, feeling shy and uncertain, then returned to my book. It wasn't long before I heard the sound of a chair as it scratched against the floor. Footsteps headed toward me. I tried to concentrate on the page in front of me, but I started thinking about guillotines. I jerked my head up. The cute woman with the big Afro stood opposite me, the table a welcomed barricade. I clutched the edge of the table with both hands, trying to draw it into me. It was too heavy. Instead, I slid down a bit in my chair. The woman stood there, looked at me hard, eyes narrowed. I watched her too. I thought maybe some fatal blow might transpire. My fingers tightened even more around the table's edge trying to force the whole thing forward, but it still would not move. I was scared, but I managed a smile as I whispered a quivering, "Hello" to those big, cute, brown eyes. I guess, deep down, I was still the polite Southern girl.

"Sky Valentine?" the woman asked. "Your name is, Sky Valentine, right?"

"Yes," I said as I slid down another fraction of an inch.

I'd heard many horror stories about New York, the Bronx in particular. Now, I feared, I was to become part of one.

"I thought it was you! You don't remember me? Ola. Ola Prioleau, from St. Catherine's."

I studied her face a little harder looking for memories.

"You don't remember me, do you?"

She pulled the chair out on her side of the table and sat down as if the proximity would immediately jog my memory. It did. I pictured her in a blue and white uniform with purple sneakers. Two thick, black braids hung down her back. She had on glasses. They were purple too.

"Ola Prioleau, from St. Catherine's?" Slowly, I sat up in my chair armed with recognition and no longer afraid. "Oh my God! Yes, I remember you now. You look different. My goodness, that was what…ages ago!"

"Yes, yes, it was, but it's so good to see you again."

She touched my hand accentuating her words and smiled like sunshine. Her smile and touch warmed me.

"So, what are you doing here?" Ola asked.

"Just checking out some books."

"No, no, no." She let out a little laugh. "I mean, what are you doing *here*, in the Bronx?"

"I live here now. Been here for a couple of weeks."

"A couple of weeks! Damn girl, you just got here, but you sound more like a New Yorker than I do." She laughed outright and hit the table.

"Well, I went to college in Rhode Island, so I lost a lot of my accent during those years and I guess just being here, now, I'm losing more of that Southern drawl every day." I laughed out loud, but the humor was really for myself.

"I do hear just a little," she said as she leaned forward. "Don't sweat it though."

She looked at me again, took hold of my other hand, and then squeezed it, and I let her. It felt good to be touched.

"Sky Valentine, I still can't believe it's you. You looking good too. No more glasses I see."

"I can say the same about you," I said, feeling my face flush and grow hotter.

"Remember, it was you, me, and Kathy Christmas. They used to tease us and call us…"

"The See-n-Eye Sisters!" we both yelled.

The librarian, young but stern, turned and frowned at us. We covered our mouths and laughed.

"So, I gather, you live in the Bronx, right?" I said, mouth still fixed in a smile.

"Yes, I've lived in the Bronx a long time now. My folks moved here after I graduated from St. Catherine's. My junior high is near here. Sometimes I come back and visit the area, see old friends, you know."

"I see."

"Look here, I'm having a get-together this Saturday at my place for my birthday. Would you like to come?"

"Sure," I said, trying not to sound too eager, too desperate. For some reason, I wanted Ola to think that I was okay, even though seeing her made me realize I was lonely.

"Great!"

Ola picked up the pen I had on the table, reached into her knapsack, and tore a slip of paper from a pad. She began to write.

"Here's my address and telephone number. The party starts at eight. If you need directions or a lift, give me a call, okay? Or better yet, if you don't mind and if I can find someone to do it, I'll send someone over to pick you up. Is that okay? I mean, I'm sure you haven't figured out all of the streets and stuff yet. Unlike Manhattan, which is basically just a goddamn grid, the Bronx can be hard to navigate with all of its street names."

"Okay," I said. Then I fumbled around in my bag until I found a scrap of paper. I scribbled my address on it and gave it to Ola. "Here's my address, just in case."

I glanced at the address Ola had written. She was right, I had no idea where the place was, but I was excited to be going to my first Bronx party, excited about the possibility of making new friends, and excited about spending time with an old one.

"Well, it was great to see you again, Sky."

"Yes, you too, Ola."

I stood up and held out my hand. Ola looked briefly at it frozen in midair. She grabbed my hand and held on to it as she stood, walked around the edge of the table, and gave me a big hug. Her body pressed flush against mine. I hadn't hugged another woman in this way since I broke up with my ex-girlfriend, aka my college roommate. It felt good to be in the arms of a woman again.

CHAPTER SIX

Seven forty-five and I still couldn't decide what to wear to the party. Storm clouds, all puffed up and threatening, had fought it out two hours ago. They'd released torrents of rain with every blow and had drenched those who were unfortunate enough to have been outside. But now the sun owned the sky again and, although it sat lower on the horizon, it flexed its muscles radiating every bit of heat it could onto the waning day.

A tepid breeze blew the bottom half of one of the flimsy, yellow curtains I had hanging over my bedroom window. It was so humid that I almost expected to see large droplets of water fall down from the seams. Living close to the ocean or the sea or whatever type of body of water the Long Island Sound was, was scenic and soothing, but you *definitely* paid a price.

I stood in front of the small closet wondering if the party would be air-conditioned or if a cheap fan would blow hot air around all night. I didn't know and every second I stood there I became more obsessed with the improbability of proper ventilation and I began to seriously consider staying home.

I wanted to meet new people, make new friends, but…I was hesitant. I guess I was just nervous. I sat on the edge of my bed. A city bus came to life with a Jurassic wail. I listened to sparrows as they argued about earthworm ownership and if said worm should or should not be lifted from the ground and brought up into the warmth of the nest. People walked by, laughed, and exchanged greetings with the security guards at the gate. In that moment, I felt like I was a long way from home, but there was no time to brood because the telephone rang. Startled, I plucked the phone off the base attached to the wall and pressed the receiver to my ear.

"Hello?"

"Hello, this is security. There's a…What's the name again, Ms.?"

"Grace. Grace Webster."

"Yes, hello, there's a Grace Webster here to see you," the guard relayed.

"I'm sorry. You must have the wrong house. I don't know anyone by that name."

I listened as the guard told the visitor what I had said.

"Tell her Ola sent me," the female voice said.

The guard dutifully repeated her words to me.

"Oh…okay, send her in."

I hung up the phone and rushed into the bathroom to get my bathrobe. As I threw my bathrobe on and looked at myself in the bathroom mirror, I recalled what Ola had said about maybe sending someone over to pick me up. It had sounded tentative to me, so I had doubted that anyone would show up and had put the thought out of my mind.

I took off the rubber band I had wrapped around my locs, shook out my hair, and headed downstairs. As I reached the bottom step, the doorbell rang. When I opened the door, a tall, lanky woman with big, beautiful, bedroom eyes the color of peach pits stood before me. Her hair was short, very close to her head, but not flat. It was springy with soft curls. A purple peacock feather hung from her right ear and it swirled and twisted in a semi-circle in response to the hot July breeze. Her face, the color of golden graham crackers, glistened with tiny beads of sweat.

"Hi, I'm Grace. Told the guard already, but wanted to reiterate it because…well…you never know who's knocking on your door. Can't be too careful. Okay, so, I'm rambling."

She was. She was also jamming her hands deeper and deeper into the pockets of her beige chinos. They were very baggy so there seemed to be a great deal of room for hand jamming.

"Ola sent me to pick you up for the party," she said.

"Why didn't Ola tell me you were coming?"

I opened the door wider and motioned for Grace to enter.

"Probably forgot. She's busy setting up and getting things together. I sort of volunteered to come out here. It was either pick you up or stack cans of Budweiser in the refrigerator. No-brainer there."

Grace wiped the sweat from her small, square forehead, looked around, took in my living room, walked over to my orange, secondhand couch, and plopped her narrow hips down on it. I hadn't decorated much since I'd arrived because decorating costs money and I was trying to save what I had until school started.

In addition to her tan, baggy chinos, Grace had on purple sandals, and a long, purple, sleeveless shirt with a picture of two women standing back-to-back with their arms folded across their chests. They were encircled with the words: "Sisters United Can Never Be Defeated." She looked at me.

"So, you're Sky."

"Yes, I'm sorry. How rude of me. I'm Sky. Sky Valentine. Nice to meet you."

I stuck out my hand for a formal shake. Grace took it. Her hand was thin and long and her palm, like her face, was moist. Her mouth was small and neat, but her eyes were big and layered with long, heavy lashes like miniature wings.

"Sorry I'm not dressed. I wasn't really expecting anyone to show up. In fact, I was actually thinking about just staying home."

I gathered my robe around myself and sat down across from Grace in my mother's old, rose-colored, reupholstered Queen Anne chair she'd found at a flea market.

"Stay home?"

A small smile pinched around Grace's lips forcing out a sharp tuft of air wrapped in laughter.

"Sorry, Sky, but that's not an option."

I narrowed my eyes. "What do you mean, 'That's not an option.' I can stay home if I want to."

"True, but you'll regret it because the party is going to be fly. Now get out of that ratty bathrobe looking like old man Spencer and put on something to rival this heat and humidity."

It was my turn to laugh.

"Did you really just refer to me as a character from *Catcher in the Rye*? What are you, an English teacher?"

"Ah, so you've read it. No, not an English teacher. I'm a sign language interpreter, but I did a stint at the public library a few weeks ago entitled, *Interpreting the Classics*, and *Catcher* was on the list."

The slow batting of her eyes while she spoke was hypnotic, like pendulums turned on their sides. I sat deep in my chair, my heart quickened, and my body felt limp. I was mesmerized. I felt like I was in that movie, *Desert Hearts*. I was Vivian Bell and Grace was Cay Rivers, the wild one who'd come to pull me back out of the closet and set me down firmly on the path of lesbianism. I wanted to hear her talk all night—eyes like half-moons, lips like pale rose-colored buds in need of watering. Which reminded me.

"Can I get you something to drink? Water? Juice? Sweet tea?"

"God, yes. I'm so parched. Water will do."

I unfolded my legs and headed into the kitchen.

"So, Ola said you two grew up together in North Carolina."

I got the pitcher of water out of the refrigerator and poured two tall glasses. The condensation was almost immediate.

"Grew up…uh, not really. We went to the same elementary school."

I glanced at Grace through the open space beneath the kitchen cabinets.

"Lemon?" I asked, holding up the small, yellow oval. The lusty tartness of it already rubbed into my fingertips.

"Please," Grace said. Then she added, "What brought you to the Bronx?"

"A job, this place." I motioned my free hand in the air to reference my apartment. "And I was in need of a fresh start."

I handed Grace her glass. Her fingers wrapped around mine briefly while she held my gaze. Her eyes were like kryptonite weakening me. I turned away quickly and tried hard to avoid her. Was she flirting? I couldn't be sure. Instead, I gulped down large mouthfuls of water accompanied by tiny, slimy lemon seeds that were slippery on my tongue. I chased the seeds around my mouth with my tongue. I wanted to spit them out, but I couldn't pull out a napkin and just start spitting. That would be totally gross and would make a bad first impression, so I swallowed the seeds while I kept my focus on my glass. I wanted to look up and into Grace's beautiful face, but I was afraid. There was an energy between us, a pull, a magnetic attraction that began, for me, in her downward gaze. I wondered if she felt it too. Wondered if this was why she'd held on to my hand.

"Hmm, sounds intriguing. What job?"

I raised my eyes a little to watch her as she took small, measured sips from her glass.

"Kindergarten teacher at a school not too far from here," I said, quickly then gulped a little more water and another slimy seed.

"Funny, my sister teaches kindergarten too. What a coincidence, huh?"

"Wow, crazy!" I said.

Grace looked at me and smiled. I smiled back, feeling the coolness of the water fade as it collected inside of me. Sweat, released from my armpits, ran down toward my hips. I pulled my robe tighter as I wiped at it. Grace's eyes took in the now exposed part of my leg that was once covered by my robe. Awkwardly, I smoothed the silky material back into place. But

Grace's eyes never left my leg and my eyes were trained on her. Slowly, she licked her lips, looked up at me, placed her glass on the floor beside the couch, and then slapped her hands against her thighs and stood. The sudden noise was an ax that sliced away the moment.

"So, party clothes. We should probably get moving. Everyone's expecting you so you can't back out. I can help you pick out something to wear if you'd like. As you can see from my outfit, I'm a bit of a fashionista."

I looked at her purple and tan outfit. When my gaze finally found her face, we looked at each other and started laughing.

"I think I got this one," I said and reluctantly headed back upstairs on my own.

CHAPTER SEVEN

It was exhilarating being driven around the Bronx at night! A hot, sticky breeze clung to my face as I stuck it out the window to see what was going on. I no longer had a car. Odeta took the van I'd rented to come to New York back to North Carolina and I had decided not to rent a car since I hadn't officially started working. But maybe I will once I do.

Luckily, Grace was not in a major hurry to get back to the party. Instead, she offered to take me to see some of the more popular sights to be found in the Bronx. It turned out to be more like pointing out the sights as they zipped by, but it was more than I'd seen since I'd arrived. The Bronx Zoo, the Botanical Gardens, Fordham University, Pelham Bay Park, City Island, Orchard Beach—all just a small part of so much more I needed to explore. The excursion had solidified for me that I had made the right choice when I'd left North Carolina.

We drove up to a small apartment building—only three floors—with large plots of grass on either side of it. In the light of the streetlamps, I saw rows of what looked to be large heads of lettuce and plump tomatoes to the right of the building near a colorful sign that boasted, "Community Garden—We Stand BUY Our Produce." On the left, there were two stone benches and three empty easels of varying sizes that jutted into the dusk like scarecrows. A paint-spattered tarp lay like a discarded Jackson Pollock painting on the ground.

The building itself was just a dull, shit brown color like so many other buildings in the Bronx, except it looked like every tenant had left the Christmas lights on in each of their windows and each window was framed by a jolt of fluorescent color, painted, I assumed, onto the building's brick face. Each window frame appeared to glow in the night like a carnival with multiple entrances.

I followed Grace as we walked by some people who were sitting on the front steps smoking and laughing. Inside the building, the lobby was open and airy. There was no elevator, so we took the stairs to the second floor where we were met by a massive crowd of mostly women of various sizes, shapes, and colors. Drinks were either in their hands, propped up against walls, or sitting in wait between their feet. Most of the crowd sported plaid shirts which were either worn on top of solid colored shirts or tied around waists or strapped down under overalls along with their Doc Martens high-top boots. A few of the ladies wore the "lingerie as outerwear" style following the new music sensation, Madonna, or the "one shoulder on one shoulder off" style like Jennifer Beals in *Flashdance*. One girl had piercings that ran down the length of her ear—top to bottom— like a small spiral notebook. I felt like a Plain Jane with my little yellow sundress and my hair stacked on top of my head in a neat bun. It was like I was headed to church while everyone else was headed for…well…a party.

Ola's apartment was spacious enough. There were huge photographs of people in various stages of undress on almost every wall. Some of the photographs were black and white, while others were bright with color. I wanted to look at them closely, but it wasn't the right time.

Large rainbow-colored pillows were piled high in several corners of the room. Others were used as bouncy backrests by women who leaned into them as they drank their beers or sat and rocked to the heavy bass as it pounded its way out of the huge speakers and thumped along the floor. I felt the faint coolness of the air conditioner, but being that the door was left open to accommodate an overflow of guests, the coolness was more like a spirit—a ghostly chill and then gone.

Grace, who had walked into the apartment ahead of me, stopped beside a woman who wore a tight red dress that squeezed and massaged her curves over tattered black fishnet stockings. The woman's hair was inky black and cut into a Cleopatra bob that shifted and covered some of Grace's face as she whisper-yelled into the woman's ear. The woman shook her head then leaned in toward Grace's ear, whisper-yelled something back, then righted herself and pointed toward another room. Grace turned to me and mouthed something, but just then Prince's new hit song, "Kiss," started to play. Everyone shouted and jumped up to dance, so I couldn't hear a word Grace said. When she moved toward the other room, I took that as my cue and followed.

We walked into a kitchen. It was small, but well-lit and organized. Several women—some standing, others seated—were talking and laughing.

"I have arrived," Grace said as she entered the room, but then she turned to me, made a small gesture toward me with her hand, and said, "Sorry, *we* have arrived." She smiled at me.

I felt somewhat exposed. My face would have reddened had I been of a lighter complexion, instead, I became invisibly but unbearably hot. I tried to fan it away with a wave hello to the group. A woman in a beautiful red, yellow, and blue turban with a design on it that resembled blooming flowers made from African ankara fabric shouted, "Grace! What took you so long?" Some of the other ladies chimed in, "Yeah, Grace, what took you so long?" They spoke to her, but their eyes were on me.

"Well, it was almost a mission impossible, ladies. I had to really twist her arm to get her here," Grace said, then turned and quickly winked at me.

A stocky black girl with a humongous nest of dreadlocks atop her head, bigger than I'd ever seen on any real person, said, in a British accent, "What's the matter dear, not in the mood to party?"

I smiled. I'd never met a black person—or anyone really—who spoke with a British accent, and I'd definitely never met anyone who sported locs before. Not in North Carolina. Not in college. Not anywhere. I was always the only one with the style and most of the people I knew weren't into it, so to come in contact with someone who rocked locs and had an accent made me feel a bit worldly and validated. I took it as another sign that I'd done the right thing by extricating myself from that box called "Durham."

"She's only kidding," I said. "I couldn't wait to get here."

"That's good to hear," someone behind me said.

I turned around. It was Ola. She had on a long, tight, black dress that caressed her hips and skimmed the floor. The neckline, low and scooped, exposed the tops of her breasts, which bounced around a bit as she stepped toward me. I was mesmerized by them and by how beautiful she looked. She'd caught me staring. She cradled and pushed at the sides of her breasts then ran her hands down her body seductively before she reached out to embrace me.

"Hey, Sky. I'm so glad you came."

"Thanks again for inviting me."

Ola grabbed my hand then turned to face the group.

"Everyone, this is Sky Valentine, an old friend from elementary school. Once upon a time we both lived in North Carolina. Now, crazy as it seems, history repeats itself as we both find ourselves here, in the Bronx. Amazing. Can you believe it?"

"It's a small world," said a white lady who wore rainbow glasses and spoke with a slight Southern drawl.

She looked older than the other ladies, like she could have been around thirty, thirty-five years old.

"I'm originally from Charleston, South Carolina, and, yet, here I am," she continued.

"Poor, Sky," another girl said. "Just when you thought your days with Ola were done, she shows up again!"

Everyone laughed. Ola, playfully, stuck her tongue out at the girl then turned to Grace.

"And you, Ms. Webster. What took you so long? Your story seems to be a bit 'dodgy' as Katherine would say."

"I only speak truths. You can direct all questions and suspicions toward your guest."

Ola and Grace looked briefly at each other. I wasn't sure if it was tension or attraction that wafted between them, but I didn't want Grace to be in hot water, so I spoke up.

"You can't blame Grace for our delay, I was…I was having trouble deciding what to wear," I said.

"Well it's a good thing Grace was there with you, love. She can give loads of advice when it comes to clothing," Katherine, the lady with the English accent, said and again, everyone laughed.

Grace fanned away their laughter as she walked toward the refrigerator.

"Don't worry about it," Ola said. "I just like to bother Grace since she's always giving us a hard time."

"Oh, here," I said, handing over the bottle of red wine I'd been holding all along. "Just a little gift to say happy birthday."

"Thanks! Look at that, Grace, a gift," Ola said as she pressed her lips firmly together and widened her eyes at Grace.

"Such a great gift. Thank you for remembering. You see that Grace? *Sky* remembered."

Then the music changed.

"Oh, my God! That's my song!" Ola said. She thrust the bottle at Grace who took it and then she grabbed my hand and yelled, "To the dance floor!"

There was no time to resist. Ola led me to the living room where several ladies were already dancing, hands in the air, feet moving about. I watched the new dance steps that I'd yet to learn being performed around me. I noticed some of the girls had their arms draped across the shoulders of other girls. There were girls who had their behinds pressed into the crotches of other girls. Ladies who firmly held the hips of others while delivering gentle or ferocious kisses to the nape of another lady's neck or mouth. I was excited by their displays, but frightened too. Would the place be raided by police because some neighbor called and complained about the lesbian activity? Would they barge in and start busting heads? Things were progressing in the world for gays and lesbians. Four years ago, in 1982, Wisconsin had outlawed discrimination on the basis of sexual orientation and two years after that the city of Berkeley, California, was the first to offer its employees domestic partnership benefits. But not all cities—and not all people—were enlightened. The party was a safe space, but how long would it remain as such? Despite my worries, the whole thing was still extremely thrilling. I had never been to a party with so many lesbians before! Did this mean that Ola was a lesbian? It was her party after all. She'd invited these people. And what about Grace? Maybe she *had* been flirting with me! I didn't know. I wasn't sure as to the proper etiquette when it came to inquiring about one's sexuality.

A new song began, and more people crammed onto the dance floor. The room vibrated. Ola and I were wedged in tight. I felt the suppleness of her breasts against mine and the firmness of the girl's rear end who danced behind me. Every time Ola jumped up and down, the tops of her ample bosom grazed my chin. I wasn't sure if she was aware of this. I tried to back up, give her more room, but there was no room to spare. When Ola jumped again, she nearly toppled over, probably from the long dress she was wearing, but I caught her in time. Then I realized that she was headed toward drunk—drunk and giddy. But it was her birthday, so she was allowed.

When the next song started, it had a much slower pace, which helped to clear the dance floor some, but not drastically. I turned to leave, but Ola grabbed me around the waist and pulled me toward her.

"Where are you going?" She had a sly smile on her face and her words sounded fuzzy as they fell from her mouth, but her grip was strong.

I wasn't expecting to be pulled into a grind with Ola. I was a little uncomfortable and I felt a bit trapped. I'd never had any romantic thoughts about Ola even though she was very good-looking. When I looked at her now, my only thoughts were of scrawny legs and glasses.

"I thought I'd get something to drink. Maybe try out the wine I bought."

"After this song, okay? I love Sade, don't you?"

I did love Sade, but I didn't want to slow dance with Ola. With Grace, yes, but not with Ola, especially since she was manhandling me. I didn't want to make a scene, so I relented, but I took her hands from around my waist and held them firmly in my own. With a quick flick of her wrist, Ola's left hand was free. She pulled me deeper into her embrace. Then I felt pressure on the small of my back and her hand on my ass. She was like a drunk, touchy octopus. I looked around to see if anyone was watching. I did not want to be the object of attention, or to be made into a spectacle. I realized in that moment that although I had been ready to step out of that box called "Durham," I really had only one foot in the box called "Lesbian." I felt exposed and fearful. Maybe if it had been Grace groping me, I wouldn't have felt this way. I felt like I would have welcomed her touch. But maybe it was just all the eyes that I imagined were watching. Being my lesbian self was new to me, so being my lesbian self in public was a bit scary. I needed to ease into the process, not be thrown into it. I looked around for Grace, hoping she would save me, but I had no such luck. So I grabbed Ola's hand again, held it even tighter, and danced.

As soon as Sade whispered her last note, I freed myself from Ola's embrace and headed back toward the kitchen. The women were still talking, laughing, and replenishing their drinks. Grace was sitting in a corner looking out a window. I walked over and sat down in the empty chair beside hers. She turned and looked at me.

"Did you enjoy your dance?" Her face was neutral, but her tone screamed annoyed.

"She's drunk," I said. "And I uh…I didn't know she was uh… gay."

"Is she?" Grace asked.

I had the feeling that she was being snide or condescending or both, but I wasn't sure. Was she pulling my leg?

"Well, she was practically grinding me down during Sade's song! So, yeah, I'd say she is."

"Maybe," Grace said. "You'd have to ask her." Then she turned and looked out the window.

A minute later Grace questioned me, "Did you like it?"

The question hung there in the air for a bit. I didn't know what to say. Was this some sort of test? If I said yes and Grace happened to be straight, then where would that leave me? If I said yes and Grace happened to be gay, then she might think that I had feelings for Ola and decide I was off-limits. If I said no and Grace happened to be gay, then she would most likely think that I was straight. So, I did what I tend to do in situations where I wasn't sure about the response I was supposed to give, I answered her question with a question.

"Did I like it? What do you think?"

"I don't know, that's why I'm asking. So, did you?"

I thought about Ola manhandling me, trying to make a scene, making me feel uncomfortable.

"No. No, I did not like it."

Grace turned away from me again. She looked out the window, up at the night sky.

"You must be thirsty," she said as she got up from her seat avoiding my eyes.

"Yes," I said. "I'll have vodka with a twist of lemon, thanks."

Grace nodded, but she still wouldn't look at me. As she moved to walk away, I grabbed her hand. She stopped, turned, and finally looked at me.

"What about you, Grace?" I asked.

Her stare hardened as if she were weighing and measuring something deep inside of me. When she was satisfied with her findings, she squeezed my hand and patted it like clergymen sometimes do to old and cherished congregation members.

"Have no fear, my dear. I'm just me. Now let me get that drink for you."

Our hands fell apart as Grace pulled away. Instead of heading to the refrigerator, Grace walked out of the room and disappeared into the crowd. I moved over into her seat by the window. I looked outside into the night. When I looked up, I could see the sky. Ola's window faced the back of the building. It was dark and quiet outside. I could see the large, shadowy plot of grass that hugged the square brick structure like a moat. The moon was high and halved, like a giant white grin laughing at my naivety, chuckling at my fear. I put my head into my hands unsure about the waxing and waning of my life. How much do I share? How much do I give away?

CHAPTER EIGHT

It had been two weeks since Ola's party. She'd called and left messages on my answering machine, but I didn't respond. I couldn't. I didn't know what to say to her. People do crazy things when they're drunk, I knew this, but I believed that these behaviors came from real feelings, wants, and desires. What if Ola wanted me? Kissing Ola, my childhood friend, was not something I wanted to do. When I saw her at the library, before I knew who she was, I'd thought, maybe. But now, it just didn't feel right, and I didn't want to deal with it. So I hid and didn't respond. I didn't want to hurt her feelings. Didn't want to lose her friendship.

I hadn't heard from Grace either. She had given me her number that night, before we'd left to go to the party. I had called her several times during the last two weeks, but she'd chosen not to respond as well. I looked down at the torn piece of paper I held in my hand that had her phone number on it. The numbers were slanted and crooked as if written in haste and I recalled that they were. We had been coming up with a rag-tag itinerary, a "get it in quick" tour of the Bronx, before embarking on partying. I recalled that even then Grace seemed a bit reluctant to write her number down. I crumpled up the tiny scrap and threw it toward the wastebasket. It tapped the rim and bounced back, landing on the floor. My ability to acquire new friends was turning out to be a big miss as well.

I searched around my bedroom closet until I found my photo albums. I pulled out one and flipped through the pages. Shots of me in high school on the senior trip and at the prom flew by, but I was in search of a specific picture, one that held special memories for me. A picture of Zenobia, my college roommate, first girlfriend, and first love.

I found what I'd been searching for: proof of the one who got away. Zenobia looked back at me with large, brown, doe eyes. Her lids heavy and her smile suggestive. Her shoulder-length hair curled up in vast waves that encircled her head. She was like a black Farrah Fawcett and I smiled to myself as I recalled the sweetness of our lovemaking, her perfect hips, the way we cuddled and slept as one on the twin beds we had pushed together in our dorm room. I remembered our crazy, ridiculous fights, the drinks thrown, the fear that the world would discover our secret. But I also remembered the insatiable passion we had for each other, the deep connection we shared, and the whirlwind feeling of finally being in love.

I had gone out with guys before Zenobia and a few after Zenobia in an attempt to be "normal" in society's eyes, but I'd never felt for them what I'd felt for her. Unfortunately, fear had spread like ivy onto our relationship and had destroyed the little we'd known about being in love. It had torn us down, tendril by tendril.

Maybe I should have told Grace the truth. But I was afraid. I was still waiting for her to confirm her sexuality. I wanted her to say the magic words that would set the light to go. I remembered after college, when I'd gone back home, I had a huge crush on Siobhan, a girl who had moved in down the street from my mom's house. We hung out all the time. We confided in each other about many things. I thought I'd read the signs correctly, but when I had finally gotten up the nerve to tell her that I wanted to be with her, she'd slapped me hard across the face and threw me out of her family's home. Luckily, she didn't tell anyone, or at least I didn't think she had. Maybe she thought it would reflect badly on her. I didn't know the reasons for her silence, but I knew that I didn't want the same thing to happen again. I couldn't bear it.

The phone rang. Startled, I dropped Zenobia's picture and jumped up to get the phone.

"Hello."

"Hello, dear. How are you doing?"

"Oh, hi, Mom. How are you?"

"I'm fine, dear."

"How's Dad?"

"He's good. He's out back practicing his archery."

"He hasn't hit anyone, has he?"

"No. No. Actually, he's got quite a shot," she said. "Sky, I called to see how you're doing. How are you really?"

"I'm a little lonely, but school starts in three weeks. I'll be fine until then."

"I knew something was wrong."

"Mom, I didn't say anything was wrong. I just said that I'm a little lonely. But I'm making friends."

"You are?"

"Yes, in fact, do you remember Ola Prioleau? We went to elementary school together?"

"Yes, the Prioleau family, they lived near the church. If I recall, they were from Louisiana originally. Nice people, but a bit wild for my taste."

"Yes, well, Ola lives in the Bronx now too. I ran into her at the library a few weeks ago and we've been, ah, keeping in touch."

"Well, that's good, dear. Tell her to tell her mother I said hello. They moved away so long ago that her mother may not remember me, but it's good to be polite."

"I'll tell her."

"I spoke to Delbert yesterday."

"Oh, Mom, not again!"

"He likes to call, honey. What am I supposed to do, tell him to stop?"

"Yes! That's exactly what you're supposed to do!"

"I can't do that, Sky."

"Can't or won't? When will you and Delbert finally accept that it's over?"

"Me? I'm just relaying a message. He said he has some business to take care of in New York and would love to see you."

"Well, I don't want to see him. You need to tell him to stop harassing me…and you or I'll get my thug boyfriend to break his arms."

"You never told me you had a boyfriend, dear. What's his name?"

"I don't, Mom! I'm just talking nonsense. Look, forget it. Don't tell Delbert anything. I have to go."

I was ready to scream! The ghost of Delbert past kept rattling his chains and my mother, in her quest to have me "set for life," was always there pointing the way.

"Where are you off to today?"

"I'm going to Alexander's. They have school supplies on sale. Look, Mom, I have to go."

"Okay, I won't hold you. Call me later if you still feel lonely. That's what I'm here for."

Would she go back and tell Delbert that I said I was lonely? I hoped not, but I wasn't sure she wouldn't.

"Sure, Mom."

"Goodbye, dear."

"Bye."

I had to stop myself from slamming the phone down. Delbert. It felt like I couldn't get away from him. He was like that invisible spiderweb that you got on your face when you walked down a garden path on a hot summer's night. It clung to you, refusing to let go no matter how many times you swiped at it and prayed it was gone.

CHAPTER NINE

I was still livid, so I tore up my apartment until I found my old phone book with the number to Delbert's business in it.

"Good morning, Sample Incorporated. How may I direct your call?"

"Delbert Sample."

"May I ask who's calling?"

"Sky Valentine."

"Thank you. Please hold."

I was happy no stupid soundtrack came on while I was on hold. I used the silence to try to calm myself down.

"My goodness, *Ms.* Valentine. To what do I owe the pleasure?"

I pictured his big teeth staring down at me. S-M-U-G was written across the front four. I wanted to kick them in.

"What makes you think this call will be pleasurable?"

"Just hearing your voice gives me pleasure, Sky. Always has. Always will."

"Only psychopaths obtain pleasure from a dead relationship."

"I didn't say our *relationship* gives me pleasure. I said hearing your voice does."

"Whatever, Delbert. I didn't call to play a semantics game with you."

"Why did you call?"

"To tell you to stop calling my mother and harassing her!"

"Harassing her? Never. I simply call her to say hello and to find out how she's doing. There is no malice in these attempts, Sky. Your mother is a nice woman. I care about her well-being."

"Yeah, right. Stop calling her and she will be well. You're just calling her to sneak around trying to find out what I'm doing."

"Sky, I'm a busy man. I run a business. I don't have time for sneaking around."

"Look, just stop dragging my mother into your schemes, okay. Just stop."

"No schemes, Sky. Both of us are just trying to make sense as to why you left me standing there like a fool at the altar. She wants to know just as much as I do."

"This is all about your wounded pride. No one could possibly leave Delbert Sample. You're such a great catch. Everyone thinks so. Well, surprise, that's just what I did, Delbert. I left you. I don't owe you an apology or an explanation. Stop expecting one. It's over. I'm gone. The end. Move on and leave me and my family alone!"

I heard Delbert chuckle. "Sky, Sky, Sky, just as I thought, you still want me."

"Oh my God, did you not hear what I just said?"

"I heard you, but I'm listening to what you're not saying. I know you, Sky. You wouldn't get so passionate, so emotional if you didn't care. You still have a lot of passion about us."

"Delbert, you seriously need help. Get counseling and get a life."

"I have a life, Sky. Oh, and I'll tell Odeta you send your love."

"What?"

The line went dead. If only it were Delbert. And what was that about Odeta? Why had he mentioned her name?

I toyed with the idea of calling him back, but decided against it. Mentioning Odeta's name was most likely a ploy, a ruse to get me to call back. I would not take the bait. I put the phone down and gathered my things for my outing. I refused to be a pawn when I could just as easily be a queen.

CHAPTER TEN

Eleven thirty Monday morning, Alexander's overflowed with merchandise and people. I stood at the bottom of the escalator waiting for the head of the serrated step to birth itself. The metal handles of the blue, plastic shopping basket that would eventually dig fervently into my arm were now light and cool against my skin. I felt the weight of my wallet in my bag. It was fat with the hard-earned, long-saved dollar bills I'd brought with me from North Carolina. My heart raced. My pulse galloped. Sweat seeped into my bra. I was ready for the high known as "shopping."

I walked up and down a couple of aisles. Every school supply I saw—pencils, markers, paper, folders, erasers, tape, glue, reinforcements, rulers, everything—went into my basket. I enjoyed the fixes, the hits, the adrenaline rushes that spending money brought, but I didn't just throw money away. I always searched for the bargain, looked around meticulously for the deal.

I was comparing prices on college-ruled spiral notebooks when I heard someone beside me say, "Well, look who it is."

I looked up and saw Grace. I smiled and threw both notebooks into my basket having forgotten about bargain hunting when faced with the surreal surprise of her presence. I was nervous but tried my best to appear cool and collected.

"Hey. What are you doing here?" I asked.

Grace shoved her hands into her pants pockets, hunched her shoulders, and rocked gently from side-to-side with a big, silly grin on her face. It made me laugh. I thought it was something a child would do.

"I'm here with my sister hoarding…I mean shopping for school supplies. You gals just can't get enough! Buy, buy, buy," Grace said.

"I guess so," I replied. "I'm new at this, so everything is fair game. Don't want to get caught out there needing something crucial right in the middle of a lesson."

"I hear ya."

"Where is your sister? I'd like to meet her."

I looked around the store briefly scanning faces in hope of finding someone who might somehow resemble Grace.

"She's about two aisles over looking at some toys to bribe those badass kids with," Grace said as she cocked her head in the direction of the aisle where her sister was.

We laughed.

"Maybe I should head in that direction. I'm sure she knows more about these New York City kids than I do."

Grace made a sweeping gesture with her hand. "After you," she said.

I wanted to bring up the party and the ignored phone calls, but I didn't want to mess up the moment, so I put it all on hold, on layaway, and focused on the pleasure of our interaction.

We made our way to the toy aisle. On the way, Grace picked up a Halloween mask, put it up to her face, looked at me, and gave an unenthusiastic, "Boo." I playfully rolled my eyes and shook my head at her silliness.

When we'd reached the aisle, we stopped in front of a girl who had Grace's face, Grace's eyes, her nose, her mouth, and the same body type as Grace. She was Grace's twin!

"Sky, this is my sister, Hope. Hope, this is Sky."

Unlike Grace, Hope's hair was long, black, and curly. She wore soft red lipstick that reminded me of the inside of watermelons and black eyeliner rimmed the underside of her light brown eyes. Her eyes were broody and sexy like Grace's, but the black eyeliner made them severe, and her flowered sundress was pretty much like my own. No baggy pants with pockets to shove her hands in when nervous like Grace did.

Hope waved and I saw that her nails were not the same as Grace's either. They were long and shiny and black like her eyeliner.

"So, you're Sky."

Hope smiled as she spoke her greeting and I realized that her smile was Grace's smile. It was as if it had been cut and pasted onto her face.

"Grace has been telling me a lot about you." Hope looked at Grace then at me again.

I was surprised to hear this. "She has? Really? Uh, good things I hope."

"Isn't that accent charming?" Grace asked her sister.

"Accent? What accent? I don't have an accent," I said.

"You know, I once fell in love with a guy simply because he had an awesome Australian accent. I loved listening to him talk. Of course, I had to dump him after a while. He talked too damn much!" Hope said.

"Everything in moderation," Grace retorted and they both laughed hysterically.

I watched them. I didn't pretend to know the joke. Instead, I watched the expanding gaps of their mouths as they cried out in laughter, slapping their thighs, shoulders hunched forward in mirth. I watched their eyes tighten and water as they became wet with secrets. Eventually, they managed to pull themselves together.

"Grace tells me you're a teacher."

"Yes, I'll be teaching kindergarten."

"Which school?"

"P.S. 138 on Lafayette Avenue."

"Oh my God! That's where I teach. You must be the new recruit."

"I guess I am."

"You're taking Paula's spot. She moved to Poughkeepsie, got tired of the city. Grace, you remember Paula, don't you?"

"Yes, I do."

"She was a good teacher. Her students loved her," Hope said.

"Looks like someone has some big shoes to fill," proclaimed Grace.

Both Hope and Grace stared at me.

"I'm ready for the challenge," I declared. At least I felt that I was ready.

"Hey, why don't you two go pay for your stuff and then we can all go and get a bite to eat," Grace suggested.

"Sounds like a plan," Hope said.

"Okay, but I still have a few more items to get." I hadn't yet attained my shopper's high.

"Go and get them," Hope said.

"We'll hold a spot for you in line," Grace and Hope said simultaneously and eerily in the same pitch.

"Twins. We can't stay out of each other's heads," Grace quipped.

I shook my head. "I see."

Grace took the bulging basket out of her sister's hand and held on to it. They turned, and headed toward the down escalator, then Grace turned back.

"We'll meet you downstairs. Don't take too long now, ya hear."

She'd said the last part in a fake and pitiful Southern accent. I guess she still heard the lingering of an accent in my speech, but I didn't hear it at all. I had tried hard to leave that part of me behind, box it away. It was not the focus of who I wished to become.

Hope had already stepped onto the down escalator. She looked at me, but it seemed to be more of a glare. Her eyes seemed cold and distant. But maybe I was mistaken. Maybe it was the distance or the lighting. I couldn't be sure, but I got the feeling that she was not happy.

CHAPTER ELEVEN

The sun hit me like a car with faulty brakes as soon as I stepped outside of Alexander's and into the light of day again. The icy layer that had formed on the back of my neck and shoulders from the frosty air that blasted from the air-conditioner inside the store had immediately sloughed off like dead skin. I welcomed the heat. It felt magical. I looked over at Hope. The frost had not left her eyes.

"Where would you ladies like to eat?" Grace asked.

"I don't know of any place that serves good food around here, so whatever you suggest will be fine," I said.

"Actually, I'm not really that hungry," Hope said. "And I just remembered that I'm supposed to meet River downtown at two thirty, so I better get going."

"River is here? From Chicago?" Grace shielded her eyes to better see her sister.

"Yes, she's visiting for a few weeks. I told her we'd get together today."

"I wish you would've told me. I'd like to see her too."

"Well, maybe you should go with your sister to see your friend. We can have lunch some other time," I said, but I thought, the visiting long-lost friend, how convenient!

Graced sucked in a breath and let out a deep sigh. Her face was serious while she contemplated and weighed her options.

"No, no, it's okay. Just make sure you tell River to call me. Think you can remember to do that?"

Hope looked briefly at her sister and then rolled her eyes.

"Of course. Anyway, I gotta go."

Hope turned and was about to walk away, but she turned back around.

"Oh, and it was nice meeting you, Sky," she said with a hard look on her face.

"Yeah, same here," I said.

Empty words. I'd always considered myself a good judge of character, so it was clear to me that there was no hope of any kind of friendship between Hope and me. Too bad. It would have been nice to have an ally at work.

Hope embraced her sister, kissed her on both cheeks, and then went on her way. Grace and I stood, immobile, beside a huge row of glistening silver shopping carts as we watched Hope head to the bus stop down the block.

"So, where to now?" Grace asked.

"I don't know. Where do you want to go?"

"I don't know."

Grace wiped at the moisture on her forehead. The sun was beaming down on us. The periodic blasts of cold air that escaped from Alexander's every time someone entered or left the store did nothing to assuage the heat dealt by the sun.

"You know, it's almost too hot to eat," Grace said.

"How about a salad?" I asked.

"Salad?"

Grace looked out over the large parking lot as she thought about my suggestion.

"Okay, that sounds doable, but where are we going to find a salad bar around here?"

"I know just the place. Follow me."

We walked along an extended narrow path that edged its way around the shopping center.

"Where are we going?" Grace asked.

"To the supermarket."

Grace looked confused. "There's a salad bar in the supermarket?"

"No, but there are salad items. We can pick up some things and make a salad at my place. It's not far from here. Besides, we'll be more comfortable there and we won't have to worry about tipping a lousy waiter."

"Good point. Good point. Uh, and your salad making skills…any good?"

"I'll have you know I'm an excellent cook! And, we will be making this meal *together*."

I handed Grace a medium-sized, green shopping basket and pulled her toward the produce section.

We made an enormous fruit salad using practically every fruit we'd found in the store. The multitude of colors glistened and the juices from all of the fruits mixed together into a wonderful liqueur that sloshed around the bottom of the large glass bowl we'd put the salad in. I'd also made mango lemonade with the last ripe mango we'd purchased from the store. It was fruit overload, but it was better than a hot meal.

We ate our salads outside in the shade of a big purple umbrella that was attached to the small round picnic table in my backyard. The yard was small and cozy, with a patch of bright green grass and a large, red rose bush that grew in the southwest corner where my neighbor's fence met mine. It was the perfect spot for a romantic meal, but this was *not* a romantic meal, or, at least, I was determined not to let it morph into one.

I could admit to myself that I liked Grace, but I had also assessed that communication was most likely an issue for her. Communication *and* commitment since she'd up and left me at the party. She'd just disappeared and never came back with my drink and didn't bother to return my phone calls either. All of these things spoke volumes as to who Grace really was.

"It's nice back here," Grace said when she stepped out of the condo and into the backyard.

She pulled out a chair and sat on the edge of the seat, which caused the seat cushion to stick up a bit behind her. She surveyed the other condos within proximity of where we sat while she plopped succulent squares of bright red watermelon into her mouth. Her lips were wet with the watermelon's sugary juices and I thought she looked so sexy as she licked the nectar from her lips. *You're not here for that,* my brain reminded me. I silently agreed with my brain, so I reached across the table and handed Grace a napkin to clean her mouth.

"Thanks," she said.

"Yes, it's nice now. Wait until the planes start coming in. La Guardia Airport is over there." I pointed in the direction of the park that bordered the edge of the gated community. "When the planes come in, it won't be quiet anymore. They come in so low sometimes it feels like they're on your head."

"Wow, you can see the planes as they come in for a landing? That's cool!" remarked Grace.

"I guess. When we're finished, we can go over to the park if you want. You'll be able to see the control tower from there as well."

"That's a plan!" Grace exclaimed, and I thought her enthusiasm to see planes land and take off was downright cute.

I looked at Grace, her big bedroom eyes, her long, lean fingers, her feathered earring spinning lazily in the tepid breeze. I felt a war between my mouth and my brain being waged. My mouth wanted desperately to tell her that she was right about what she had insinuated at the party. Upon further soul searching, I concluded that I'd sort of liked the sexy dancing with Ola, but it creeped me out because it felt almost incestuous since we'd practically grown up together. I wanted to tell her that I was not, in any way, freaked out about lesbians, obviously—or maybe, not so much so. I *was* fearful of gay and lesbian bashing and being ostracized, but I felt like with her, I could be a bit braver. My desire for her and need to be with her almost rendered all onlookers transparent and thereby inconsequential. I wanted to tell her these things. Instead, I drowned them in a large mouthful of mango lemonade. I needed to hear more from her first.

"How is Ola doing?" I asked.

I'd never meant to bring up Ola, it just slipped out. Most likely because I'd just been thinking about her. Still and all, I could've kicked myself.

"Ola? She's good, I guess. I haven't spoken to her today."

"She's called me a couple of times, but I haven't returned her calls."

"Why not?"

"I don't know. It's stupid really. I just feel awkward, not sure of what to say."

I looked down into the small, red bowl in front of me. Three kiwi slices sat under two big chunks of pineapple. I felt Grace's eyes on me as she reached for her glass of lemonade.

"You mean, because you think she's gay?"

"Well…yeah because what if she tries to hit on me again? She's like a sister to me!"

"Sky, Ola was extremely drunk that night. *If* she hit on you, as you claim, you shouldn't take it personally. She probably hit on twenty other women as well. It's not a big deal."

"I didn't say it was a big deal."

"No, but you're not answering her calls, which *is* making it a big deal. Be brave. Answer her calls and pop the question. Curtail your infatuation already!"

"I am *not* infatuated with Ola. If anything, I was…am… repulsed."

Repulsed was definitely too strong a word, but I still wasn't sure about Grace's sexuality. I was pretty sure she was gay, but she had never confirmed this. I wanted her to be the first one to say, "I am a lesbian" before I put myself out there. Was it impolite to ask? I wasn't sure as to the protocol when it came to asking about one's sexuality.

"Repulsed, wow, that's serious. Are you a homophobe?"

"What? No! Are you serious?"

"Very. Usually it's homophobes who, once they find out someone they know is queer, automatically assume that person has an interest in them. It's extremely presumptuous. I know gay people find this very annoying," Grace said as she threw another head onto the pile of strawberries she had already beheaded.

"Well, hey, the girl was grinding on me."

"Why didn't you stop her? Why didn't you walk away?"

"She was holding me rather tightly."

"How tightly could a drunk girl have held you? Are you sure it was Ola doing the holding on?"

"Look, I don't know why I didn't stop her or walk away. I mean, I finally walked away, but I don't know why I didn't do it sooner. I guess I didn't want to cause a scene. Anyway, let's talk about something else."

I stood and started gathering the soiled napkins and plates.

"Getting too hot for you, Sky?"

"Yeah, let's go inside. It's too hot out here."

Grace laughed and pushed out her chair. "Yes, too hot indeed."

CHAPTER TWELVE

Inside, the house was cool. I'd kept the shades down to ward off the afternoon sun and I was rewarded.

Grace sat on my orange couch and thumbed through the old May issue of *People* magazine on the coffee table. On the cover, people held hands and flashed megawatt smiles while they got their pictures taken for the charity event of the year—Hands Across America.

I was still in the kitchen when the drone of the first incoming plane slightly shook the sides of the condo. I dried and stacked the last bowl into the cabinet, then Grace suggested we head out to the park to watch the planes. I grabbed my keys off a small red plaque that hung on the wall next to the phone; the word "love" was spelled out across its tiny iron middle.

It was around three thirty in the afternoon. The park was empty except for a goose or two that ignored us and kept pecking hardily at the emerald grass that grew in the park's marshy land. A warm, almost tropical, breeze batted at the leaves on the trees and as they swayed, they made a sound like a hollowed-out cassava filled with tiny grains of rice.

The Manhattan skyline was to the right of us. The airport's control tower was set down in the middle of our view. The Whitestone Bridge jutted up into the sky on our left. Large rocks and a crooked wire fence tightly hugged the periphery of the park and kept the Long Island Sound at bay. We contemplated walking around the track that was stamped into the middle of the park, but, instead, we opted to sit on a bench that faced the water.

"It's nice out here," Grace said.

"Yes, it is. I come down here often, to think."

"What do you think about?"

"Everything and nothing. My parents. My old friends. My new job. Stuff like that."

"Do you miss North Carolina?"

"Sometimes, but it's good to be away."

"What brought you to New York anyway? Are you running from something or…maybe…someone?"

"Isn't everyone dying to come to New York?" I asked.

I was focused on some geese droppings. I turned a few white and green turds over with the front edge of my sandal. When I looked up, I didn't meet Grace's gaze. I kept my eyes peeled on the water. There was a huge sailboat making its way toward Manhattan. Its large white sails puffed out fat like baby's cheeks.

"Hey, why didn't you tell me you had a twin sister?" I finally looked at Grace when I said this.

"Okay, so you want to change the subject. I get the hint. I didn't tell you I had a twin because, well, really, it's of no relevance. What I mean is, why would I go around telling people that I have a twin?"

"I don't know. It's kind of interesting. You don't meet twins every day," I said.

"How would you know? Twins usually don't go around advertising their situation. Sure, there are those who dress alike all the time and go everywhere together so they can be seen, but most twins, I suspect, want to be known as individuals."

"Well, I get the feeling that your sister doesn't like me."

"What makes you think *I* like you?" Grace laughed. "I'm just kidding."

I laughed too, but it trailed a short distance behind Grace's statement in search of the truth. Was this a true thing said in jest? I wasn't sure.

"Seriously, though, what makes you think Hope doesn't like you?"

"In the store, when I was talking to you and she was standing by the escalator, she gave me this look. Then she cut out on us as fast as she could."

"She had to meet up with a friend."

"Wow, you believed that? Come on, she made that up. She was pleasant until she heard that I would be teaching at her school."

"Maybe it has to do with Paula, the teacher you're replacing. She and Hope were very close."

"Maybe," I said.

A strong breeze blew in off the Long Island Sound. I looked out at the water trying to spot the sailboat that had passed earlier. It was gone and the water formed tiny spikes along the path where it had been. When I looked back at Grace, her feather earring was twirling in the breeze. It spiraled and whipped around like a miniature version of those big brushes at a car wash.

My locs blew across my shoulders and the sensation sent a small shiver down my spine. Behind us, a huge green and white jet smashed through the air. We both looked up to see the word "Delta" scribbled across the underside of jet's belly plain as day as it passed over us and headed out over the water. If I'd thrown a ball into the sky, I'm certain it would've hit the bottom of that airplane with ease.

We sat on the bench for a while, watching as one plane after another headed toward the airport to disembark. I imagined each passenger breathing a sigh of relief as they got on with their lives. It made me think about Ola and about how foolishly I'd behaved, and I wanted to make things right.

"I guess I should give Ola a call," I said. I sat up straight and pushed my shoulders into the hardened slats of the bench.

"I don't see why not, but only if you want to. Not because I've talked you into it."

"No, you're right. I was being silly."

"I'm not sure 'silly' is the word I would use."

"Silly, stupid, moronic. You know what I mean."

"I was thinking asshole," Grace said with a sarcastic smile planted on her face.

"Hey, wait a minute, I wouldn't go that far!"

"Of course not, most homophobes wouldn't."

I looked at the sky. The last plane from the lineup roared above our heads then advanced toward Queens. I waited until the noisy assault died down before I responded.

"I'm *not* a homophobe!" I yelled, growing weary of the accusation.

"Really, have you ever been attracted to another woman?" Grace asked as she eyed me suspiciously.

"Now *that's* a silly question. What does that possibly prove? My response, whether it be yes or no, would not indicate homophobia. Dumb question," I said.

"Yeah, yeah, yeah, you're stalling. Why are you stalling, Sky?"

"Have *you* ever been attracted to another woman?" I asked, hoping she would finally confirm my suspicions.

"Aren't all women attracted to other women? I mean, we spend most of our time scrutinizing each other—look at her hair, her butt, her breasts. What is she wearing? That shirt is too tight. She has nice legs. She's pretty. She has great abs—and on and on. I'd say we look at other women more than we look at men. My point is a woman would be lying if she said she has *never* been attracted to another woman."

"So, what, that was a trick question? If I'd answered no you would have thought me a liar?"

"Well…yes and no. Yes, because like I said, I believe every woman has had, to some extent, an attraction to another woman. And no because generally, women don't label these behaviors as attraction. But, if you ask me, that's exactly what it is."

"So, have you been attracted to other women, Grace? Stop stalling and answer the question."

"Sure, I have, plenty of times," Grace said.

"Really? Anyone I know?"

But who did I know here, in the Bronx, besides Ola? I was still curious though about the tension I thought I saw between the two. Was there something to it? Was Grace about to say Ola's name?

"Yes, as a matter of fact. Someone you know very well and not at all."

I gave Grace a puzzled look.

"Think about it," she said as she hopped down off the back of the bench. "Come, let's walk back to your place."

CHAPTER THIRTEEN

We walked back to my place in silence. Grace took in the view while I thought about our conversation. She didn't have to say it, I *knew* she was attracted to Ola because of all of the tension between them and with how upset Grace was with me after Ola and I had danced. She had walked out on me! Didn't even get the drink she had offered to get for me! But why the guessing game? Was it weird for her to admit her fondness of Ola to me because of my friendship with Ola? My experiences with female relationships have been complicated, but they became even more complicated when attraction, love, and sex were involved. The more I thought about it as we walked back to my place, the more I felt I really didn't need to know who Grace was attracted to. I mean, did it really matter? Would it change anything? Probably not. I just wanted for us all to remain friends.

When we arrived at my front door, I unlocked it and stepped aside to let Grace in first. As soon the door was closed, I blurted out, "It's Ola, isn't it? You're attracted to Ola."

I couldn't help myself, couldn't hold it inside anymore. Curiosity had gotten the best of me, and it didn't help that Grace did not respond right away. Instead, she shucked her heavy sandals by the door and dropped down on the couch like a discarded watermelon, as if the short walk back to my place had actually been twenty miles. Then she slid her body into the nearest corner of the couch and put her feet up on the backrest pillows so that the top of her head faced me.

I slipped off my sandals. The coolness of the linoleum floor penetrated my feet and toes. The sensation brought me back to Durham, to the sharp, cool edges of freshly cut grass after my father had mowed the backyard. I sat in the opposite corner of the couch from Grace. Her lips were slightly upturned as if she were holding back a smile.

"Good guess, but wrong," Grace said. "At least not now anyway. Ola's old news."

"So, you *were* attracted to her?"

"Yes, but like I just said, that was in the past. Now, we're just great friends—most days."

"Was there more than just attraction?" I wanted the whole scoop.

Grace got up and walked to the screen door where she stood and looked out onto the gardens the co-op maintained. I couldn't see her face.

"No, no, nothing more."

I couldn't see her hands either. They were stuffed into her pockets again. I wondered if she had her fingers crossed, like children did, as a way to dispel the lie they had just told.

"Really?" I asked.

"Really," Grace said.

"Well, if not Ola, then who?"

I had gotten to my feet. I was in the kitchen getting some more mango lemonade for us when Grace said something that I couldn't hear because I had turned the water faucet on full blast.

"Wait, I can't hear you," I yelled.

I shook the excess water from both of the tall glasses, added a few pieces of ice, and then poured the drinks. The ice cracked and split and rounded at the edges when the lemonade raced over it. I took a quick sip from my glass before heading back into the living room where Grace was now seated in my mom's old chair.

"Please repeat what you said. I couldn't hear you from the kitchen. Who are you attracted to?" I said as I handed her the glass.

Grace gulped down her drink. Her eyes peered into mine over the top of her glass as she drank but were lifted away as she tilted it upward. When the last drop of lemonade rolled down the side of the glass and disappeared, so did Grace's eyes. She kept her head down and her eyes on her lap.

"You," she said. "I'm attracted to you."

I couldn't believe it. It was what I had wanted to hear, but at the same time, not what I was expecting to hear. I was excited and somewhat terrified at the same time because after the whole slow dancing episode with Ola and not knowing how to appropriately handle the situation, I realized that I was not ready for a relationship. Not yet. I felt like I still had some fears to work through. But then I realized I was jumping the gun. Grace has only stated that she was attracted to me. According to her theory, every woman was attracted to another woman, so really, her whole admission amounted to a hill of beans.

"Me? Wow, umm, I don't know what to say."

"There's nothing to say."

But I thought I saw something in her eyes when she finally raised her head and looked at me.

"I think I need to add some vodka to this," I said, raising my glass.

I walked over to the small cabinet next to the window in the kitchen. I drank about a third of my lemonade and refilled the space with vodka. I didn't drink often, but this was definitely a moment where some spirits were needed.

"Want some?" I called out from the kitchen.

"I'll take a little."

I walked back into the living room with the bottle of vodka in my hand. Slowly, I poured some into Grace's glass, my hand shaking noticeably the whole time. Clear liquid splashed onto the chair's arm and Grace chuckled.

"I actually drove you to drink," she said smiling. But when she looked at me, her smile faded a bit.

I put the bottle on the coffee table in case we needed another hit and sat on the couch that was parallel to Grace's seat.

"What are we going to do?" I asked.

"What do you want to do, Sky?"

I am not ready to go down this path yet. I am not ready to go down this path yet. This was the message that I kept on loop in my head. I repeated it over and over again as I sat there. Then I thought about something else. She'd only said "attraction". She hadn't admitted to being gay. She hadn't said that she wanted to sleep with me. She had only admitted to there being an attraction.

The tinkling of the ice jarred me away from my thoughts. I watched as one piece of ice melted and fell squarely onto another piece. The frost and condensation on the glass made it cold and wet in my hand. I switched the glass to my other hand and wiped my hand on the bottom of my shirt.

"Don't sweat it, Sky. I'm not in love with you or anything. I just, well, I dig you."

"You dig me?"

"Yes, I dig you. I enjoy your company. I like hanging out with you. You're smart, funny, sexy, and pretty. There's also an adventurous spirit that shows its head every once in a while. And dare I say it? Yes, I dare. You've got a great body."

"I do?"

I was flattered but I also felt the flames of embarrassment grow hotter and higher by the second. I chugged down more of my drink in an attempt to extinguish the flames. *I'm not ready to go down this path yet. I'm not ready to go down this path yet.* I started my mantra again.

"Yes, you do," Grace said. "In fact, to be totally honest with you…I can be right? Totally honest with you?"

Apparently Grace had been asking rhetorical questions because she did not wait for my response.

"I'd like for us to make love."

I think my head snapped back like a shot. I felt like I'd just gotten hit with an "I'm a lesbian" fastball.

"What?" I yelled.

Grace poured more vodka into her glass then set the half-empty bottle back down on the table. She stared at me from her spot in the chair. Her big peach pit-colored eyes, heavy and hooded. Bedroom eyes, Odeta would have called them, like she had once heard her mother say about Smokey Robinson's. When I looked into those bedroom eyes, my stomach fluttered. I had to admit, I wanted her. There was no denying it. I just felt that now was not the time. I needed to sort things out. I needed time. I needed...I needed...I stood up and took a step toward Grace. She smiled. I took another step toward her, my eyes on her full lips, her sultry eyes. Grace slid to the edge of her seat. Her hands were open and lifted to welcome me. But I walked past her, unlocked the screen door, and held it open.

"I think you should leave," I said. "I...I just need some time to think this through—alone."

I looked over at Grace, but she hadn't turned yet to look at me. Instead, she kept her eyes focused on the unblemished white wall the couch backed onto. Her hands had fallen to the tops of her thighs and her head was lowered between her shoulders. You have humiliated her, I thought. I hadn't meant to, had no intention of doing so, but it had happened just the same. But I did need time to think and I needed to do so without distractions, so Grace did need to leave.

Grace finally turned toward me. "What are you going to do now, Sky? Sit here for three months trying to figure it all out? I don't even know why I told you. I knew you would freak out. Look, forget about it, okay. Forget everything I said."

"I can't forget something like this."

"Why not?"

"Because...I can see it in your eyes and because...because...I feel the same way about you. I just need some time is all. I need to think."

"Well, then, I guess I'd better get going."

Grace stood and walked toward the door. She stopped right in front of me, placed both of her long, thin hands on top of my shoulders, and looked me square in the eyes.

"Stop running. Stop playing hide-and-seek with yourself."

I dropped my head. My eyes found the floor. A tear sprung from my eye and watered my big toe.

"I'll call you," I murmured into my chin.

"Yeah, I'm sure, just like you called Ola."

Grace's hands dropped from my shoulders and she pushed her way out the door and down the front steps.

I watched her back through the screen door netting as she moved along the front path. Watched as she shoved her hands into her pockets and walked farther away from me. I thought about calling her back, back into my arms, into my dreams. But I didn't. I couldn't. I felt empty inside because the woman I wanted was outside, but so was the cruel, harsh world.

I locked the screen door, walked back to the couch, sat, and poured myself another drink. Vodka, straight this time. Drinking was not going to solve my problems, but, at least for a while, I could forget.

CHAPTER FOURTEEN

Three weeks had passed. I hadn't seen nor spoken to Grace, but school had begun. My days were filled with way too many kindergarteners in one classroom, which made teaching a major juggling act. My nights were filled with creating lesson plans and looking for art projects that coincided with stories I'd read to the children and figuring out ways to teach concepts to students who had difficulties recalling the curriculum. Hard work, yes, but I loved every minute of it. All of these activities and as busy as I was, I still thought about Grace. She was constantly on my mind. Having Hope around every day served as a constant reminder that I hadn't called Grace as of yet. As a result, I spent my mornings, lunch hours, and after-school hours avoiding Hope so we wouldn't have to broach the subject. Thus far, it had worked out well. It seemed as though Hope was trying her best to avoid me as well. I'd noticed several times when she had seen me in the hallway or out on the school playground, she would look straight at me, then turn around and go back the other way or she'd rush over to another colleague and pretend to have a dire need to converse. I knew it was all bullshit. I was actually thankful for these moments, because if she hadn't retreated, it would've meant that I'd have had to. I didn't know what to say to Grace or Hope. I couldn't even manage a simple, "Hello." How lame.

It was Friday. The beginning of my lunch hour. In order to elude Hope, I always ate my lunch outside in the park across the street instead of on the bench in the school's playground area where most of the other lower grade teachers congregated. Before I exited the building, I needed to relieve myself and wash away the dried smudges of clay and paint that had accumulated on my hands from the classroom assignments I had completed so far. I decided against using the first-floor bathroom because I was sure I'd run into Hope there. Instead, I went upstairs by way of the rear staircase, which was always empty. I pushed open the bathroom door. The stall and sink areas were empty. I breathed a sigh of relief, then walked in and stood at the sink. Too much sun and not enough water had dried my lips once again. I'd continued to reapply lip balm over and over again during the day, but it didn't do any good. I was visualizing placing reminders around the classroom that would instruct me to drink the water I'd brought religiously every day but inevitably sat unopened, when Hope walked in. Nervous, I dropped my lip balm into the sink and held onto the smooth, cold edge of the sink for support. It was as if shockwaves had ripped through the ground, traveled up my legs, and buckled them. Hope seemed to fill the doorway. The air that was trapped between us churned, popped, and sputtered, then quickly evaporated. With all of the warmth seemingly sucked out of the room, a heavy coldness rose up and seemed to fill the space. The ghost of Grace perhaps.

I made the first move. I grabbed my lip balm from the center of the sink where it had fallen. I rubbed off the top layer and continued to reapply the sweet, sticky substance to my dried lips. I fought to focus on my lips in the bathroom mirror, but I saw Hope, eyes hard as she looked at me. When she spoke, I heard the hatred in her voice.

"Sky," Hope said.

I wasn't sure if the acknowledgment was a greeting or an accusation, so I replied in kind, "Hope."

But was there any hope that we'd be able to come to some kind of understanding? Hope that one day we might actually be able to eat lunch together? Hope that someone would build a few extra floors onto the school to make our game of hide-and-seek a bit more challenging?

Hope walked over to the sink next to the one where I stood, looked in the mirror, and pretended to fix her hair even though it was already perfect—not a strand out of place. I checked myself out again in the mirror above my sink and pretended that I needed more lip balm. It was obvious to me that Hope had something to say, so I was willing to endure wax buildup to hear what it was.

"How is teaching here working out for you?" Hope asked.

I pursed my lips a bit because I knew that my contentment with the job was of no real concern to Hope. Her motives were all about bait and switch. Her question was the pat on the shoulder that preceded the knife in the back.

"The job is great. The kids are great, eager. I'm enjoying myself immensely."

"That's nice," Hope replied as she smoothed out her eyebrows with a sharp-edged, precious pink-painted pointer finger.

Her voice was icy, hard and I watched in her mirror as she pushed her hair around her head without really moving it at all. It was like shaking out a sweater. I'd thought about keeping the conversation going just to see what she would do next, thought I'd ramble on about some project or the other that I had the kids working on while I waited to see how long before she presented her blade. But Hope's patience had worn thin almost immediately.

"Why haven't you called my sister?" She turned and faced me, a deeply creviced scowl on her face.

I stared back at her. Not directly, mind you. I used my mirror as a buffer this time. Here we go, I thought. My scalp tingled and I felt my face become flushed.

"Why hasn't she called me?" I squished up my face in anger, in an attempt to appear appalled, then swung around from the sink with my hand on my hip. A tried and true defensive gesture.

"Call you?" Hope chuckled with a mouth like that of an angrily carved jack-o-lantern. "*You're* the one who threw her out of *your* home and now *you* want *her* to call *you*? Not even! She is devastated, humiliated, and now you want her to lower herself even further by calling you? You are definitely buggin'! Why would she do that, Sky? Would you do that?"

Hope's face was twisted like a big pretzel and her neck was rolling around her shoulders like a blender. I didn't know what to say, but she was definitely becoming a bit too loud for my taste. We were at work for God's sake!

Of course, I didn't really expect Grace to call me. Hope was right, why would she? But on some other crazy level, I thought, hoped, that maybe, just maybe, she would. Maybe Grace knew and understood my struggle and felt some tinge of sympathy and would reach out to tell me that everything would be okay. That she understood and had herself at one time been afraid to take that initial step "out" into the world of lesbianism. That she, too, had once grappled with the same fears. But that was just wishful thinking. As I stood there coming to terms with this realization, I knew I couldn't explain any of this to Hope. She wouldn't understand, so I just mumbled the few words that came to mind.

"I…I don't know what to say."

"Well, you need to think of something and soon because my sister did not deserve to be treated like that."

"I didn't exactly throw her out on her ear for God's sake. I politely asked her to leave."

"You humiliated her. She poured her heart out to you and you stepped all over it!"

"Okay, now I think you're being a bit dramatic. She didn't pour her heart out to me. The whole gist was more like, 'Hey, I'd like to screw you.' If she considers that pouring her heart out, then she should have poured it on someone else's living room floor. I don't find that romantic at all. Thus, the reason why she needed to bounce."

"Thus? Thus? Sky, this is not some school paper you're writing. This is my sister's life, her dignity. But you don't care do you? If you did, you would have called her by now."

In her enthusiasm and sisterly chivalry, Hope had ventured a little too close to my face. I heard a click in my head as my mind switched to fighting mode. My blood percolated, my heart rate quickened, and my fists were curled into tight tiny ham-shaped balls. It was about to be three o'clock on the playground, but in the bathroom! The only thing missing was the jeering of the crowd. At that moment I was grateful for the heavy thickness of the large, brown bathroom door. It may not have been soundproofed, but I hoped that it caught and held our voices so only pressed ears would hear our confrontation.

This is a new job, a little voice in my head said. You don't want to lose it. The voice was right. So instead of hitting Hope, I grabbed my lunch bag off the ledge that jutted out from the bottom of the bathroom mirror and headed for the door. I chose flight not fight and I felt good about my decision, mature. Let Hope think what she wanted to think. Really, this whole thing was between Grace and me, and I wanted to leave it like that.

As I pushed open the bathroom door, I turned to Hope and said, "I don't know about you, but I'm hungry. Catch you on the flip side!" I yelled a corny phrase from my childhood that seemed a very appropriate way to end our confrontation.

"Go! Go eat your stupid turkey sandwich, you turkey!"

But Hope was all wrong about me. I was a vegetarian.

CHAPTER FIFTEEN

After school, I headed straight to the gym where, for three hours, I released my anger and frustration by executing every exercise imaginable. I ran, kickboxed, lifted weights, biked, climbed stairs, everything. You name it and it was done. By the time I finished sashaying around in the fast-paced African dance class, I was calm, sore, and very tired. But all the drama of the day was forgotten and forgiven. So, Grace made a pass at me, big deal. I mean, secretly, I was extremely flattered and totally over the moon about her interest in me, but I wanted to keep these feeling under wraps. Why start something that I knew I'd be too afraid to finish? And if I was being honest, Hope rushing to defend her sister was totally to be expected. If I had a sister, I might have done the same. The more I thought about it and exercised on it, the more foolish I felt for not returning Grace's or Ola's calls, two women who befriended me when I had no one. I couldn't believe I'd acted so poorly, so immaturely. The whole reason I came to New York was to be my true self and, yet here I was hiding and acting like a green country girl all frightened. I remembered I'd read a book once that had a great acronym for fear—False Evidence Appearing Real. At the time, it had stuck with me, but it seemed that I'd forgotten it as of late. No more fear-based living for me!

By the time I made it back to the Bronx from Manhattan, the sun was beginning to set. Clouds that resembled the fluffy backsides of woolly sheep ran horizontally across the sky as they absorbed and reflected the sun's reddish rays and turned the rooftops and building facades the color of freshly splattered blood. The air was warm and still, and the Bronx, unlike Manhattan, allowed space to move around. That was what I loved about the borough; as I strolled down the streets, I was able to walk *and* swing my bag. I was able to twirl and even skip if I wanted! No one bumped into me. No one walked directly behind me, accidentally stepping on the back of my heels. I didn't have to dodge people who insisted on walking three abreast along narrow city streets. Yes, the Bronx had many vacant lots overrun with bushes, trees, and wild grasses, but as I passed them, the abundantly sweet smell of plant-generated oxygen filled my lungs. In the many parks I passed on my way home, I witnessed children playing on swings and scooting down slides while their mothers sat on park benches gossiping, holding other children lovingly on their laps. I also loved the Greenways. As dusk approached, I knew that rabbits, wild turkeys, bats, and opossums, which I'd often seen on the nature trails, would either be rushing out to acquire their last meal of the day or groggily waking to face the night head on. I wanted to stop by a trail on my way home to watch the frenzy, but I was too tired, so I headed straight home.

Along the path that cornered my neighbor's yard and blocked the view of my condo was a bank of mailboxes. I stopped to open mine. Inside there were several envelopes. One in particular caught my attention because my name was scrawled across the front of it in handwriting that was vaguely familiar to me, but I couldn't pinpoint to whom exactly it belonged. I flipped the envelope over and searched for a return address. There was none. I closed my mailbox, walked toward my place, and continued to study the envelope and the handwriting on it. As I neared my stoop, I looked up. Grace sat on the top step, forearms pressed into her thighs, her thin hands clasped tightly between her knees. The redness of the setting sun showed up in her skin and gave her eyes a fiery glow. She appeared to be burning. I was rooted to the spot, set aflame. Grace smiled, stood, and walked toward me. I smiled back and threw my arms out to embrace her as I flung fear aside. Grace clung to me and I to her. We held each other tight. I felt passion, apprehension, and desire surge through me, but no fear. No false evidence. Everything I felt at that moment was real.

"It's good to see you," Grace said. Her chin moved up and down on the top of my shoulder.

"It's good to be seen," I said and gently pulled away to look at her.

"How are you?" I asked tentatively, afraid of the angry words she might say.

"I'm fine. I heard about today with you and Hope. I wanted to apologize. She had no right to accost you in that way. I wanted you to know that I did not put her up to it. Hope tends to be overprotective. I'm sorry."

"Please, don't apologize. I'm to blame. I should've called you. I'm so sorry I asked you to leave that day. It was rude and I hurt your feelings. Hope may be overprotective, but she was right. I should be the one apologizing, so please, please forgive me. I acted like a jerk again. I'm so, so sorry."

Grace gently squeezed my arms. "Apology accepted," she said.

We hugged again and as Grace pulled away from me, her hands slid from around my arms to around my waist. Her fingertips burned and vibrated desire into my hips.

"Does this mean we're friends again?" I asked as I fought to maintain a cover of cool composure.

"We're more than friends," Grace replied, which immediately piqued my interest. "We're friends who have survived a spat," she said.

"That's true. Maybe we should celebrate," I said.

"Maybe," Grace said, a sly smile on her face. "Shall we go inside?"

CHAPTER SIXTEEN

I set Grace up with two wineglasses and the remainder of a chilled bottle of chardonnay before I went upstairs to shower. When I came back down, we drank, talked, listened to music, and played Boggle, Upwords, and Rack-O, for several hours. Grace won practically every game of Rack-O. I was convinced she was cheating but I couldn't prove it, so I got up and went to the kitchen for more wine, vowing to exact my revenge upon my return. Grace laughed as she shuffled the stack of cards again.

I felt light and airy as I grabbed the second bottle of chardonnay out of the refrigerator by its thin neck and set it down with a "plop" in front of me. I slipped a Grace Jones compact disc into the player on my way back from the kitchen. Sexy French words slid out of Grace Jones's mouth as if they were on ice—gliding and backpedaling to the tempo.

I looked at Grace Jones's picture on the cover of the disc. Androgynous, dark, and beautiful, with cheekbones high and sharp enough to cut someone's heart out. I swayed my way back to my spot on the hard linoleum floor in front of the coffee table. Just as my rump touched the floor, the telephone rang. I flopped back at the thought of having to get up yet again. The wine rushed to my head and sloshed around in my belly. Tipsy was passing the baton to drunk and I had trouble getting myself up off the floor again. Grace, who sat there and witnessed my struggle, laughed at me which, in turn, made me laugh and fall back down to the floor.

"Do you want me to get that?" Grace asked. Her speech sounded slurred. I found this to be hilarious and laughed harder. The phone rang two more times. It sounded angry as it rocked in its cradle like a baby left in its crib. It screamed and the vibrations undulated through the thin kitchen wall.

"No, no. I'll get it."

With much focus and help from the edge of the coffee table, I managed to stand and answer the phone by the sixth ring.

"Hello," I said, hip pressed against the kitchen counter to hold me steady.

"Hello, dear," my mother replied.

I wanted to laugh at her timing, at the way she always seemed to know, even across several state lines, that I'd broken one of her rules. I tried to pull myself together because according to my mother, ladies did not drink and if they did, it should be no more than a sip. I was way over the limit.

"Hi, Mom. Wassup?"

I turned to see what Grace was doing, but she wasn't sitting where she'd been before. I looked around a bit more, but I didn't see her. I stopped my search because I was getting dizzy and I figured she'd gone to the bathroom or something. I turned my face to the wall and focused solely on what my mother was saying.

"Sky, it's your father. There's been an accident."

The room dipped then spun into the shape of a half moon. I struggled, but I managed to hold the contents of my stomach down. I did not want to hear another word, but I held the phone in my hand as tight and as steady as I could. The cheap wine climbed higher along the walls of my stomach, and my mom's ominous words rang over and over again and again in my ears—*there's been an accident.*

"Accident?" My voice shook. "Oh, God, please tell me he's all right."

"The doctors aren't sure yet. He's still in critical condition. They're saying he had a minor heart attack."

Crazy, but I breathed a sigh of relief. Not dead. I thought. Not dead.

"Minor heart attack? What does that mean, Mom? I'm sorry, but there is nothing minor about a heart attack."

"Well, the doctors are calling it minor. I guess they mean it could have been worse."

"He's in critical condition, Mom! That's not good. Not good at all!"

"Sky, calm down. I know it's not good. Please stop yelling."

I shut my eyes against the tears, balled up a fist.

"I just don't want them to label it minor and then treat Dad as such. Please don't let that happen. Keep on top of them. Have you been able to see him?"

"I saw him a few minutes ago. He's not talking, but he's being monitored. I'm keeping watch over him, don't worry."

"Oh, Mom. I'm so sorry I'm not there with you. I'll come home. I'll make arrangements."

I wiped my eyes as I wondered which airline to call, which flight to take, what to tell the school.

"No, no. I'm okay. You stay put. Your brother's here."

"No, Mom. I'm going to head home."

"No, there's no need. Henry is here and he's been very helpful. He's really been a great comfort to me."

"Are you sure?"

"Yes. We will keep you posted if anything new develops. Okay?"

"Okay, Mom. Tell Henry I said, hi. When you get the chance, give Dad a kiss for me. Tell him that I love him. And Mom?"

"Yes, Sky?"

"I love you too."

"I love you too, dear. Take care of yourself. Talk to you soon. Good night."

"Good night."

At the sound of the click the phone became an elephant, too heavy for me to lift. It dropped from my hand. I pushed my hot forehead deeper into the cool kitchen wall and cried.

"Sky? What's wrong?"

Grace stood behind me, her hands placed gently on my waist, unsure. I was so glad she was there with me. So glad I was not alone. But I couldn't answer her question right then. The thought of losing my father caused my heart to break and my shoulders shook from sobbing. Tears and snot streamed down my face and hung from my nose in a clear suspended line.

"Sky? Is there anything I can do?"

My feet like my father's feet. My toes like my father's toes. The floor. Everything, everything on the ground was blurred. I saw my father sitting beside me on my bed. I was five years old. My father was helping me prepare for school. My feet were propped up on his thighs. He was getting ready to put my socks on, but he stopped to examine my feet.

"You know," he said. His voice had been so full, so rich. "You look like your mother. You smile like your mother. You even walk like your mother. But you have my feet. These are my feet you're walking with. My feet that will march you into your future. Take good care of these here feet, Sky. They will support you all your life just like I will."

Then he brought my little toes up to his mouth and kissed them.

Grace held my waist a little tighter. I felt her uncertainty and her compassion. I turned and hugged her. She pulled me in close. I buried my head into her shoulder and wished that this terrible thing had not happened to my father. After a while, my tears subsided, and I was able to tell Grace about my father's heart attack.

"I'm so sorry, Sky. I hope everything will be okay. The important thing is to remain positive."

I saw mist in her eyes. "I know. I know. I'm just so glad you're here. I'm so glad I'm not alone tonight. What would I have done if I were by myself?"

"You would have called me. At least, I hope you would've. Anyway, that doesn't matter because I'm right here."

Grace hugged me again. I didn't want to let her go. I realized at that moment that I felt safe in her arms. A couple of weeks ago I couldn't have imagined that to be possible, but I found out that it was indeed possible. Or was it the wine? The comfort after the bad news? Or maybe it was just what it was. In her arms was where I belonged.

We stood in the kitchen holding on to each other for a while. I smelled the faint scent of raspberry as it escaped from Grace's armpit. The scent of cocoa butter, which smelled a lot like chocolate, emanated from the area around her collarbone. Her shirt was soft to the touch and my hands felt large and brutish as they held on to her slender frame. The tiny tip of her feathered earring brushed gently against the top of my head. I thought about denial. Denial of who and what I was. As I held on to Grace there, in my kitchen, it dawned on me how our embrace was a visual metaphor for how I needed to stand up and embrace myself, my life, and who I loved. My father's condition forced upon me the realization that I needed to accept who I was before it was too late.

Grace held me and stroked my back. She showed and shared her love for me in that moment and I knew if I let her, she would continue. I grew warm and my face burned with shame at the memory of having thrown her out, this woman who stood here with me without malice and who whispered softly in my ear how everything was going to be all right.

I looked up at Grace. With the back of her hand she wiped away the trails of tears that streaked my cheeks. The gesture was simple but powerful and passionate, and my heart swelled.

"Kiss me," I said.

Grace looked at me steadily, questioning.

"Sky, I don't think you need that on your plate right now. You have enough to contend with."

"Please, Grace."

"Seriously, I really don't think that's a good idea. Right now, I mean."

"But I've wanted to feel your kiss, your lips against mine for a long time. Not just because of what's happened here tonight."

"Really?"

"Yes."

"Then why did you kick me out?"

I lowered my head and looked at the floor for a bit before I met her eyes again. "I don't know. I was...frightened."

"Frightened? Of what?"

I turned away from her and walked back toward the living room. The empty wine bottles and game cards littered the floor and the top of the coffee table. Some wine had spilled and left a dark circular stain beside a lopsided stack of game cards and the sharp edge of the small white box the cards were housed in.

"Sky, frightened of what?"

Grace followed me a short distance into the living room, then stopped and leaned against the wall that divided the kitchen from the living room as if she knew that my response required distance.

"Of...of getting involved with another woman."

I stood in front of the coffee table and stared into the dark-ringed center of the wine stain.

"*Another* woman? But you told me you weren't attracted to women."

"Actually, I never answered your question. Anyway, at Ola's party you told me you weren't a lesbian. Then suddenly you tell me you want to sleep with me."

Grace rubbed her chin then rubbed her hands together. Then she shoved them into her pants pockets.

"Yeah, okay, I lied to you at Ola's party, but only because I saw how disturbed you were when you put two and two together about Ola. I didn't want to scare you away. I like you. I like spending time with you."

Grace walked over to me and put her hands on my shoulders.

"Hey, even if we never sleep together, I'd still like to hang out with you. I don't want you to feel pressured into being sexual with me. I'm here because I want to be here as a friend. I'm not here just to get into your pants."

Grace's eyes were soft and wet. I noticed her lips looked soft and wet as well.

"Thank you. That's good to know," I said. "And it's all the more reason why I want you to kiss me."

I tilted my head upward. I parted my lips and opened my mouth in offering. Grace looked down into my eyes. I ran the tip of my tongue slowly across my bottom lip. I quivered in anticipation.

Grace's voice was heavy with desire when she spoke. "Are you sure there won't be any regrets in the morning?"

Her large golden eyes had drooped to half-mast.

I glanced at the clock. "It's already morning and I have no regrets."

"Maybe you will when we're done."

"Maybe," I said and then ran my tongue across Grace's upper lip.

Grace raised an eyebrow in question. She lifted her head a little away from my protruding tongue.

"Maybe," I continued, "I'll regret that we didn't do this sooner."

Grace smiled.

I stretched my neck toward her again and gently kissed her lips. They were deliciously soft, sweet, and bruised with wine.

Grace pulled my body into hers. The music had stopped a while ago, but our hearts knocked a wild rhythm against our chests. Mine first, then hers responded. I was drunk with passion and desire for her. Her eyes said she felt as I did. When she spoke, her voice trembled with longing.

"Let's go to bed," she said.

I kissed her again. Harder and deeper. I wanted to devour her.

"Yes, let's," I murmured.

CHAPTER SEVENTEEN

Saturday morning and the world had changed. Everything was brighter and sharper. Too bright. Too sharp. The sunlight that snuck into my bedroom through the sheer yellow curtains that hung from the window was so effulgent it stabbed me. I closed my eyes against it, but the yellow rays banded together, sat on top of my eyelids, and bore their way in. I turned and tried to pull the sheet over my head, but ran into a lump called Grace. She was in my bed beside me. She sucked in and released soft puffs of air, and the sound made her presence beside me more real, more special. I wanted to think more about what had happened between Grace and me the night before, more about my poor dad, and more about my future, but my head felt like it weighed five thousand pounds. Every movement, every thought punched me in the belly and caused my mouth to sour.

"Sky? Are you awake?" Grace asked as she pulled at the blanket, but I couldn't respond. I didn't want to move anything, not even my mouth.

"Are you awake?" Grace asked again.

Grace turned her long body toward mine. The bed bucked and rocked like a boat on the wild seas and I wanted to throw Grace overboard to stop all the movement. I reached behind me, felt around for a bit, then firmly put my hand on her leg to stop the ruckus.

I managed to burp up a small, "Yes," to her question. My voice was scratchy due to extreme dryness.

"Are you sure?" Grace asked.

"Yes, but can't talk. Major headache."

"So…you're okay with what we did last night? I mean, no regrets or anything? No plans to toss me out on my ear again?"

"I'm fine."

Grace let out a sigh of relief. "Whew!"

Grace seemed excited. She moved about so much the bed felt like a boat caught in a storm. I squeezed the sheets tighter for fear of capsizing or throwing up, whichever came first. From the increased sour taste in my mouth, I'd say it was the latter.

Grace leaned toward me and semi-whispered in my ear. "We did drink a lot of wine last night. How many bottles was it?"

"Can't talk. Feel sick," I replied.

"Yeah, I'm a little hung over myself. Don't worry. I'll go make some breakfast. That should fix you right up."

Grace kissed me on the cheek and got out of bed. For that, I was grateful. I slowly pulled the sheets over my head and eased into a shallow breathing pattern, which helped me fall asleep.

When I awakened again, it was one thirty in the afternoon. The room was warm and the house was quiet, but the scent of onions and garlic danced deliciously around my nose. I sat up, pushed my feet into my slippers, and was about to get up and venture downstairs when the phone rang. My head wasn't pounding anymore, but the sound of the phone shaking in its cradle was loud, nonetheless. I picked it up on the first ring to avoid hearing the clamor a second time.

"Hello?"

"Hey, Sky."

"Henry? How's Dad?"

"Much better, but they want to keep him for some more tests."

"How's Mom doing?"

"She's good, hanging in there. Well, she puts on a good front anyway. If she bakes anything else for me to eat, I'm going to end up in here myself with type two diabetes!"

I chuckled. "That's Mom—Miss Betty Crocker. You can definitely count on her baking a cake or a pie or something anytime she gets nervous or upset. Right now, I'm sure she's both, so just take a few nibbles and give the rest to the neighbors."

"Yeah, I'll do that. Odeta's been asking about you. Said you haven't written or called her yet. Said you left town and forgot about everybody."

"Oh please, Odeta's just being dramatic. I'm busy with my new job. Tell her I'll write her soon or, hello, she could pick up a pen and write me!"

"Yeah, I'll tell her."

There was a brief bubble of silence. Then it popped.

"Delbert came to the hospital."

"I bet he did."

There was annoyance in my voice that I did not want to be there. I was tired of becoming upset every time Delbert's name was mentioned.

"He bought Dad a massive bouquet of flowers and he had another huge bouquet that he gave to Mom. Is that something men give to other men when they're hospitalized?"

"I don't know, but flowers are expensive and that's what Delbert wants you to notice."

"Oh, okay. I didn't know that. Anyway, he seems like a nice guy. I mean, I don't know much about him since I wasn't around much when you two were an item, but he seems nice. A little lonely, maybe, but not bad."

"Sounds like you two should get together," I said.

"I'm just saying."

"Yeah, I know what you're 'just saying.' Please, say no more. I made a decision that I am very happy with, thank you. I just wish everyone would respect it. Look, I have to go. Tell Mom and Dad I love them. I'll call tomorrow."

I was about to hang up when I heard my name.

"Sky," Henry said.

Here it comes, I thought. The "how could you leave such a good man" speech.

"Yes," I replied, nearing exasperation. Tension had made its way into my voice.

"If you're happy, I'm happy for you," Henry said.

I was shocked and then extremely grateful to have my big brother by my side. "Thanks, Henry." I smiled into the phone and hoped Henry felt my gratitude.

"And Sky."

"Yes, Henry?"

"Just make sure you really are happy."

"Goodbye, Henry!" I yelled and slammed the phone down.

I should have known he was going to say something backhanded. And actually, he had no right to try to lecture me on the certainty of my happiness when everything he did in life was out of obligation—the Navy, his marriage, his job. Henry wouldn't know happiness if it walked up to him and danced on his head! And he didn't know much about my relationship with Delbert because he was never around. He was always too busy doing God knows what to spend time with his little sis. As I thought about these things, I became more upset, so I was glad I'd slammed the phone down in his ear. Hypocrite!

I went downstairs and was headed toward the kitchen when I spotted yesterday's mail stacked on the arm of the couch. The letter with the familiar handwriting sat on top of the pile and I was still unable to place the penmanship, but I knew I'd seen it before. After Henry's comments about Odeta, I thought it might have been her hand. Maybe she had written me after all. I ripped open the envelope and read:

> To My Dearest Sky,
> I will be in town soon on business. I would love to see you. Maybe we can have dinner? See a movie? Have a drink together? Or maybe you'll let me into your new place of residence? I still love you, Sky. Deep down, I know you still love me too. We were good together. Have you forgotten that? Was our leap toward marriage too fast for you? Maybe we should have waited then

you would still be here with me. I'm willing to wait for you, Sky.
Fool around in New York, but come back to me. I'm willing to
wait so we can try again. We owe it to ourselves to try again.
   With all my heart.
   Delbert

Fucking Delbert! I didn't want to be pissed off, but he just pushed me there. What was wrong with him? I tore the letter and the envelope into tiny pieces and crumpled it all up into the ball of my fist. I would have burned the whole damn thing if I had a match.

I was starting to get stalker vibes from Delbert. I thought about who had given him my address because I was not listed in the phone book. I made sure of that. Most likely, he'd wrestled the information out of my mom. Or maybe, she'd just given it to him, him being a "good man" and all. Anyway, it didn't matter because I knew that if Delbert showed up on my doorstep he definitely would not get the same treatment as Grace.

CHAPTER EIGHTEEN

"I smell garlic and onions. Are you still working on breakfast?" I asked as I entered the kitchen.

Grace stood at the stove, her head perched over a sizzling frying pan. I walked over, stood behind her, and held on tight to her waist.

"Breakfast? No, you slept through that. This, my dear, will be brunch."

Grace straightened her stance, turned, and kissed me. The pungent smell of garlic combined with the tangy smell of onions mixed with the sweetness of her kiss was delicious.

"Well, whatever it is, I can't wait to have some of your home cookin'. Will there be biscuits and gravy?"

Grace swiftly chopped off the bulbous heads of the mushrooms with steady pressure from one of my sharp knives.

"Well, well, so, you are Southern after all," Grace said with a smile.

"Yes, I am."

I let go of Grace, walked around the corner to the living room and picked up a pale wooden stool from under the kitchen counter overhang that protruded into the living room, brought it into the kitchen, and sat down and watched as Grace finished chopping and slicing unsuspecting vegetables.

"Was that phone call news about your father?" Grace asked.

"Yeah, my brother, Henry, called. He said my dad is getting better. He said…he said my…uh, my uh ex bought these humongous bouquets of flowers for my father and my mother. He wanted to know if that was something men got for other men when they are hospitalized."

I was hesitant, but I knew, at some point, I'd have to address my past. I wanted Grace to know that my ex was male. I wasn't sure how she would feel about this information, but I put it out there anyway. I noticed that she took some time to respond. She grabbed more eggs, cracked them, and proceeded to scramble the yolks in a steady and thoughtful manner. I watched her face, then her hands, then I looked back at her face. She was steeped in an aura of concentration. Most likely thinking and measuring her words as carefully as she had folded and mixed the egg yolks. Finally, she let out a sigh.

"Um…I'm not sure as to what men get other men when they are hospitalized, but maybe flowers are appropriate. Who knows?"

"Yeah, maybe," I said, relieved that her reply addressed only the flowers.

"So, I just want you to know that I usually don't move as fast in a relationship as we did last night. I'm guessing, hoping, you don't either."

Graced had tried to make her statement seem like a statement, but I knew it was a question in disguise. A poor one.

"No, no, I don't either," I said.

"Good. We should've discussed a lot of things before we jumped into bed together such as you being bisexual. Sometimes the moment becomes bigger than us and we forget things."

"I'm not bisexual," I said.

"How so? Before you told me you were with a woman and now you're telling me your most recent ex is a man, so it seems to me that you are."

Grace divided the cooked eggs between the two plates that were on the kitchen counter then put the hot pan in the sink. It hissed loudly at first, then quieted just as the brown heads of toast popped up from the toaster.

"Well, I'm not, but if I was, would that be a problem for you?"

"I'm not sure," Grace said.

We were both silent for a bit. Grace buttered the toast and I sat staring out of the kitchen window as I thought about my life choices and how to explain them. And why I had to.

"What about you? Have you ever been with a man?"

"No, I haven't," Grace replied.

She poured orange juice into my cup, then pushed my meal in front of me.

"Eat up," she said with a dour face.

I got up and grabbed a fork from the drying rack. Grace stood opposite me. She cut her toast into tiny pieces, then dug in, sending tiny crumbs of dry bread tumbling to the floor.

Grace tore a section of paper towel from the roll situated in the corner of the kitchen counter and wiped her mouth.

"Did you love this guy? How serious were you two?"

"No, I didn't love him, but, um, let's see, how can I explain this? Let's just say he was a safe choice. He was like the quintessential man to have by my side so everyone would look at me and think, no *see* that I was normal, that I wasn't some deviant."

"So, are you saying lesbians are deviants?"

"No, I'm not, but other people do, especially in the South."

"So, this guy was your beard."

"My what?"

"Beard. You know, he was this like false front that you used to hide the true you underneath."

"Wow is that what it's called? A beard. Yeah, then, I guess so. My mother, God bless her, but she can be a pain in the butt and very meddlesome. She had gotten it into her head that this guy was 'the one' for me. She started talking marriage every time he was around, and he grabbed on to the idea like it was his own and then poof everything was planned and paid for. My protests fell on deaf ears. My mother insisted that she knew what was best for me and in the end, I'd thank her."

"Wow! No shit!" Grace exclaimed then sipped her juice.

"No shit," I said.

"How did you get out of that?"

"I was what we call in the South a runaway bride."

Grace pressed her hand to her mouth in an effort to stop an outburst of juice.

"No shit! You ditched him at the altar? Oh my God! Very gutsy move."

"I had to. I just couldn't go through with it. I mean, yes, he's well-off. He has a mini mansion, owns his own company, and drives a nice car, so it's true, I'd probably want for nothing, but I felt like I was dying the whole time I was hiding behind this image of 'normal.' For a long time, I've been afraid of what my family would think of me, my friends, society. To be honest, I'm still afraid, but I took the first step toward shedding that fear by moving up here, to the Bronx."

I drank the rest of my juice and put down my glass. Grace filled it up again, then raised her glass. "Cheers to the runaway bride!"

I smiled and raised my glass. We toasted to my bold act, then sipped our drinks.

"You were afraid, Sky, but you have to know that that took guts. Leaving someone standing at the altar, that's badass! I'm sure he was pissed."

"Very. He still hasn't accepted it. He keeps trying to get in contact with me, keeps doing things for my family. It bugs the hell out of me."

"His ego is bruised. He's feeling less manly."

"Yeah, I guess so, but it's still extremely annoying."

Grace gathered the plates, forks, and glasses. She scraped the remaining bits of food into the trash and placed everything in the sink.

"I'll wash them," I said.

I got up, walked over to the sink, and turned on the hot water. I tested the water's warmth as I moved my hand into and out of its downpour. Grace stood beside me staring at the refrigerator lost in thought.

Finally, she uttered, "You know, he'll probably try to get you back in order to prove his manliness. I like you a lot and I'm hoping we can be more than just fuck buddies. Is this something I need to worry about?"

I held a soapy fork in my hand.

"More, as in being together, together? Like a couple?"

Grace smiled then laughed.

"Yes. Okay, wait, let's make this official."

Grace got down on one knee and grabbed my soapy hand in hers.

"Would you, Sky Valentine, like to be my girlfriend? Think carefully before you respond and remember, there's nowhere for you to run."

I laughed. She looked so sweet down there on one knee. Half of her face glowed as the sunlight waned.

"Yes, Grace. I'd love to be your girlfriend."

I leaned over to kiss her, but she stopped me, holding my face in her hands. Her eyes looked serious and deep.

"Are you sure?"

"Very," I said.

Grace let go of my face and we kissed long and hard. My groin stirred and my nipples hardened.

"Let's go upstairs and celebrate," Grace said in a sultry voice.

I rinsed the soap from my hands and turned off the water. Tiny bits of brunch lay bunched up beneath the soapsuds that remained in the sink.

Grace held my hand as she led me up the short flight of stairs and into the bedroom. The scent of onions, fried eggs, and toast lingered on the top floor of the condo, and butter had been slathered onto the air.

The sun burned through the sheerness of the curtains and left the room feeling very warm. I walked toward the pedestal fan, switched it on, and pressed the button that stated "high." A million kisses of forced air flew out and marched across my face, cooling it, and burning my eyes before the fan turned its dark, round head.

Grace had on the same T-shirt she'd worn the day before. Today it looked tired as it hung crooked and loose over her thin shoulders. She gathered the material that billowed under her arms with both hands and slowly pulled the shirt over her head. Her torso was a highly polished brown color, almost bronze. Her breasts were high and full, regal-looking with nipples that were small, black, and pinched to perfection. When she removed the pajama bottoms I loaned her the night before, I saw that her legs were long and lean, but not overly muscled. The dark tangle of hair that puffed out between them looked thick and quite dense compared to my own. I wanted to touch, see, taste, know the mystery beneath it all. All of these things, all of her beauty I had missed the night before in my drunken stupor. We had fornicated in a frenzy like bees eager to taste the first nectar of spring. I saw the woman, but I had missed the beauty she was composed of. Now, I wanted to hold her, to touch her, to fondle the full orbs of her breasts that absorbed the late afternoon sun and made her skin shine. I wanted to kiss her succulent lips and smell the warmth that encircled the base of her neck. I wanted to love her, to make love to her in slow motion, to feel every sensation, every vibration. I wanted to listen fully to every sound she'd make, to the beating of her heart as it grew rapidly into a gallop. I imagined the taste of salt on her skin as my tongue passed over it. I wanted us to make love as slow as sloths in summer. I undid the belt that fastened my robe and revealed myself to her.

"Come," Grace whispered.

I walked toward her. My robe fell softly to the floor and I felt the cool air from the fan dance across my naked back and bare ass. I put a hand on her shoulder. With my other hand, I cradled her head cupping the soft small curls that coiled loosely there.

Grace held the sides of my face with both of her hands. Her eyes were dreamy, heavy, and so sexy. Pressed together, our bodies swayed and pulsed with desire and so much longing. I pulled her head toward me as I leaned into her. Our kisses, all lips at first, then tongues slipped and searched, transferring what we felt in our hearts. Grace's hands ran down the length of my back, then moved toward my ass. She caressed its fullness, massaging and gripping its roundness. This ignited my clitoris and caused my hips to gyrate against her pubis. Her great triangle of hair tickled my thighs and sent sparks toward my pussy that fed my flame.

Grace parted my legs with her own. Immediately, I began my slow ride and like a well-oiled lock, we fit together perfectly. I grabbed her ass, backed her up against one of the bedroom walls, tongued her like she was a lollipop, and pinned her arms up beside her head. Our breathing intensified. The air around us was hotter than it had been before. Grace's tongue was deep inside my mouth. Our legs were intertwined, and our hips and clits sought sexual satisfaction amidst our shared wetness. Grace gyrated and my body responded as I leaned fully into her, riding her faster and faster like a train about to jump the track, the conductor lured to the beauty of the edge.

"Oh, yes! Yes! Give it to me!" I shouted.

Grace lowered me to the floor and situated herself between my legs at just the right angle to allow our vulvas to rub against one another. I felt her clit hard against my own and the warmth of her wetness brought me to the brink of excitement. I burst through the tunnel of love into an explosion of light and sound and emotion. I grabbed Grace's hands, grabbed her hair, grabbed her neck, and held her tight. Seconds later she had her own explosion and bucked wildly against me, flooding me with her juices. She wrapped her arms around me and moaned, squeezing me as sweet orgasmic spasms rolled through us.

CHAPTER NINETEEN

It was early evening when we decided to get out of bed and go out on the town. I lent Grace an old T-shirt that had a picture of Michael Jackson on it. He had on a black and red outfit with the name of his album, *Thriller*, scrawled in thick red letters under his feet. I also let her borrow a pair of black pants I'd recently bought that were too long for me. The pants were a bit too big in the waist, but I slapped a belt on her and we headed out to Greenwich Village. I hadn't been downtown much since I'd arrived and didn't really know my way around, so Grace was the designated guide.

We took the bus, the BX 39, to Hugh J. Grant Circle, which was located in a neighborhood called Parkchester, in order to get a train that would take us downtown. I had heard about the New York City subways, so I was expecting the train to be underground, but it wasn't. The train platform at Hugh J. Grant Circle was an aboveground—elevated—train. It was massive and long and it reminded me of a prehistoric creature that had been preserved, domesticated, and was now used by hordes of people.

Inside the station, I saw a sign taped to the Plexiglas booth the train worker was sitting in stating that the cost of a train ride was one dollar. I dug around in my bag to find some coins to pay for my ride. I had four quarters in my hand, and I walked toward the stairs that led, I assumed, up to the train.

"And where do you think you're going?" Grace called after me.

"Upstairs. That's where the train is, right?"

Grace coughed out a laugh. "Yes, the train is upstairs, but you need to pay down here."

"Oh," I said and walked back to where she stood.

She was in a short line behind a light-skinned girl who wore a gold chain around her neck with a nameplate that read, "FLY" in large gold letters. Her hair was slicked back into a long, shiny black ponytail and she had ferreted out her baby hairs and plastered them down along the sides of her head with grease that was visible from where I stood.

"And we're in this line because?" I asked.

"We need to get tokens."

"Oh, so we can't just give our money to the train conductor when we get on the train?"

Grace laughed again. "No, love. It doesn't work like that." She pointed to the woman inside the booth. "She is a token booth clerk. We give her our money, she gives us some tokens, we put it in the turnstile, and then we go frolic near the tracks. See, simple."

I thought it would be a lot simpler to just pay on the train, but what did I know. Grace gave our money to the clerk. The clerk counted it and handed Grace back some coins. Grace then, in turn, handed me a dull, scuffed, gold-looking coin with a round bull's-eye in its center made from a silver-colored metal. We walked over to the green and silver turnstiles and Grace instructed me to drop the token into the slot on top of the turnstile and push through. I did as I was told, then we went up two long flights of stairs to wait for the train.

Five minutes later, the train platform began to vibrate beneath my feet and within seconds a brick-red train thundered down the tracks and blew my hair and Grace's earring around with gusto. We boarded and I found a small corner seat for two where Grace and I sat looking at the closed door of the conductor's booth. Someone had drawn a large, red heart around the keyhole on the conductor's door with a permanent marker. Inside the heart, right above the keyhole, the person wrote, "RW + LP."

I pointed to the writing. "I guess RW loves LP, huh," I commented.

"Looks that way," Grace replied. "Key to someone's heart."

"Hey, where's all the graffiti? I thought the trains in New York had layer upon layer of graffiti on them?" I looked around the train and from where I sat, I didn't see much. Someone had spray-painted three windows with the words "Boogie Down Bronx"—one word per window. And on one of the advertisements, which were located above the metal handles people held on to, someone had drawn a large, handlebar mustache on the older woman in the advertisement and had written in the speech bubble that was drawn beside her picture, "I just can't handle this." Other than that, I didn't see much graffiti, but my view was blocked by the impressive number of people who had boarded the train car along with us. As I looked out at the almost crowded train car, I was more than glad I had a job that I could walk to and that I'd be able to avoid the long journey to the train every morning and all these people.

"Yeah, the MTA cut the plug on that a few years ago, so you just missed it. New York City has cleaned up its act…almost."

"Almost?"

"There are still trains covered in graffiti in the poorer sections of the city. They haven't received their letters about the upgrade as of yet, if you know what I mean."

I didn't really know what Grace was talking about, but I nodded my head up and down and replied, "Yeah."

We tramped around Union Square Park, urinated at Barnes & Noble, and got a couple of appetizers at Zen Palate where I was introduced to scallion pancakes. We approached the humongous white arch that marked the entrance to Washington

Square Park, walked under it, and sat on the rim of the stately fountain located in the center of the park as the wind blew droplets from the cascading fountain water onto my face and neck. We watched a middle-aged, black comedian yell and fool around and work the crowd for change. Meanwhile a young, white guy in a dingy white sailor's shirt with a yellow bandana wrapped around his head played his guitar on a bench near the children's playground. The pungent smell of marijuana wafted through the air toward me and I spotted a large rat as it ran from under one bench to another just as the sun was on the verge of vanishing from the sky. The night doled out stars that the bright lights of the city obscured, but I was still able to find the Little Dipper and I pointed it out to Grace.

Around nine o'clock, although it was still relatively early, I began to feel tired. I guessed I had not fully recovered from last night's hangover.

"Should we call it a night? Head back uptown?"

Grace looked at me like I'd said some bad words.

"Head back uptown? No way! Let's go and have a drink."

Grace stood and pulled at my arm to get me to stand too. I tumbled forward off the fountain's rim.

"I don't know," I protested. "I'm still trying to get rid of my hangover from last night and what if my mom calls with news about my dad?"

Grace stood in front of me, holding me at the elbows as if I were in danger of losing control. I was. I felt like grabbing her and kissing her all over her sweet, kissable face, but my enthusiasm was curbed by the crowd of possible onlookers.

"Sky, I don't mean to sound insensitive, but you have an answering machine. Your mom will leave a message. I promise to remind you to check your messages when you get home, okay?" Grace looked at me all doe-eyed and eager.

"Oh, okay," I relented.

When we entered Pandora's Box—which sat on the corner of Grove Street and Seventh Avenue, catty-corner to a place called the Sheridan Square Restaurant—Grace informed me that it was a small, predominantly black and Latina lesbian bar. She said it was called The Grove and Duchess years ago, but now it had new owners.

The place was practically empty, and the lighting was almost as scarce as the people. There was a long bar by the door, a couple of wooden tables placed haphazardly along the walls, a decent-sized dance floor, and what appeared to be a small stage in the rear. Nothing gleamed or glistened, not even the bar that was constantly being wiped down by the bartender. But the music was excellent.

"Grace! Hey, how are you? Haven't seen you around in a while," the bartender said with long fluid motions of her rag across the mirrored bar top.

"Hey, Suzy. I'm good. Keeping busy."

Suzy looked at me with a sly smile and a roving eye. "I see."

Grace laughed and turned toward me. "Sky, this is Suzy. Suzy, Sky."

"Hello," we both uttered in unison.

"Sky…is that your given name?" Suzy asked.

"Yes, it is."

"Hmm, nice. Welcome to Pandora's. Your first time right? I don't recall seeing you in here before."

"Sky just moved to New York from North Carolina," Grace offered.

"Got tired of the country, huh?" Suzy inquired.

"Something like that."

"I know all about it. Louisiana born and bred. How's New York treatin' ya?"

"Pretty good so far," I said.

"Nice. New town, new friends, how about trying a new drink? You two can be the first ones to try my new mixture. I'm calling it Suzy's Sunshine."

Suzy handed us two tumblers filled with bright yellow liquid.

"If you like it, it's free. If you don't, you'll have to pay," Suzy said teasingly.

Grace took the first sip. I really didn't feel like drinking again, especially if it was gonna taste like crap, but I wanted to be polite. I watched Grace's face. She smacked her lips, smiled, and took another sip. A good sign. I took a sip of my drink. It was sweet, like citrus mixed with a little coconut. And there was a hint of mango in it too.

"This tastes great," I said.

"Exceptional," said Grace.

Suzy smiled. "Now, do I make a mean drink, or do I make a mean drink?" Suzy asked. The merriment behind the question seemed to sharpen Suzy's blue eyes and they appeared brighter amid the dimness of the bar.

"Which question do you want us to answer first?" Grace asked.

We all laughed and then Suzy shooed us on.

"You ladies better get a table before the place gets packed."

We took our glasses of sunshine and found a table away from the large speakers. The music wasn't too loud, so we were able to talk to each other without shouting.

There were two women across from us who were engrossed in conversation. At another table, there were four women laughing, drinking, and talking. Prince's "Kiss," came on and two of the women headed for the dance floor. There was one woman there alone. She sat at the end of the bar looking down into her drink. Most of the women looked like your average, everyday women—hair done up, nails painted, some in flowing dresses with brightly colored lipstick smeared across their lips. There were two or three women who fit the "dyke" stereotype with short, short hair, plaid shirts, and construction boots, but that was it. I was surprised. I had expected more of the latter. It was nice to see that variety was accepted and I was comforted to know that there were no expectations, no molds to be filled.

Grace finished her drink five seconds before I finished mine.

"I think we need another round of sunshine," she said.

I nodded. Grace got up and headed for the bar. I looked around the room again. The two women who had been talking before were now holding hands. Their conversation had morphed into tender kisses and I noticed that I was the only one gawking at them. The other ladies were doing their own thing, as if the sight of two women openly kissing was an everyday occurrence. As if it was no big deal. It was a big deal to me! Very big! So I gawked a while longer and wondered if I'd grow to be so cavalier, so blasé upon witnessing two women holding hands and kissing and sharing the affection they had for each other with the world. Would I acquire their boldness, their seemingly blatant disregard concerning the opinion of others now that I was Grace's girl? That's who I was now, who I'd become: Grace's girl. I was a lesbian in a lesbian bar waiting for her lesbian lover. I glanced at Grace. She was standing at the bar, one foot up on the ledge that jutted out about two inches from the bar's bottom, her elbows pushed hard into the thin wood at the bar's edge. The sleeves of my long-sleeved T-shirt flopped down just below her wrists. I couldn't help but smile. I really liked Grace. She was smart, caring, funny, educated, good-looking, and very sexy—many of the qualities I sought in a lover, a girlfriend. But was it enough? What about my family? What would they say when I eventually told them about Grace? What would they think of me? What would they think of Grace? Would they see her like I see her? My mom would probably bake herself right into her own bakery. And my dad? Oh, my dad. How would he take the news? Anyway, everything was all so new. I didn't even know if it would last, so there really was no rush to tell anyone about anything at this point. No need to jump the gun.

Grace returned to the table with our drinks. We finished those and had a few more rounds of Suzy's Sunshine, then I needed to use the restroom.

"Where's the outhouse?" I yelled.

Grace pointed toward the stage. "To the right of the stage and down the stairs. It's crowded in here now, so there's going to be a line. Good luck," she yelled back into my ear.

She was right. The place was now packed, and the music was blaring. I squeezed and squirmed my way through a lot of women in an effort to reach the stairs that led down to the bathroom. I walked down three of the six steps and stopped. A line had formed and there appeared to be five women ahead of me. I stood behind a brown-skinned, heavyset woman with a short Afro who popped her gum and snapped her fingers to the loud beat of the music that filtered down from upstairs.

I felt a tap on my shoulder. I turned around and saw a light-skinned woman with dark brown freckles scattered across her cheeks and nose. Her lips were pink and juicy, and her smile was bright.

"I like your hair," she said.

"Thanks," I replied.

"How did you get it to lock? Was it a hard process?"

"No, just kept twisting it. My hair sort of naturally coils, so it was sort of doing it on its own anyway."

"Oh," she said. "Reminds me of Whoopi Goldberg."

I tossed my head to the side a bit and raised my eyebrows. "Yeah, I hear that a lot," I said. Then it was finally my turn to use the bathroom.

On the way back to the table, I noticed my seat was occupied. I could only see the back of the person's head, but I noticed the huge smile on Grace's face and what looked like major merriment in her eyes.

"Here she is. I thought I might have to head down to the bathroom to fish you out," Grace said as she stood and pulled out an empty chair for me to sit in.

"Well, well. Look who's in the Box. Thank you so very much for returning my calls."

It was Ola. She tried to make her statement sound like a joke, but I knew better. I also knew that she definitely had a right to be upset with me.

"Hi, Ola," I yelled over the music. I leaned toward her. "I am so very sorry that I did not return your calls, but I can explain," I pleaded.

Actually, I couldn't really explain because my response to what had happened was irrational, but I thought I could buy some time to think of an explanation instead of saying something stupid like, "Finding out about your lesbian status freaked me out." It just wouldn't really jive with where we were. It would have seemed totally hypocritical and dumb, which, indeed, it was. But I was the first to admit that sometimes I did dumb things. Not responding to Ola's calls was high up on my list.

"No need to explain, Sky. In fact, everything will be forgiven if you dance with me. Right here and right now."

"Oh, uh, I'm not a good dancer. Remember?"

"From what I can recall, you were a pretty good dancer, and, oh, listen…they're playing my song. Let's go! I want us to make amends. Don't you?"

From what I recalled, practically every song was Ola's song. But I did want to make amends. I looked at Grace.

"Do you mind?" I asked, hoping she was astute enough to see that *now* was the time to 'fish me out' of a situation.

"No, not at all," Grace said with a big shit-eating grin on her face.

"Thanks," I mouthed. She waved at me as Ola pulled me onto the small dance floor.

As soon as Ola and I made it to the dance floor, the thumping beat of House Music was replaced with the funky sounds of Prince's song, "Another Lover Hole N Yo Head."

"Ow, that's my jam!" Ola squealed.

It was my jam too, but I didn't share that with Ola. Instead I commented, "It seems you have a vast array of favorites." I almost laughed at what I had said because it reminded me so much of something Grace would have said. The sarcastic overlay was perfect.

"Yes, in fact, I do," Ola said. "I love music. So, you and Grace are an item now?"

"Are you asking me or telling me?"

"Asking? Is there something wrong with asking?"

Ola stopped dancing and looked at me with her face screwed up.

"Didn't Grace tell you? I saw the two of you talking and laughing at the table when I came back from the bathroom."

"Have you slept with her yet?"

"I thought we came out here to dance?"

Ola looked at me. Her expression was grave. I saw a hint of Odeta in her eyes and posture. It made me think about my past. Red dirt and collard greens. Sunshine, slow times, and small minds. Things I came North to get away from. I turned away from Ola, but I continued to dance as I turned toward Grace and hoped to catch her eye. Maybe she'd see my distress and save me.

Another woman, thin and bald with huge, gold hoop earrings that dangled above her shoulders like door knockers occupied my seat at the table. Grace had a smile on her face that was bigger than a slice of watermelon. Ola came up behind me. I felt her crotch against my ass. She grabbed me around the waist with both hands, leaned into me, and whispered in my left ear, "She's going to play you."

"What?" I pretended not to understand the local idiom, but I got the drift. Although, sometimes it helped to be perceived as the country bumpkin.

"She's going to play you. You know, cheat on you," Ola said as she swayed her hips back and forth against my ass.

"And why would you say that?"

I pushed her hands off from around my waist while I kept my eyes locked on Grace and the stranger.

"Because she cheated on me," Ola said.

What! I thought. I spun around fast and looked at Ola. It was as if she were someone new.

"You and Grace were a couple?" I asked with a major amount of incredulity in my voice.

"Surprised?"

"Sure am."

"So, she didn't tell you?"

"She told me there was attraction, but no involvement."

"Really? I thought you knew about us and that's why you were avoiding me because…you know…guilt."

"Oh, my God. I'm so sorry, Ola. Can we talk for a minute over there?"

I pointed to an empty spot along the wall near the end of the bar.

"Sure," Ola said.

Again, I was faced with the fact that I really didn't know that much about Grace's history except that she had a twin sister and was a sign language interpreter. I wanted, needed to know more.

"How long were the two of you together?" I asked. There was a lull in the music, so we didn't have to shout.

"A little over a year, but we broke up a couple of times during that year then we got back together again. She cheated on me, oh, I'd say about three times. But to be fair, I cheated on her too. But only once!"

"How long ago was this?"

"Hmm, I'd say about six months ago we broke up for good."

"Not that long ago," I said.

"True."

"What do you know about her family?"

"She has a twin sister, Hope."

"Yeah, that I know. I met her not too long ago."

"Watch out for that one. She's a real pain in the ass. Always trying to tell Grace what to do and who to see. Meanwhile, her girlfriend up and left her ass. I guess she got tired of Hope's shit."

"Wait, Hope's a lesbian too?"

"Yes, girl. Grace didn't tell you that either? Hope used to go out with one of her colleagues. It seems like one day the woman just up and left; moved to Poughkeepsie."

"Paula?"

"Yeah, that was her name. Look, Sky, Grace is cute, charming, and decent in bed, but she's a wanderer. She's always looking for the next conquest. I probably shouldn't have sent her to your house that day to pick you up, but it was a last-minute decision. No one else wanted to go and I wanted to make sure you made it to the party."

"I wondered why you sent someone without informing me."

"Informing you about what?" Grace asked.

Ola and I whipped around simultaneously. We looked at Grace who was practically standing directly behind us. Guilt and surprise must have been quite apparent on our faces.

"Are you two talking about me? You both have that deer in the headlights look right now."

"No," Ola and I said in unison. Grace gave us a look that said, "Yeah, right."

"Anyway, I came to get, Sky. It's getting late and we have a long ride ahead of us."

"Since when do you care about the time?" Ola asked.

"Since I found a respectable woman," Grace countered.

"Oh, no, you did not," Ola said with a finger in the air and a hand on her hip.

"No, no, Ola, Grace is right. It is late. I have to get home. My dad is sick, and I need to get home to call my mom, see how they are doing."

"Well, if you must go. As long as it's something that you want to do," Ola said. Her finger was now pointed at me.

"It is. I'm tired. Give me a call soon. I'll be sure to answer the phone this time. Promise."

"Sure thing. Tell your mom I said hello. I hope your dad feels better soon."

"Thanks, and I will."

"Goodbye, Grace," Ola said, her lips tightly pursed and her eyes rolled upward toward the ceiling.

"And good riddance," Grace retorted as we headed toward the door.

CHAPTER TWENTY

I couldn't stop thinking about the two of them together. I thought about it all the way home on the train. Thought about Grace lying to me. Why didn't she just tell me about her and Ola? Why was she trying to keep it a secret? It didn't make sense because, eventually, I was bound to find out. Someone would have spilled the beans, and someone had! Maybe her plan was to play me like Ola warned. Whatever her reasons, I couldn't help but feel betrayed.

The bedroom was cold. I had unplugged the fan and put the air conditioner on full blast before we left the house. I pulled the comforter up over my ears and watched as the curtains bobbed up and down trying to run away from the torrent of air that poured from the machine.

Grace was still in the bathroom. I was tucked tightly under the covers, but my head was in the clouds grasping for the right words to confront her. I heard the water that poured from the faucet of the bathroom sink stop. The light switch clicked and Grace stepped into the bedroom. She was still dressed.

"What are you doing? I thought you were going to take a shower," I said.

The room was almost dark, but a large streetlamp just outside of the house was bright enough to allow slivers of light to enter the room through the curtains. Lines of light illuminated Grace's eyes making them glow like cat eyes. She's so beautiful, I thought. Then I recalled that I was supposed to be mad at her.

"Yeah, well, I've been thinking."

"About what?" I inquired.

"I think I'll stay at my place tonight."

I sat up. "Really? Why?"

"I'm not sure about this, about us."

"Really? Since when? You seemed very sure just a few hours ago," I said. "Oh, wait, I see, the chick with the bald head and big earrings changed your mind, huh?"

I folded my arms across my chest as I tried to control my anger and disbelief.

"Bald chick with big earrings? Who are you talking about?"

"Don't play dumb, Grace. The woman who sat at our table at Pandora's. The one you were chatting and laughing with while I danced with Ola, which you so conveniently condoned."

"You mean, Yvonne?"

"I don't know her name, but I saw you smiling like the cat who ate the canary while the two of you were yukking it up."

Grace laughed softly. "I've known Yvonne for years. And, no, she is not the reason. You are."

"Me?"

"Yes you," Grace said.

She walked over and sat at the edge of the bed, her back toward me.

"What on earth did I do?"

"I'm just...I'm feeling weird about what you told me this afternoon."

"And what did I tell you?"

I was puzzled. We'd been drinking so much over the last few days that I was not exactly one hundred percent sure about anything I might have said or done.

"About you being married."

"Almost married!" I yelled a little too loudly.

"Yeah, well, almost married. But you stayed with that guy for a while though, right? I mean, you said you were just with him for appearance's sake, trying to pose as straight and that you were, no, wait, you are afraid to come out to your family. I just…I'm just not sure I'm ready to go back there again."

"Back where again?"

"Back to dealing with someone who's not ready to be who she is. Someone who can't stand tall and proud and tell the world that she's gay."

"Oh," I said.

I felt the tears as they gathered inside of me. Grace stared at the swatch of floor between her feet, then she put her head in her hands.

"It's just that now, at this point in my life, I'm used to being with women who are totally out."

"And I'm used to dealing with people who are totally honest. Why did you lie about your involvement with Ola?"

"What?" Grace asked. Her head snapped in my direction. "What are you talking about now, Sky?"

"Ola told me that you two were romantically involved. It wasn't nothing, like you claimed it to be. She said you two were together for around a year."

I needed to fight fire with fire, let her know that I knew and that I wasn't an idiot pushover that she could play.

"Romantically involved, huh? Is that what she said?"

"Yes, she did."

"There was nothing romantic about it," Grace huffed. "We were just friends with benefits."

"Well, that's not Ola's version of the situation."

"Who cares what Ola said? One thing has nothing to do with the other. I need for you to be clear about who you are and what you want. I don't want us to say we're a couple and then a few months later you turn around and tell me that you're in love with some guy."

"I wouldn't do that."

"I'm sorry, but right now, I feel that is a huge possibility. It's also possible that your ex-husband or whatever he is will try to track you down and win you back. You said life would be easy with him. He has money. He can give you things I can't. Who knows, things could get hard for you here and he'd be your ticket out."

"So, that's what you think of me? That I'm looking for an easy way out?"

Tears rolled down my cheeks. I was sad and angry at the same time. I wanted to hit Grace and hug her, then tell her that I was crazy about her. But she walked to the window.

"I'm not saying you're weak or that there is a certainty that that's what you'd do, but I am saying that I'm a little uneasy about the whole thing. I need time to think."

Grace's words hurt. I'd uprooted my whole life, left everything behind, and was here taking a chance on everything. I hadn't taken the easy way. I had rolled the dice and made my move. But I guess in the end, for Grace at least, it just wasn't enough.

I lay down and slipped back under the covers.

"You can let yourself out," I said.

My voice was shaky yet stern. Grace was quiet. She didn't say anything, nor had she made a move for several seconds. Then I heard her as she quietly moved toward the bedroom door.

"Good night, Sky," she muttered softly.

"There's nothing good about it!" I shouted back.

CHAPTER TWENTY-ONE

Sunday morning, I woke up with a major headache. Between the Suzy Sunshines and Grace's sudden change of heart, it was definitely warranted. I pulled myself out of bed and searched the medicine cabinet for some relief. I popped two shiny blue pills in my mouth, swallowed hard, then crawled back into bed.

I thought about being a high risk. Grace no longer wanted to deal with me because she felt there was a high risk that I'd go back to Delbert. Boy was that funny! Delbert, who I so hated. The man I wanted to punch the crap out of. The man I wished would just disappear. She was so wrong in her assessment it was laughable. But I didn't laugh. I cried. Cried because according to Grace, and possibly others, I wasn't lesbian enough. There was a smudge on my record. I was a high risk. I had been involved with a man. Almost married one. I'm sure, according to true lesbians that would make me a category three, a red alert, a flip-flopper. I had not only slept with the enemy, but walked down the aisle and almost agreed to share my life with him too. I was an outsider, a sympathizer. True lesbians would ask how

I could believe in or fight for lesbian rights when I had shared my bed with a man? Women who knew that they were gay when they were three, four years old have little patience for us late bloomers. If you weren't toting a rainbow flag by the time you were five, you were questionable, suspect. You were a constant reminder of all the girls who turned them down. Who kissed them, then later proclaimed, "Sorry, I'm not like that" or "I was just having fun" or "I really like boys." You were a constant reminder of their pain, their frustration, their embarrassment. I understood it all because it had happened to me too—rejection from girls who just wanted to see what it was like to kiss another girl. Girls who had strung me along while I fell deeper and deeper in love, only to eventually be told they had boyfriends or they weren't "funny," so please leave them alone. I understood. I got it. It's what had happened with Siobhan and, although I vowed never to put myself out there again, I ended up falling for Lisa. She was gorgeous beyond belief. She attended North Carolina Central as an English major, but she worked at Piggly Wiggly as a cashier to make some change. She strung me along just like Siobhan did, then hung me out to dry. I was angry and embarrassed, but I never held it against either of them. Never felt like I needed to banish them to the outer rims of existence, nor felt the need to punish them. But could I have? The world was on their side, so in the end, whatever I had felt was on me. I chose to let go of the anger. To let go of the categories. To let go of measuring out someone's life in order to slap a label on them and put them in a box. I didn't want someone measuring me, labeling me, packaging me. I just wanted to be me, not a fill-in-the-dots rendition of me. But, maybe, that's not possible. Maybe that's too scary for the real world.

All that thinking made my head hurt even more. I crawled out of bed again, popped one more shiny blue pill into my mouth, chased it with a sip of cold water I collected in the palm of my hand from the faucet, dragged myself back into bed, put the comforter over my head, and focused on sleeping.

CHAPTER TWENTY-TWO

I spent the next week worrying about my life, thinking about Grace, and creating lesson plans. School was in full swing and the days flew by. September was dwindling away. There were little pieces of it tucked into every yellow leaf that fell to the ground. The air had become crisper, sharper, letting us know that October was fast approaching.

My mother had called several times a day updating me on my father's condition. Those calls meant I had the opportunity to talk to my brother more than I had in prior months. He seemed to always be around; I was sure my mother had found his close proximity very helpful.

"So, Mom's not baking as much anymore now that Dad's feeling a little better, and I hate to say it, but I kind of miss her gooey chocolate chip cookies."

"Henry!" I said.

"What?" He laughed. "Ah, come on, you know I'm only joking."

"Yeah, yeah. Tell Mom to give your wife the recipe. I'm sure June wouldn't mind whipping up a batch or two," I said.

"Girl, now you know June burns everything. She can barely boil water!"

"Well, who doing all the cooking then?"

I heard a little Southern charm in my words. Talking with Henry always brought out the down home in me.

"Hell, I'm cooking most of the time. It's okay though, 'cause I enjoy it. But baking ain't my thing."

"Mm," I said.

"How are you doing? Things going well for you up there?"

"Things are good," I said, my voice flat.

"You sound like you a little down in the mouth. You sure you all right?" I heard concern in his voice.

"Henry, what would you say if I told you...if I told you..."

"If you told me what?"

I wanted to tell him about me and Grace. Get the opinion of my big brother as to what I should do next. Wanted him to tell me that she was a fool for leaving me and that she'd come back, but I wasn't sure if Henry would sympathize with me.

"If I told you that I'm going to try to come home for Thanksgiving," I said with a forced brightening of my tone.

"I'd say that's great! Bring your butt on down here for the holidays. Get away from all a those weirdos and freaks in New York. Plus, Dad would love to see you. Maybe he'll be home by then."

"What weirdos and freaks? New York is basically the same as North Carolina except North Carolina has more grass," I laughed.

"Yeah, well, North Carolina's not infested with all a them homos and guys running around in dresses and thangs, like in New York. I know you musta seen 'em by now. From what I've seen about New York on TV, they're everywhere! They not bothering you are they?" he said. "You can always come back home, Sky, you know. I'll help you find another place or maybe...maybe Delbert could help you."

"You know, Henry, I gotta go." And I hung up on Henry once again.

He is so not ready, I thought.

I called Ola to see if she wanted to meet for brunch. It was Sunday. I had gotten up late and hadn't had breakfast yet, so we made plans to meet at The French Roast down in the West Village.

It was cold and a bit windy, but the wait for a good table to open up inside the restaurant was too long, so we opted to sit outside. Luckily both Ola and I were dressed appropriately.

I took off my sunglasses, glanced at the menu, decided I'd order the same thing I always ordered at The French Roast—a vegetable omelet with hash browns and two mimosas—then shoved my sunglasses back in place. Ola continued to hem and haw over her decision until she settled on mimicking my order. Except she wanted two Bloody Marys with her meal.

"Have you heard from Grace?" she asked.

She handed both menus to the waiter without looking at him. I was checking out the hot women who passed by our table. Many of them were gorgeous with long legs, hair twisted into perfect angles, trendy shoes with clunky heels that punished the pavement as they walked, and clothes that made them sparkle and shine, but they held no interest for me apart from aesthetic. They were not Grace.

"No, I haven't. Have you?"

"No."

"What am I supposed to do, Ola? What am I supposed to do to show that I'm *all* lesbian? To prove myself?" I asked.

The waiter brought us one drink apiece "to start," he said. I grabbed my mimosa and sucked it down.

"What can you do? You are who you are."

"Yeah, well, tell that to Grace."

"Look, Grace is on some holier-than-thou shit for some reason. That's her problem. Don't let it fuck with your head. Anyway, I know for a fact that some of the women she dated before were not gold star lesbians."

"What's a 'gold star lesbian?'"

"A lesbian who has never slept with a man and has no intention to do so."

"Oh," I said. "Wow, I guess that makes me what, a bronze star? Tin?"

"Sky, you really have to stop beating yourself up over this. People's lives are generally messy. Those of us who know what we want and who we are at a very young age are few and far between. I've always envied those kids who knew since they were three years old that they were going to be doctors or ballerinas or lawyers. I didn't know. I tried med school—didn't have the stamina or the stomach. I tried teaching in a traditional setting—hated it. The kids lacked passion and the schools lacked funds. Then I took a photography class and the whole world opened up for me. Then I knew. Am I beating myself up about those lost careers? No. I wish I could get all of that time back, but other than that I figure that was just my path. Everyone has their own path and we must respect people's paths because your path makes you who you are."

"Yeah," I said.

I sipped at the rest of my mimosa. The champagne bubbles engulfed each of Ola's words and carried them straight to my brain where they helped to clarify her point. My path shaped who I was today, just as Grace's path helped to shape her. It wasn't fair that I should be punished for my journey while she held high court because of hers.

"Hey, you're right!" I shouted. "I'm going to tell Grace that just because she's a gold star doesn't mean she's better than me!"

"Exactly," Ola said and put up her hand to give me a high-five. We slapped hands and I smiled. I felt a lot better about things. The waiter came with our food and suddenly I was famished. I'd barely eaten all week worrying about Grace.

"Why are you so into her anyway? Maybe you should find someone new. Someone who understands you and your path more. And remember, she's a liar. She likes to bend the story to make it seem like you're the one with the problem, just like she's doing to you now. Maybe you need to take Nancy Reagan's advice and 'just say no.'"

"Yeah, about that. You told me that you and Grace were an item, like you were really into each other and you dated, but Grace said you guys were just friends with benefits. So, which is it, Ola?"

"Is that what she said? Ha!"

"So, Grace is lying?"

"I recall us being hot and heavy, but, uh, truthfully, I was thinking about it and…I uh…I was uh…actually seeing someone while Grace and I were fooling around."

I stared at Ola with hard eyes. "'Fooling around?' You told me you were an item! That things were serious between you two!"

"Things started off serious, but Grace didn't want to commit. She just wanted to fool around."

"Uh, maybe because she knew you already had a girlfriend. Did you ever think about that?"

"Look, I'm sorry. I was sitting around the other day and I recalled more details about what went on between Grace and me. I guess I've been upset at her for a while because I wanted more, and she didn't. I guess it hurt my pride."

"So, Grace was telling the truth."

"I guess so, in a way. I remembered we were on-again, off-again, because she didn't want me like I wanted her, and the rejection really fucked with me. It tends to spill over into Grace and my relationship to this day, but I'm working on letting it go. Recently, I started seeing a therapist and I'm working on my shit, so I'm sorry about what I said. But Grace didn't tell you about Hope and Paula either. Why did she keep that a secret?"

"Ola, that's minor stuff. Maybe she thought if Hope wanted me to know she was in a relationship with a woman she would tell me herself."

"True. True. Okay, I messed up, Sky. I'm sorry. Like I said, I'm working on things, trying to be a better me."

"That's good."

"You never answered me though, why Grace? Why are you so into her?"

Ola cut off a large piece from her omelet, laid it on top of the buttered toast she had on the small plate beside her big one, bit off a corner, and looked up at me.

"With her, it just feels right. We just click—or so I thought. She just feels like the yin to my yang. I love her eyes, her smile, the way she talks, her body. People usually don't get my jokes, but we laugh at the same things and make each other laugh. I think humor is very important in a relationship. I love to laugh. Most people tend to make me feel sad."

"Oh, you mean like Grace has." Ola donned a sarcastic smile.

"Ha, ha," I said.

"Kidding. You know, I hate to say this, but maybe you two really are the perfect couple. I mean, you seem really into her and maybe if I wasn't being vindictive, you two wouldn't be fighting right now. Maybe she's afraid of what she's feeling for you. Either way, I'm going to be on the side of love and say that you shouldn't give up. You need to fight for her. Show her that she's making a mistake. Win her back. Knowing what I know about Grace, she most likely feels that you're the right one for her too and she's freaking out about it. I read that sometimes people sabotage a good thing because they think they don't deserve good things. Maybe that's the case here."

"Maybe," I said as I sucked up the last of my second mimosa. "I must say, Ola Prioleau, that therapy is working." We laughed.

"Oh, and Sky, me being in therapy is our little secret." Ola pointed her fork at me, and her face was serious.

"Yes ma'am," I replied, then I moved my fingers across my mouth to show I had zipped my lips.

CHAPTER TWENTY-THREE

I thought about what Ola had said off and on for a whole week, weighing the pros, cons, and rebuttals to her theories. I had practice conversations with Grace in my bathroom mirror while steam clouded her fictitious face. The Grace in the glass was kind, patient, forgiving—everything I hoped the real Grace would be when I spoke to her. I dialed her number. The phone rang and rang. Then the machine kicked in: "Hey, if you need me leave a message. I'll get back to you as soon as I can. Enjoy."

It was nice to hear her voice all throaty and extremely sexy, but I didn't want to leave a message begging her to call me. I hung up the phone. Then I remembered Ola's advice that I might have to fight for her if I didn't want her to get away. I wanted to fight for Grace, but I wanted her to want me too, and it was difficult to put my pride aside.

Wednesday, hump day. At work, I bumped into Hope during the kindergarten teachers' professional development meeting. She was all rouged and glistening tucked up under the assistant principal like an awkward appendage. How I hated brownnosers!

"Hello, Sky. Have you met our new assistant principal? Ms. Parker, this is Sky Valentine. Sky, Ms. Parker. And how fabulous is it that you're both fairly new to the school. Yay, newbies!"

Hope cheered, guffawed, and made a slight horse-like sound, then smiled wider than a Colgate pinup girl.

"Ms. Parker," I said and shook her hand. "We met a week ago in the front office."

"Yes, we did. Good to see you again," Ms. Parker said.

Almost immediately, poor Ms. Parker was pulled over to another section of the room where Hope-like minis waited to deflower and devour her, but before they tore her away completely, she squeezed my hand tight and looked me in the eye.

"It was really nice to see you again, Sky."

She smiled and revealed a small gap between her two front teeth. It was…sexy, confident. It made me think of a secret place, a curtain pulled.

I smiled back at Ms. Parker and released her hand. The meeting was about to begin. I walked to the opposite side of the room—away from Hope, her flunkies, and Ms. Parker—and took a seat.

The meeting finished on time, which was surprising since the teachers usually liked to spend an extra twenty minutes complaining or comparing notes about why certain aspects of the curriculum would definitely fail. Maybe Ms. Parker was a godsend. Or maybe they decided to go easy on her since it was her first meeting. Whatever it was, I was glad it was over and I could head home. As I gathered together the abundant amount of handouts I received during the meeting, Hope approached me.

"So, what do you think?"

"I think forming a book club for kindergarten is a great idea. Very cute," I said as I straightened out the books and papers that I held cradled in my arm.

"Funny," she said. "I'm not talking about that. I'm talking about Ms. Parker."

"What about her? She seems nice, effective."

We both looked across the room to where Ms. Parker stood by the door surrounded by women who wanted a piece of her, a tiny nod of approval. Ms. Parker was their rock star.

"She's more than effective. She's like one of the up-and-coming major players in education."

"Oh, okay. Well that explains the fawning."

Hope whipped her head around and looked at me. I saw a look of disgust on her face. She huffed and then moved her stack of handouts from one arm to the other.

"I get it, you plan to be a kindergarten teacher forever, huh?"

"I didn't say that and, anyway, don't delude yourself into thinking that kissing up to Ms. Parker will land you a position with the chancellor, because I'm sure it won't," I said.

Hope stared at me. "You know, I don't know what my sister sees in you."

"Apparently nothing since she hasn't called me in a while."

"Have you called her?"

"Yes, several times. She refuses to pick up the phone."

"She hasn't picked up the phone because she's not home. She's been out of town at a conference in Chicago for a week and then she planned to hang out with our friend, River, who lives in Chicago, for an additional week. Did you leave a message?"

"No, but I...I wanted to talk, really talk. Not leave messages."

"And how is she supposed to know that? She's many things, but a mind reader isn't on the list. Don't be a jerk, Sky. Leave a message like normal people do. Talk about country bumpkin," Hope said.

She turned on her heel and stormed out of the room. All I could do was smile.

Later that night, before bed, I called Grace. Again, I got her answering machine, but this time I did not hang up. Instead, I talked and talked about how I felt about her, about me, and my past. I put the things Ola had said in my own words and I told her that too. I talked and cried and talked some more until I was all talked out. I hoped all the tears and words would eventually erode some walls.

CHAPTER TWENTY-FOUR

There was no response from Grace the next day or the day after that, but someone called then hung up when I answered, so I was hopeful.

Monday was gray and muggy. As the temperature went up, more rain came down. The puddles that had formed in the morning grew to the size of lakes by the afternoon. I stood in the entrance of the school with my raincoat on, but open because I felt too warm when I buttoned it up. My large, expensive umbrella was useless against the downpour and gusting winds. I snapped it shut and held it by my side as I contemplated the best route to take home.

"Lots of rain. High temperatures. Gusting winds. If we were in Florida, we might be worried about tornadoes right now," the assistant principal said.

I was so focused on the weather and figuring out how not to get drenched that I didn't hear her walk up and stand beside me. I glanced at her, then back at the rain.

"Thank God we're not in Florida," I said.

She laughed. I didn't. My mood was volatile like the weather.

"Not a rain lover, huh? Me neither, but in everyone's life a little rain must fall—as the phrase goes."

"I don't think the phrase is referring to actual rain," I said.

"I don't think so either. I'm talking about that sad look on your face and in your eyes. All of that emotion can't be because of a little rain. Are you okay?"

Educated, sexy tooth gap, good-looking, and perceptive. Too bad she's my boss, I thought.

"I'm…great…fine. I'm fine. Trying to plot my course home is all."

"No car?"

"No. I don't live that far away. I'm just not relishing the idea of getting drenched as I dodge or jump over tiny lakes as I walk home. It's too windy for my umbrella and too warm to close my raincoat properly so…"

"So, commence drenching."

"Exactly," I said.

I gathered the lapels of my raincoat together creating a small barrier around my neck against the wind. "Well, I better get going." I stepped one foot out the door.

Ms. Parker caught and held me by my elbow. "Wait. Don't get drenched. I'll drive you. Wait right here while I'll get my keys." She turned and began walking toward her office.

"No, that's not necessary. I'll be fine," I said to her retreating back.

"Nonsense," she said and kept moving.

"Buckle up."

Ms. Parker smiled at me, then gunned the engine. I clicked my seat belt in and pressed my back into the seat, hoping to minimize my nervousness. Ms. Parker smoothly pulled the black Bentley out of the parking lot. The dashboard radio icon lit up and "Take the A Train" ricocheted its way around the inside of the car. I jumped and covered my ears as Ms. Parker's hand shot out to turn down the radio.

"Whoa! I'm sorry. It never sounds as loud in the morning as it does in the afternoon."

I uncovered my ears and smiled. "I'm sure," I said.

Ms. Parker fiddled with the dial, adjusting the volume until she thought it was perfect.

"So, where can I take you?"

"Oh, uh, Saturn Lane. It's in…"

"Shorehaven. Yes, I know. Had a friend who lived there and, as I recall, all of the streets have either nautical or astrological names. It stays with you. You sit back, relax, and enjoy the music. Hope you like jazz."

"Yes, I do. And thank you so much for the lift, Ms. Parker."

"Valerie. You can call me, Valerie. We're not on school grounds anymore, so I think it's safe."

She had a big shit-eating grin on her face that made me laugh. "Valerie," I said.

I wiped away the last bit of condensation on my window and stared outside. The rain was still coming down in buckets, but the car rode smoothly, and the jazz was a mellifluous buffer against the outside sounds.

"Nice car," I said. "Sturdy." I was terrible at small talk.

"One of the few things I insisted on taking after my divorce," Valerie said.

"Good choice."

"Yes, very. Are you married?"

"Me? No."

"Divorced?"

"No, never been married or divorced," I said.

"That's good. Single then?"

I laughed. It felt a little like being interrogated, but she was still the boss, so I played along.

"Yes, I'm currently single," I said.

"Must have been a recent breakup, which would explain the sadness I saw before in your eyes."

"Very recent."

"Well, things will get better. They always do."

"I hope so," I said.

I decided to turn the tables. Learn some more about the esteemed assistant principal.

"What about you? How long ago was your divorce?"

"It'll be five years in a few months."

"Oh, okay. Are you single or did you jump back on the saddle again?"

"No more saddle jumping for me. I've remained single. It's hard to find a good woman to be by my side since I'm always working. Very hard."

What! I felt my heart jump and my head explode—did Ms. Parker just come out to me? I needed more clarification.

"So, you're a…"

"Lesbian, yes. As they say nowadays, there's no shame in my game. I'm thirty-five years old, no more hiding who I am. I hope you're not offended, and this doesn't upset or pose a problem for you. I just feel so much power in owning who I am."

"No, no problem at all."

"Good. I was right about the vibe I got from you."

"Vibe?"

"Yes, you're not like the rest of the flock that was gathered around me a few days ago at the meeting," she said. "Anyway, here we are. I'll take you through the guard's gates."

"Okay," I said. Resistance was futile.

I showed the guard my identification. He looked at it briefly, then looked back at my guest and me. He opened the gate slowly.

"Right turn at the corner, correct?" asked Valerie.

"Yes, that's right."

She made the turn, drove a short way, and stopped the car at the curb without making the second right that would have left me directly in front of the condo I was renting.

The wind had died down a bit, so I was able to use my umbrella.

"Thank you so much, Ms. Parker." She gave me a look. "I mean, Valerie."

"You're welcome, Ms. Valentine. I mean, Sky." She laughed. "Anytime. Really. Please don't take this the wrong way, but it was nice spending time with a beautiful woman even if it was a short time."

I giggled like a schoolgirl at the compliment and got out of the car. I pushed the door shut and waved. Valerie waved back, mouthed "good night," then zoomed off. I walked to my mailbox and opened it. Empty. Closed it and turned the corner, headed to my place. I climbed the stairs and opened the screen door, and a small white envelope fell to my feet. I bent to pick it up. When I got inside I opened it.

Saturday, 11:00 a.m. My place. Let's talk.

—Grace

CHAPTER TWENTY-FIVE

The week crawled, and with every second that inched by I grew more and more anxious. Spilling my guts to a machine was easy; face-to-face was a different story. I went to the gym a lot after work to squat it out and relieve some of the tension, but then nerves would put a box of chocolate cookies in my hand, which canceled out the whole workout.

Friday night came around and I was throwing outfit after outfit out of my closet and onto the bed trying to find the perfect thing to wear. Something that said "Take me back I'm worth it" without seeming too desperate. I decided to dress simply: simple white shirt with a nice pair of black pants, black shoes, black leather jacket.

The next morning, I got up early since, instead of sleeping, I was just lying in bed making up crazy scenarios about the day ahead. I decided to go for a run on the Greenway. It was early in the morning, so there was nothing but me, the trail, a view of the Long Island Sound, and a squirrel or two that scattered into the bush when they heard me coming. I took a long, hot bath with lots of bubbles when I got home, then made green tea with honey to sip as I got dressed. I had taped an episode of the new talk show with the African-American woman host, Oprah Winfrey, on my VCR, and I sat and watched a few minutes of it, but I couldn't really focus on the show, so I turned it off. I still had time to kill, so I walked the mile and a half to the train station in Parkchester instead of taking the bus.

When I got off the train in Harlem, I had to walk a few blocks that curved downhill to get to Grace's apartment. I pressed the buzzer outside her building. Five seconds seemed like five minutes as I waited. I was about to press the buzzer again when the door hummed. I pushed the heavy iron door and let myself into the building.

The lobby was quiet and big, with lots of wood paneling. It was an old building that was probably grand in its day. I took the elevator up and thought about the first time Grace and I were in this elevator together. It was our fourth date, and we were all over each other. The thought brought a smile to my face. I was glad the elevator was old because it lacked cameras, which meant no one saw what we did except us. Today, however, I wasn't too thrilled to be in an old elevator all alone because I actually was not fond of elevators, so I was very happy when I made it to the fifth floor without incident.

Someone was cooking bacon. The smell tempted as it wafted through the air. As a vegetarian of many years, I hadn't eaten bacon in a long time, but I still found the scent of it being cooked alluring. Beneath the bacon smell was the smell of coffee—strong and pungent like a one-two punch. I was not fond of coffee either.

When I got to Grace's apartment door, I stopped. I checked my hair and my clothes, and applied more lip balm to my lips. I was in the process of applying a second coat when the door sprang open.

"Are you going to stand out there all day?" Grace asked.

The words sounded serious, but her body language seemed relaxed.

"I was just putting my lip balm away," I said.

"I see. Come in," she said and handed the door off for me to catch and close.

I hadn't been to Grace's place in a while. The last time I was here was in August. We had been hanging out on the pier listening to music, relaxing by the water, and getting frisky with each other when the cops came and chased everyone away. The Preppy Murder case, where Robert Chambers strangled his girlfriend Jennifer Levin in Central Park, meant tighter police restrictions. Grace suggested we take the romance to her place since she lived closer than I did. I agreed and we had a great time. Now, as I stepped inside and looked around, I saw that nothing much had changed since that night. There were still books everywhere and more books on top of those books. The apartment was already small, so the multitude of books made it feel even smaller. There were two good things about the place—all of the natural light that poured in from the massive front windows and the fact that she kept everything extremely tidy. Each book mountain was impeccably formed.

Grace had cleared a big, blue, overstuffed armchair, which I assumed was for me to sit in, so I sat in it.

"Can I take your jacket?"

"No need. I'll just fling it over the back of the chair."

She sat across from me on a high wooden stool that gave her the advantage of looking down on me. A power play. I became aware that she had done some planning, some scene setting of her own during the week.

"Do you want something to drink, eat?"

"No, I had tea before I came. I'm good."

Grace looked down at her feet as she shoved her hands into her pants pockets. I took a deep breath in and started talking.

"So, obviously you got my message. I didn't know you were out of town until your sister told me."

"Are you responsible for all of those hang-ups? Someone kept calling me and hanging up."

"Yeah. I'm sorry. I wasn't sure about what I wanted to say. Plus, I thought you were home, but ignoring me. Anyway, I didn't want to leave a message at first, but then, I did since... since Hope said you were going to be out of town for a while. I couldn't keep all of those thoughts to myself any longer."

"Let's talk about the things you said."

Deep inside of me a wall had begun to erect itself in preparation for the blows I was sure were about to be administered.

"Okay," I said.

I sat up straighter in the chair, wanting to look brave and unafraid. I tried to foster a *do your best* look and attitude.

"You said that I was being unfair judging you for the decisions you've made thus far in your life and something to the effect that those decisions have made you who you are."

"Yes, I believe I said something like that. And it's true just like the decisions you've made in your life have made you who you are. I'm not trying to punish you for that."

"I'm not trying to punish you either, Sky."

"Really? It feels like you are." I rolled my eyes and glanced at the windows. The sun had shifted further west as noon approached. The apartment felt warm and my chair was a little too soft. I heard children as they screamed and chased each other down the sidewalk outside.

"You're right," said Grace.

My head snapped back toward her direction.

"What?" I asked.

"I said you are right. I have been acting extremely judgmental toward you and it's not fair or polite. I'm sorry, Sky. I'm an ass. I really wasn't trying to punish you, but I can understand how you might see it as such. Forgive me."

"Wow!" I said out loud without really meaning to. I just couldn't believe that she understood where I was coming from. "Thank you."

"Why are you thanking me?" Grace asked.

She removed her hands from her pockets and adjusted herself on the narrow square of the stool seat. One long leg dangled free while the other was bent and formed a right angle with the bottom rung.

"Because you got my point without us having to have a knock-down, drag-out fight."

"Violence is not the answer," Grace said and smiled.

A diminutive dimple I'd never noticed before formed a very meager cave-in at the center of her left cheek. I smiled back.

"So, where do we go from here?" I asked.

"Nowhere. You made your point and I apologized. End of story."

"Oh," I said.

I put my head down. I didn't want her to see the tears that had sprung up in my eyes. I felt like a fool.

"Uh…well…I better get going then."

I grabbed my jacket and practically ran for the door. I felt like such an idiot. I didn't know what made me think Grace wanted me back. I guess I'd hoped for it so much it had begun to feel like a possibility. No, a certainty.

"Sky, stop. Don't go anywhere. Please, wait there."

I stood by the front door drying my eyes quickly while I shrugged into my leather jacket. Grace had made her way to either the kitchen or the bathroom. I wasn't sure which. I just wanted to be out of there. I felt totally humiliated. I reached for the doorknob.

"Sky, wait. Here," Grace said.

I wiped away more tears and straightened my jacket, then smoothed it down in the front before I turned to face her.

Grace's arms were outstretched and in them was a spray of petite pink roses wrapped in shiny silver wrapping paper that seemed sort of folded and tucked away like so many miniature kisses. I cried outright when I saw them.

"Oh my God, they're beautiful," I said as I took the flowers from her hands and smelled them.

Their scent was soft, supple, like something born of spring. I petted them, just barely, felt the tightness of each petal as it held on to another and I hoped this was Grace's plan—for us to hold on to each other.

"I love you," Grace said.

It was the first time she had said those words to me. I looked up at her, and tears slid down my cheeks and pooled at my chin.

"I love you more," I said.

She leaned down and kissed me.

CHAPTER TWENTY-SIX

For the remainder of September, Grace and I clung to each other as if we were the last leaves on a rapidly exfoliating sycamore tree. She slept at my place and I slept at hers. Our clothes, books, work items, were strewn between and many had fallen into the great chasm of origin uncertainty. Was it originally mine or hers? We didn't know, didn't care. There seemed to be no separation, no she, no me, only us. We were one. Together, we cooked elaborate meals or ordered mundane Chinese that we ate curled up against each other as we watched *The Cosby Show* or *L.A. Law* on my orange couch or in her pulled-down Murphy bed. We read to each other in the bath, massaged sore feet and backs, kissed eyelids that had grown heavy in the night. I'd bought her varying bouquets of flowers. She fed me chocolates with fat bellies stuffed with more chocolate. Together we ran the nature trails puffing out solitary breaths and sucking in the cool air of unity.

Love had been mentioned again—several times, and I felt such an intense connection to Grace that it was alarming. I'd never felt so connected, so in sync with anyone before. Never. No one. *This is what love feels like* ran through my head and fueled my body day after day.

October blew in on fifteen mile per hour winds that shook leaves from trees, rapidly undressing branches, throwing their red, yellow, and faded green smocks to the ground. Once there, they were lifted, spun into circles, created funnels in midair, then, eventually, parachuted back down to the ground. Meanwhile, the smell of the sea hung in the air along with fish, algae, and wet sand. It made me think of sailing, of getting away, of taking a trip to some distant land. The furthest I could afford was North Carolina. Thanksgiving was around the corner. I'd have the time off from work, and my dad, I hoped, would be back home by then, so I figured it was time for a visit.

I pulled the blankets up closer to my shoulders, hoping to combat the cold with carefully combed cotton. Grace, who was reading her book at the foot of the bed, pulled the covers back toward her own shoulders.

"Hey!" I yelled.

"Hey, yourself. You know I'd give you anything, but right now, I'm cold too, so you can't hog the blanket like you usually do," Grace said as she pulled at the blankets a bit more.

"I do not hog the blankets."

"You do, but it's okay. Usually, I don't mind because most of the time I have on my sweater, but I left it downstairs on the couch and I don't feel like getting up to get it, so be nice, share."

"Ugh." I pushed the blankets aside and stuffed my cold feet into furry slippers. "I'll go get your sweater. You just stay here all warm and cozy like," I said and gave her a twisted smile.

Grace pursed her lips and rolled her eyes.

"Anyway, I want to call my mom. Check on my dad."

Downstairs, I put on my sweater, turned up the thermostat a bit, then grabbed the telephone that was in the living room on the side table by the couch. A ring, from either a wine or juice glass, scarred the table, leaving the wood lighter than the grain that surrounded it. I really need to buy some coasters, I thought.

My parents' phone rang two, three, four times before it was answered.

"Hello?"

"Mom, is everything okay? What took you so long to answer the phone?" My body and voice were tense.

"It was only four rings, Sky. Plus, I was doing a little cleaning. I'm trying to get things in order for when your father comes home."

"I still think you should sue either the hospital or the doctor. First, they told you it was mild, then Dad turns around and has another heart attack. That could have been a potentially fatal misdiagnosis, Mom. Definitely grounds to sue."

"He had a stroke after the heart attack, Sky. Sometimes these things happen. I'm just glad he made it through. I'm counting my blessings. You should do the same."

I sighed. "I am grateful for that, Mom, but right is right, and you'd be in the right if you decided to sue."

"How's work, dear?"

I laughed. My rage had been dismissed.

"Okay, Mom, okay. Got it. Work is fine. Honing my teaching skills as the weeks go by."

"That's great! I always knew you'd make a great teacher," my mom said.

I heard the pride and joy in her voice, and it pleased me. I hadn't heard pride in her voice in relation to me in a long time.

"I'm thinking about coming home for Thanksgiving since I have that time off from work. Dad will be home by then, right?"

"Oh, yes, Sky, and he'd love to see you. He misses you so much. We all do."

"Great! Then it's settled. I'll call you in a few days with all of the details. Okay?"

"I'll be here."

"Good night, Mom. Kiss Dad for me. Tell him I love him. Oh, and Mom, is it okay if I bring a friend?"

"That's fine, Sky. I will tell your father what you said. Good night."

Back upstairs, I handed Grace her sweater and pounced on the bed.

"Thank you," Grace said. She promptly shrugged on the sweater, then checked the pockets. She pulled out a skullcap and put it on her head. As I watched her, I measured the words I wanted to say in my head. Quickly, I made lists of pros and cons, and tried to assess my degree of bravery until, finally, I just blurted it out.

"I'm going to North Carolina for Thanksgiving. Do you want to come with me?"

Grace dropped her book onto her knees, looked at me, and then slowly slid her legs down the length of the bed. Her toes stopped where I lay across it.

"Are you serious?"

I squeezed her toes through the blankets. Her foot jumped a little.

"Yes, I'm serious. I just told my mom that I'm coming."

"Did you tell her you plan on bringing your girlfriend?" Grace asked.

"No, I asked her if I could bring a friend and she said I could. I can tell her you're my girlfriend when we get there. She'll be able to meet you directly."

"You think that's a good idea? I don't want to get shot so far from home."

"I'll hide all of the bullets," I offered.

"Thanks. That's what I like about you, so supportive," Grace said.

I laughed. "Hey, you can count on me."

CHAPTER TWENTY-SEVEN

The temperature dropped further and further as October marched bravely toward its end. The trees were nearly bare, with the bodies of dead leaves piled up beside them waiting to be broken down by rain, snow, and time and then absorbed by long, spidery, fibrous roots back into the very tree from which they fell. That same tree would eventually spit them out once again, come spring.

It was nearing Halloween and Ola had invited Grace and me to her masquerade party. We discussed costume choices for days. We thought about going as Dwight Gooden and Darryl Strawberry since the New York Mets had recently won the World Series, defeating the Boston Red Sox eight to five in game seven at Shea Stadium, but thought that would be everyone's choice. Finally, we decided to go as Salt-N-Pepa, sporting thick, fake gold chains, big hair wigs, tight jeans, and puffy, black leather jackets. We both knew most of the duo's lyrics in case we needed to recite a few for those who couldn't readily recognize who we were supposed to be.

Halloween was on a Thursday, and Ola's party was scheduled for Saturday, November second, which was great because on Halloween it rained huge cats and dogs in New York while other states experienced major, unexpected snowstorms. It seemed not much trick-or-treating would occur anywhere, but Grace had stayed at my place after work that day and we were armed with candy just in case some die-hard trick-or-treater craving sweets knocked at the door.

Grace was soaking in a bath upstairs while I finished up the last of the dinner preparations downstairs. The plates, silverware, napkins, and glasses were in place. I decided to add a bit of a romantic flair by using a fancy centerpiece for the table—a climbing vine tea light candelabra that I'd recently bought from a guy who was selling some of his personal items on the street next to Toys "R" Us on White Plains Road. Whenever Grace decided to get out of the bath and venture downstairs, I'd light it.

"Sky, I forgot to get a towel. Can you get one for me... please?" Grace yelled.

"Okay, coming," I yelled back, pushing the candelabra squarely into the center of the table.

Grace was surrounded by a huge cloud of bubbles. The window on the opposite wall was open a crack letting in wisps of air from the cool wind outside. I could both hear and smell the rain. The sky grumbled, belched, and lit up almost simultaneously. I placed the towel on the edge of the sink and sat down on the toilet lid.

"You look very relaxed," I said.

"I *am* very relaxed, but it would be nice to have some company."

"Really? Are you sure it wouldn't mess up your vibe?"

"No, not at all. I want to share this vibe with you," Grace said.

Her head was tilted back, resting on the wall with the bath pillow she'd bought me crammed under her neck for support. Her eyes were closed. She had a sweet smile on her face as she reached her hand out toward me. I couldn't resist.

"Okay," I said and proceeded to undress.

"Grab a candle or two from the linen closet. It'll be nice with the storm and all."

"That's true," I said.

I went out into the hall and grabbed two votive candles from the top shelf of the linen closet along with two clear candleholders and a box of matches that sat beside them. I plopped the candles into the holders, then put them on top of the toilet tank. I lit them, closed the bathroom door to lessen the draft, then sank down in front of Grace in the tub. She opened her legs to make room for me as the bubbles rose up around us. I rested my head near her right shoulder, and she wrapped her arms around me. Her hands fell against my stomach.

We didn't speak. We just sat there enjoying the heat from the bath and each other. We listened to the steady beating of the rain against the window and against the side of the house. The candles flickered, grew dim, then rose up again casting shadows around the room. The bubbles burst and drowned beside us.

Grace moved first, cupping the hot water into the palms of her hands then releasing it onto my breasts, stomach, and back into the bath. She did this several times massaging my breasts and stomach with every watery release. The heat of the bath combined with her caresses warmed me and beads of moisture formed along my forehead. Grace tilted her head up, which caused me to slide off her shoulder some, but she held my head, leaned down, and firmly bit into the softness of my neck. I moaned. She knew my weakness. A bolt of lightning burst and brightened the sky and Grace bit me again, deeper. A bolt of desire surged through me. I turned my head toward her. Our mouths met—warm and open. Her tongue searched around inside my mouth as she massaged my nipples, which I could feel were erect from her teasing. Then her hand slid farther south, tickling my pubes before she moved toward my clitoris, which was also erect and stiff as a lightning rod. She touched me, her fingers forming tight, tiny circles. Our kisses deepened and my legs parted, requesting more. Grace slid two fingers inside of me. My back arched. Thunder rumbled and rolled between clouds. Bathwater sloshed around like waves at sea and the wind that seeped in through the cracked window now made a howling-like sound.

Grace pulled her mouth away from mine but left her hand where it was. She looked at me.

"Maybe we should take this to the bedroom," she said.

"Yes, I think we should."

I stood slowly, wanting to hold on to the sweet feeling of surrender. Grace held on to my hips as she rose from the warm bathwater. We exited the tub, our bodies flush against each other. Grace grabbed her towel, wrapped it around both of us—as much as she could—and we walked like a four-legged woman toward the bedroom. Rivulets of water streamed down our legs, arms, and pooled around our heels. We didn't care. When we got to the bed, Grace released the towel to the floor. I turned, faced her, put my arms around her neck, and kissed her deeply once again. She broke away then pushed me gently onto the bed. She laid on top of me, kissed my mouth, cheeks, neck, breasts, and slowly made her way down between my legs where another storm was about to begin.

The rain eased up a tad around eight o'clock that night, but the wind continued to blow hard and steady. Grace and I had moved from the dining room to the couch to eat our food. We were wrapped in our warm, thick, cotton robes and buried beneath a big, heavy quilt while we chowed down on thick, succulent slices of grilled teriyaki tempeh burgers with mango sauce.

"What are we going to do with all of this candy?" Grace asked as she held onto her fork and pointed with her pinky at the large bowl of goodies on the end table beside her.

"I don't know. I guess I'll take some to school with me tomorrow. Although, the last thing those little beggars need is sugar."

"That's for sure. Twenty-five, thirty kids high on sugar in a contained setting is *not* a good thing."

"Yeah, too bad Halloween's a bust. I'm excited about Ola's party though," I said as I wiped mango sauce from around my mouth and off my hands.

"Sa-Sa-Sa-Salt and Pepa's here!" Grace said while bobbing her head up and down.

I laughed. "Push it good! Push it real good!" I said then we both laughed and pumped our fists in the air like we were on a crowded dance floor.

"Okay, okay," I said. "Save it for the party." I was finished with my meal. "Are you done?" I asked Grace, pointing to her plate.

"Yeah, I'm full."

I pushed back the quilt, wrapped my robe a little tighter around my waist, then took our dishes, glasses, and silverware to the sink. On my last trip back to the couch, I sat in front of Grace with my back against her chest. We pulled the quilt up higher and together we snuggled down into the couch. We sat there silently for a while as we listened to the wind that blew outside and whispered its way through the house. I heard drops of water escape from the kitchen faucet and plop down loudly on the edge of a plate or maybe a glass. I listened to Grace's heartbeat as I felt her chest rise and fall. I was happy, content, in love. Under the quilt Grace held my hand and then she squeezed it gently.

"You know," she said. "You know...I like...I...I love you. I just wanted you to know that."

"I love you too, Grace," I said calmly holding the reins tight against my heart.

She gave me a huge hug that felt better than any she had given me thus far. I craned my neck upward and kissed her cheek. Then we settled back into happiness. A few minutes later there was a knock at the door. We both cocked our heads in disbelief.

"Wow! I can't believe someone is actually trick-or-treating!" I said.

"Crazy!" said Grace. "Come, get the bowl. I want to see who this crazy kid is."

I grabbed the bowl off the end table. Grace and I both walked to the front door pulling our robes tighter around ourselves during the journey. When I opened the door, all we saw was a huge, black umbrella. No one yelled "Trick-or-treat." There was only the sound of wind against rain.

"Can I help you?" I asked. I reached over and felt for the latch on the screen door to make sure it was locked.

"I hope so," a voice said. "Because I really need to see you, Sky."

When the umbrella was tipped back, Delbert's face came into view.

"Oh my God," I said, rolling my eyes.

"Who the hell is he?" Grace asked.

"Her fiancé," Delbert said. "Who are you? And why are you both in bathrobes?"

CHAPTER TWENTY-EIGHT

Lightning seemed to penetrate the air directly above Delbert's umbrella. It lit up the sky and brightened the surrounding area. I was able to see a black car, with its lights on, idling in the parking area that was situated a few feet from where he stood. A gust of wind grabbed greedily at his umbrella hoping to make it its own, but Delbert tightened his grip.

"Aren't you going to invite me in?"

This was supposed to be a question, but Delbert made it sound more like a command, as he was used to getting his way.

"No," I said. "I suggest you turn back around, get in that car that I'm sure is waiting for you, and go on back to…wherever."

"I see you've lost your Southern hospitality." I just looked at him. "Open the door, Sky, and let me in."

"Why are you here, anyway?"

"I told you I was going to come. Didn't you get my letter? We really need to talk about us."

"Oh my God, Delbert, there is no us! You *really* need help. I told you before this is one prize you missed. Go collect something else, move on with your life, and leave me alone already!"

"Sky, it's not like that. You're not just another notch in my belt."

"Hey, sure. Anyway, I don't really care. Just leave me alone."

"Look, if you let me in I can elaborate further."

"Bye, Delbert," I said.

Grace and I simultaneously backed away from the screen door. I had my hand on the edge of the storm door, ready to close it.

"Who's this? Your new lover? I would've been down with that, Sky. All you had to do was say the word. She looks like she probably tastes good too. Does she taste good, Sky?"

I gave him the finger and slammed the door. He laughed as he descended the stairs and made his way down the path. A few seconds later, we heard the engine of the car roar as it raced away.

Grace and I plopped down on the couch. She in one corner, me in the other. The mood of peace, contentment, and love had dissipated—slipped out with the cracking open of the front door. I fiddled with my robe as I pulled my feet up onto the couch. I was nervous, and the silence didn't help. Grace pulled the quilt back up over her legs, then pulled more of it up near her chest. She looked down at her hands before looking up at me.

"So that's the ex, huh? The guy you almost married?"

"Yeah, that's the asshole," I said.

"He came all the way to New York from North Carolina just to…to what, harass you? I don't get it."

"He's crazy. It's like he has a target he failed to hit—me—and now he's obsessed because he feels cheated in some warped way. Really, it's like a tantrum. He wanted something, couldn't get it, and so he's acting out."

"Weird," Grace said, studying her fingers.

"Definitely," I replied.

"So, what was he saying about some letter he wrote you? You never mentioned it to me."

"No, I didn't because, honestly, I didn't take it seriously. I read it, crumpled it up, and forgot about it."

"But he said in the letter that he was going to come here to see you, right?"

"Yes, but Delbert says a lot of things to get folks riled up. You heard what he said before I slammed the door."

"Yeah, but why didn't you tell me about the letter? It just seems a little…I don't know…a little…I'm thinking weird, but I'm also thinking secretive and dishonest. Would you have let him in if I weren't here?"

Grace looked directly at me now, her face hardened as if preparing for a blow. Her eyes seemed small and mean, and her hands were tight little fists.

"No, I wouldn't have. I'm sorry I didn't tell you about the letter. I didn't think it was important. It didn't mean anything to me, which was why right after I read it I threw it in the garbage. Then I totally forgot about it, Delbert, and his madness. I'm trying to focus on my future, on you, on us—not on my past," I said.

Just like that, I felt like we were right back at square one. Right back to me having to prove myself worthy. Right back to way before the "I love yous." I could see it in Grace's eyes, in her body language. She did not trust me.

"Earlier, you said you loved me. Is that still the case?" I asked.

"Of course, it is. I just…I just don't like secrets is all. If we're going to be a strong couple, there cannot be any secrets between us, okay?"

"Okay," I said.

"Good. Now come back over here and sit with me."

I crawled across the couch and sat between Grace's legs where I had been before, only this time I felt sad.

"I'm sorry," I said.

Tears, silent and warm, fell from my eyes, but Grace couldn't see them, and I didn't want her to know that I was crying. I didn't want her to know that my love for her was massive, but it also felt extremely fragile, like a giant balloon that could be destroyed by the tiniest of pricks.

"No worries," Grace said.

But I did worry.

CHAPTER TWENTY-NINE

The day of Ola's party was cold and windy. I was glad Grace and I had chosen costumes that fell in step with the weather. Our heavy leather jackets and long pants would definitely keep us warm. I double wrapped a long, red scarf around my neck and wore a pair of black leather gloves I'd taken from the lost and found at school to combat the cold. I thought the gloves added an extra touch of toughness to my costume, but Grace said they looked dumb.

The party started at nine o'clock, but we arrived around ten because Grace was in a shitty mood and she was dragging her ass. She was still a little distant and insisted on dwelling on the now infamous letter. She'd convinced herself that I'd kept the letter a secret because I was still madly in love with Delbert and didn't want to admit it. I'd pleaded my case over and over again trying to eradicate her fears and help us get back to that loving place we'd resided in for like five minutes, but it was to no avail, so I stopped trying and switched to hoping. I hoped that she would soon come to her senses and feel the love I had in my heart for her so we could move on to a better place. But my friend Sammy, a new teacher at my school who I'd become fast friends with, informed me that Geminis with Scorpio risings tend to hold on to things.

"So, are you Salt or are you Pepa?"

Ola materialized in front of me just as I'd exited the bathroom.

"Uh, I'm not really sure. We've never really discussed it. We've just been saying that we're Salt-N-Pepa. Which one is more levelheaded and reality based?" I asked.

"Not sure. Why, what's going on now?" Ola sidled up to me ready to devour some gossip.

"Nothing, but Grace refuses to believe it and I'm tired of being made the bad guy."

As reluctant as I was to tell Ola about what was going on between Grace and me, I felt as if I would burst from not having someone who would empathize with my side of the story to talk it over with.

"What's she making you feel bad about this time?"

"This stupid letter my ex sent me."

"Really?" Ola looked back and glanced around the room quickly. "Come, walk with me so we can talk more freely."

She grabbed my hand and led me as we weaved through an undulating crowd filled with Prince wannabes, Diana Ross imitators, and a few women rocking black turbans with black and gold military gear looking just like Queen Latifah on her *All Hail the Queen* album cover.

We exited the building and found our way to the vegetable garden planted and cared for by the tenants of the building. Down from the remnants of corn husks and the empty climbing poles labeled with big signs stating "peppers" and "tomatoes" that still occupied space in the otherwise bare community garden were two wooden benches painted a neon orange color. The benches seemed to glow in the dark.

"Sit. Tell me all about it," Ola said. So I did.

"So, Grace is upset because you forgot to tell her about this letter. A letter that you didn't even feel was important, which was why you threw it out in the first place."

"Exactly! She has it in her head that I was trying to hide something."

"Well, she's going to think what she's going to think no matter what you say. Sometimes, the more you plead your case; the guiltier people feel you are. Catch twenty-two. You just can't win."

"Exactly," I said.

"Maybe she'll come around. When we were together she would get upset about little things too, like if I mentioned that some chick was cute. She'd get all uptight about it and then she'd bring it up weeks later after I had totally forgotten about the comment and the girl."

"See. That's what I'm saying. She definitely holds on to things, which causes problems."

"Yeah, but you can't tell her that."

"No way," I said, shaking my head.

"So, what are you going to do?"

"Right now, nothing. I've tried pleading my case, but that didn't work. Time heals all wounds, right?"

"Girl, you sound like some old church lady!" Ola laughed.

I chuckled at my despair.

"Give her time. She'll come around, eventually. That's what my therapist says." Ola patted my hand and let out a sigh.

"How's therapy going?" I asked.

"It's…okay. Sometimes things come up that I'm not ready to delve into, but my therapist is patient so that's good."

"Hey, at least you're working on your issues. Maybe Grace and I need to go to therapy."

"Maybe," Ola replied. "But give it time, Sky. You two seem to always be on a roller coaster—up and down, up and down. It's like my mother used to say…"

"I know, focus on the good times."

"That's true too, but my mother would always tell me and my sisters that even if we stumbled, we were still moving forward."

"Nice," I said.

"Yeah. Come on, let's get back upstairs before folks notice that we're missing. I am the host after all," Ola said.

We stood and headed back toward the front of the building. Ola stopped short in front of the entrance.

"If you need anything or if you just want to talk, don't hesitate to call me."

"Okay, I won't. Thanks for listening," I said.

I reached out to give Ola a hug. She hugged me back. As she pulled away, she kissed me on the lips. This surprised me, but I didn't say anything. I just couldn't deal with anything else at that moment, so we just stood there, arms wrapped around each other, looking into each other's eyes. Then a white car filled with guys whipped around the corner. One of them yelled out the window. "Fuckin' dykes!"

I froze, not knowing what to expect next. As the car raced past us, one guy threw an empty beer can at us that missed by a mile. But his words, for me, had hit a target. Especially after the murder of that lawyer from Houston, Texas, Paul Broussard, that had happened on July 4th—the day of my big move to New York to finally live my life and be who I was. Someone the world hated. I was scared, but Ola yelled, "Fuck you!" as the car faded from sight. After the incident, she ushered me inside.

"There you are," Grace said when we got back upstairs. "I was looking for you."

"Needed a pepper from the garden. Took Sky with me for protection. Is that okay with you, Ms. Webster?" Ola asked.

Her tone seemed a bit rough and I wondered if she was as shaken as I was from the experience we'd just had.

"Whatever," Grace said. "Anyway, I was really talking to Sky. Are you ready to go? Because I'm ready."

I was definitely not in a rush to go back outside. What if next time the guys threw more than just an empty beer can? What if they skipped throwing things altogether and decided that they would just attack us? I was scared.

"We just got here," I said.

"Well, I'm ready to leave and I'm the one who's driving," Grace said.

"I'll take you home, Sky," a voice said from behind us. Grace and I turned around.

"Ms. Parker? What are you doing here?" I asked.

"Apparently, I'm your knight in shining armor."

"Who's this?" Grace asked.

"Assistant principal from my school. Grace, Ola, this is Valerie Parker."

Ola said hello, but Grace just looked at her. Ms. Parker seemed to take no notice.

"If you still need that ride, Sky, I'd be more than happy to give you a lift."

"I'm sure you would be," Grace grumbled.

"I want to stay a bit longer, so I'll take you up on your offer. Now we're all happy because we all get what we want," I said full of facetious intent.

"Fine," Grace said and barged her way toward the door.

Ms. Parker stuck out her elbow like gentlemen did a long time ago when they were escorting women.

"Shall we?" she asked.

"Surely," I said.

The drama of the night vanished in the crook of her smile.

I waved to Ola as Ms. Parker and I edged our way to the dance floor. Before I lost sight of her, I saw Ola shake her head. There was a sly smile on her face when she mouthed the words, "You're bad."

CHAPTER THIRTY

The party was still jumping, but Ms. Parker and I called it quits around two in the morning. I knew Grace was mad and I'd probably be in for a major argument when I got in, but it was nice dancing, laughing, and just having some fun.

"Here we are, safe and sound just like I promised," Ms. Parker said when she pulled up near the condo. I was glad she let me off in the same spot she did before and not right in front of my window. I didn't want Grace to see me step out of Ms. Parker's car and get upset all over again.

"Thank you so much, Ms. Parker."

"It's Valerie, remember, and there's no need to thank me. It was my pleasure."

"You never told me how you ended up at that party."

"Oh, girl, a friend of a friend's friend. You know how insular the black lesbian community can be."

"Yes, I'm beginning to see that," I said.

"Hope I didn't fan the flames between you and your girlfriend."

"No, the flames were sort of high already."

"Too bad."

"Yeah."

"I had a lot of fun with you tonight. Maybe we can get together again sometime soon and, say, have dinner, drinks, and a movie maybe?"

"Um, I'd love to, but right now I'm dealing with Grace and believe it or not, I'm hoping that it works out."

"Okay, I can respect that. I like an optimistic woman." We both laughed.

"Good night, Ms., uh…Valerie," I said.

"Good morning you mean. Good luck!"

"Thank you."

I closed the door and she was off.

I imagined the myriad exchanges to come as I walked slowly, reluctantly toward my apartment. I even stopped to check the mailbox—nothing. When I put my key in the door and turned the knob I expected to see Grace's face all flaming and twisted in anger, but she wasn't there. It was quiet downstairs, which meant she was probably upstairs feigning sleep, readying herself for the pounce.

The light was off in the bedroom, but I could see the outline of a large lump on Grace's side of the bed. For a minute, I contemplated going back downstairs and sleeping on the couch, but this was still my place and I needed to take a stand. I walked into the room, found the light switch, and flipped it on. The lump did not move. I walked over to my side of the bed and sat down to remove my socks.

"I see you're still mad at me. That's fine, but this obsession that you have about Delbert's letter meaning something to me has to stop. It's ruining us and I don't want us to be ruined."

I pulled off both my socks and tucked them into a round little ball.

"Again, with the silent treatment. That's definitely going to help make things better."

Aggravated, I got up, turned, and looked over at Grace's side of the bed. On top of the lump was a note.

Went home since you don't want to spend time with me anyway. Have fun with the old gal. Seems old is how you like your lovers anyway.

—Grace

"That bitch!" I yelled.

CHAPTER THIRTY-ONE

A couple of days had passed since the party, but I was still angry at Grace for her stubbornness, for her avoidance behaviors, and for being rude, so I hadn't spoken to her. Maybe we could've worked out our issues if she would've stayed Saturday night. Maybe we could've been in a better place by now. Maybe. Maybe. Whatever. I was getting tired of the little dance we had going. I was tired of running after her, heart on my sleeve, apology in my pocket. Let her come to me this time.

The day was cold but clear, so my kindergarten class was allowed to venture outside for recess. The yard was right outside my classroom window and I could hear their shouts of joy bounce off the cold, shiny slide before being absorbed into the playground's thick, rubberized surface. Malachi was reciting the ABCs at the top of his lungs. I heard one of the girls say, "Malachi is being boisterous." I chuckled with pride as I cleaned the paint off the students' tables. She had remembered the new, impromptu word I'd taught the class last week.

"What's so funny, Ms. Valentine?"

Startled, I turned around. It was Hope.

"Well, hello to you too, Hope," I said, then turned and continued my work.

"This is not a social visit," Hope said as she entered the classroom and closed the door behind her.

I noticed that her voice and face were tight. Her arms were folded across her chest like she was in a straitjacket. Hope amused me. She fancied herself a thug, a crusader fighting against some imagined injustice, but she was just a waif. A little girl playing dress-up.

"Oh, well, tell me, what kind of visit is this?"

"My sister told me you were *fraternizing* with the assistant principal. That is a big no-no, Sky. You should know that."

"We just happened to be at the same party," I said.

"Yeah, but then you deliberately decided to hang out with her knowing how that would make my sister feel." She took several steps into the classroom, all puffed up with pomposity. The chip on her shoulder could crush a nation.

"Is that what Grace told you? And did she tell you all of that so you could run over here with your cape flying and set me straight?"

"Cape flying? What are you talking about?"

"If Grace has an issue with me, then *Grace* needs to approach me instead of sending someone to do her dirty work. You two are like some sort of crazy tag team. Sorry to tell you, but this is not wrestling and I'm tired of your drama and intimidation tactics," I said. "If Grace wants to talk, she has my number. Goodbye, Hope."

I turned my back on her, gathered all of the used paintbrushes that were on the tables, and walked over to the sink. She closed the door with a thud before I could turn on the water.

The next day, parent-teacher conferences were being held from four o'clock in the afternoon until seven that night. Some of the teachers had gone out for an evening meal to hang out before the parents arrived, but I stayed in my room hanging up the children's many accomplishments for their parents' perusal.

"Looks great."

I turned around and saw Ms. Parker standing in the doorway.

"Thanks. Trying to make it look nice. I want to showcase all the students' work," I said.

"Great job." Ms. Parker looked back behind her into the hallway, then glanced from side-to-side.

"I wanted to talk to you." She came into the room, walked over, and stood beside me.

"Your girlfriend, she's Hope Webster's sister?"

"Twin. That's right."

"Funny, I didn't really look at her. All I saw was the short hair."

"Why? What's up?"

I walked over to another desk where I'd stacked paintings that I needed to sort through. Ms. Parker was on my heels.

"Hope came to my office this morning and she made this sly and very subtle, umm, I don't want to say threat, but it sort of felt like one, telling me that, in short, if I was smart I'd leave you alone."

"Hope is crazy. Pay her no mind," I said as I pushed the corner of a large paper heart onto the wall hoping the Fun-Tak would hold.

"She made it seem like she'd take the matter above my head if need be. I guess she's failed to realize she works for *me*—not the other way around."

"Exactly. What sane person would threaten their boss and risk their livelihood over something that doesn't even concern them? No one," I said. "I guess since she's like three minutes older than Grace she feels obligated to play the role of big sister, protector, and all that, but really she actually causes more trouble then there was to begin with."

I stopped working and faced Ms. Parker. "Don't worry about Hope, really."

"For now, I'm not. I just wanted to know how close the two of you were, being that you're dating her sister in case I have to make some moves."

"You're the assistant principal. Do what you need to do."

"I will."

Ms. Parker turned and walked toward the door. She had a lean build and I watched as her long legs covered the distance with ease. She walked with confidence, assurance. I knew that she hadn't really come to me harboring worrisome questions and insecurities regarding Hope. She already had a plan.

Once in the doorway she stopped and turned around.

"I'm still hoping that we can do dinner one day—soon."

She had a sly, little smile on her face, and I could envision all of the things she was thinking about. Things she hoped would take place after dinner.

"You know Ms. Parker, this could be considered sexual harassment," I said.

Ms. Parker placed her hand on her hip and widened her smile.

"Why Ms. Valentine, you and I are just friends. Nothing more. Isn't that what you said?"

I tried to hide my smile but couldn't. "Yes, that's what I said."

"Then I see no problem here." She looked quickly at the watch on her wrist. "You might want to get back to work. Parents will be here in ten." Then she turned and ambled out the door.

CHAPTER THIRTY-TWO

Parent conferences went well and there were no more surprise visits from Hope or Ms. Parker, but several days had passed since then and I still hadn't heard from Grace. I was standing firm in my resolve to not make the first move. Maybe it was dumb being that I was sort of miserable, but I thought it was important.

I hit the gym again after slacking off for a while; feeling the burn and soreness in my muscles was painful, but invigorating. It felt like I was accomplishing something, like I was moving forward. I felt like growth was occurring, although not between Grace and me.

I arrived at the gym at five and decided I'd take the African dance class offered at six o'clock even though it was often overcrowded. This allowed me enough time to change out of my school clothes and into my workout gear. I was hopeful that I'd get a good spot.

The locker room was a good size, but it was packed with women in various stages of undress, all of them of varying shapes, sizes, and hues. I searched up and down the rows for a full-sized locker so I wouldn't have to fold and, ultimately, wrinkle my coat. Luckily, I found one in the last row, close to the restrooms.

I hung up my coat and placed my scarf, hat, and gloves on the top shelf of the locker, then grabbed a small metal stool so I could remove my boots. For some reason, the incident with the guy yelling "Fuckin' dykes!" and throwing a can at Ola and me popped into my head as I sat there. I was horrified after that had happened, but then so much other stuff had taken place so quickly after that I hadn't had time to reflect on it. Ola seemed to handle it well. I wondered how often she'd had those words hurled at her as she walked down the street. I looked around me at all the women seemingly at ease exposing their breasts, asses, and bushes. Would they remain at ease if they knew I was gay? That I liked breasts and asses? I was thinking about this when I felt someone standing over me. Without looking up, I scooted my stool over a little more to the left to allow the woman extra room to pass.

"Thanks, but I don't think that's going to cut it."

I recognized the voice. I looked up to see Grace. Although I was pissed at her and wanted to yell and argue with her, I still loved her. A single glance into her big, beautiful eyes threatened to wipe away my anger. But I fought with my heart and held tight to it.

"What are you doing here?" I asked, my voice and face trying hard to hold on to the edge of anger. I could have kicked myself for encouraging her to join the gym.

"Working out."

No malice in her voice. No sign of impending confrontation. This angered me more, as part of me was looking for a fight. I wanted the flames to burn high between us and shine a bright light on her hurtful accusations and festering insecurities.

"I'm glad you're here. I was going to call you tonight. I wanted to say I'm sorry. I apologize for being such a tool. I harped on your ex's letter and blew it up into some secret validating thing in my head when clearly it wasn't all that. I behaved like a jerk and I'm sorry. Please forgive me. I've missed you."

"I've missed you too," I said. "And I accept your apology."

My anger had completely dissipated like the mean witch after a good rain. She reached for me. I stood, grabbed her shoulders, and pressed her body into mine. It was good to feel her, to have her in my arms again. She hugged me tight. It was like we were both whole again.

I stepped away from her, but she pulled me back toward her and kissed me. There was an immediate rush of heat through my body. She pulled away this time and when she did I recalled where we were, and looked around. I noticed that a few women were looking at us as they passed by to go to their lockers or to the bathroom, but no one said anything. I wasn't really worried though because I felt safe with Grace by my side. It didn't make any sense really because between the two of us, I was most likely to kick someone's ass in a fight, but having her by my side made me feel courageous.

"So, what class are you planning to take?" Grace asked.

I pulled at the large, heavy blue scarf she had wrapped several times around her thin neck.

"African dance at six."

Grace looked at the large watch on her slender wrist.

"It's twenty after five now. Uh, how invested are you in this class?"

"Mm…I could be persuaded to engage in other endeavors," I said, smiling.

"Good! Let's blow this joint."

"Okay."

I shoved my boots back on, grabbed my hat, gloves, scarf, and bag out of the locker and set them on the stool. Grace snatched my coat off the hook and held it open for me as I proceeded to put my arms inside. When my arms were tucked safely inside, Grace buttoned my coat, pulled at my collar so that it stood up around my ears, and gently wrapped my scarf around my neck while I put on my hat. When we were done, she kissed me again quickly on the lips.

"Are you done with that locker?"

A young, brown-skinned woman with loose, curly hair that fell to her shoulders stood about two feet away from us. I noticed a thin, beaded rainbow bracelet around her wrist. Grace turned to face her.

"It's all yours," she said.

Then she grabbed my hand and we left, together.

CHAPTER THIRTY-THREE

Thanksgiving day and the flight to North Carolina was fast. Too fast. I spent the entire flight preoccupied with how I would tell my family about my relationship with Grace. Should I just come right out with it and let the chips fall where they may? Or should I ease into it, feel them out, see how they took to Grace first? If they liked her, maybe it would be easier to tell them? I wasn't sure, so I decided to go with the flow. Maybe some perfect situation would present itself along the way.

Grace and I both had only carry-on luggage, so as soon as we could exit the plane we did. We made our way, mostly in silence, through the airport while I kept an eye out for my brother, who was supposed to pick us up.

"Did he say what he would be wearing?" Grace asked.

"Yeah, jeans, a shirt, and jacket. Generic attire. My brother's not the type to think about those things," I said.

"Does he know about us?"

"No. I told you, no one knows yet, but I plan to tell everyone before we leave."

"Don't do that on my account," Grace said, then walked ahead of me.

I knew she was uncomfortable. The tension in her shoulders, the rigidity in her arm as she held her bag told the story, but I was nervous too. My family was old-fashioned for lack of a better word. They considered themselves "good Christians" which, when I was growing up, I took to mean "closed-minded." They believed in the stereotypical male-female roles and felt that everyone had their place. There was no rocking the boat, no changing things up. To this day, well, as far as I knew, my mother still did not wear pants because only men wore pants. We'd had a big argument about my wanting to wear pants when I was younger. End result: I was allowed to wear them, but my mother would not buy them. I had to save up the money I made from chores and working at the library to pay for my own jeans. This decision was made by my father, who was either tired of the arguing or figured I'd never get around to saving my money anyway. But because I'd taken it as a battle to be won against my mother, I saved every cent until I was able to buy my first pair of pants. I wore them every day for a whole week so she would have to look at me in them as I paraded around the house sitting in the most unladylike ways I could think of.

I spotted Henry as soon as we spun through the revolving doors. His head was turned away from us. He was probably scanning folks in hopes of finding me.

"Hey, bro!" I yelled in his direction. He turned.

"Hey!"

He smiled and walked toward me with his arms outstretched. We hugged, then he stepped back to look at me.

"Well, you look the same. Guess the big city hasn't changed you that much."

I laughed but didn't bother with a direct reply.

"This is Grace. She'll be visiting with us for four days," I said.

Henry reached out and shook Grace's extended hand.

"Nice to meet you. I'll take that," he said as he reached for Grace's bag.

"Hi, um, it's okay. It's not that heavy," she said.

"Nonsense, I can't have you young ladies walking around carrying your own bags. And you're a guest too. Uh-uh." He turned to me. "Well you ain't a guest, but still, give it here. Gotta do my civic duty."

I gave Henry my bag and Grace followed suit. Henry smiled as he took the bags and led us to his car.

"New car, I see," I said.

Henry had the trunk open wide as he put the bags inside.

"Yeah, the old one was shot. Didn't want to, but had to get a new one."

"Didn't peg you for a red man," I said.

Grace and I were standing by our respective doors—she in the back, me in the front beside Henry—waiting for him to finish up so we could all get in at the same time.

"The color was June's idea not mine."

He closed the trunk, walked around to his door, pulled the handle, and climbed in.

"June's moving you out of your comfort zone, I see. Good for her," I said as Grace and I climbed in the car and sat on the new black leather seats.

"Yeah, well, you know. She's trying." He laughed and put the car in gear, and we pulled out and into very little traffic.

The car was quiet as we rode along. I looked out the window and took in the countryside. I was calmed by the sight of the trees we passed, their tops swaying gently back and forth in the cool November breeze. The houses were modest with large plots of green grass that surrounded them. Children—some on bikes, some sitting on the top steps of porches with dusty brown dogs sprawled out beside them—looked content, but I wondered if they were. I wondered if being content was enough as we drove through the place where I grew up, the place that made me. The place I'd fought so hard to leave behind.

Henry broke the silence. "So, are you a teacher too, Grace?"

Grace cleared her throat. "No, I'm an interpreter."

"Interpreter? Wow," he said.

Henry flipped a switch and engaged the turn signal as he moved his hands counter-clockwise and guided his new Toyota Corolla into a left turn. He looked intently out the front window for a while. I noticed his face was a little rounder than it had been before I'd left. His belly, a little bigger. Henry's thirty-five years were beginning to show. He caught me staring and gave a shy smile. It was the same smile he'd worn as an awkward teenager. Then he glanced at the rearview mirror for a second, giving Grace another quick inspection.

"So, then, you know, what, Spanish?" he asked.

"Excuse me?" Grace said.

"You translate Spanish? Or do you know some other language?"

"I don't translate. I interpret. And no, not Spanish— American Sign Language," Grace replied.

"Translate, interpret, same difference, right?" Henry laughed as he glanced at me.

"Well, not really," I said. "Translators convert written material from one language to another while interpreters convert spoken material from one language to another." I looked back at Grace. "That's correct, right?"

"You hit it on the head," Grace said. We smiled at each other.

"Like I said, same difference," Henry said. "And here we are."

He had pulled up into the driveway adjacent to my parents' house. I got out of the car and looked at the house. It felt like I'd left it a lifetime ago.

The house still appeared neat and well-maintained, but it looked smaller, like it had squatted down lower somehow. The windows and door seemed like they were hidden as they were recessed behind the wraparound porch that encircled the small, white, two-story home.

"Who put in the flowers?" I asked.

I walked around the car toward the front porch. I noticed there were dainty pink and white flowers along the periphery of the house.

"Mom's taken up gardening. Looks good now, but it took her a few tries to get it right," Henry said as he lifted our bags out of the trunk.

"They're nice," Grace said. I stood beside her looking at the flowers, hesitant about making my way into the house and seeing my parents. Hesitant to be confined in a space that was now mostly memory.

Henry closed the trunk of his car with his elbow. He walked up to the house, put our bags down on the porch, opened the screen door, and held it open for us with the side of his foot as he lifted our bags again. The storm door was already ajar.

"After you, ladies," he said.

I wanted to hold Grace's hand for moral support. Wanted to feel the transfer of strength in the silence of her touch, but I didn't. I couldn't. Instead, I walked up the stairs and across the threshold alone, reminding myself that I was okay. I had made a new life for myself beyond these walls. I had a new job, new friends, and a new lover who was standing right behind me. My life was my own now. I didn't need to ask permission to live it or to be me.

CHAPTER THIRTY-FOUR

I found my mom in the kitchen—head in the oven, butt in the air—just like old times.

"Smells good, Mom," I said, coming up behind her.

Surprised, she popped up quickly and twirled around, closing the stove in the same fluid motion.

"Sky! You're here!"

"Yes, I am," I said with a smile on my face.

Mom gave me a big, long hug, which surprised me as she was never one to show affection. But staying true to my "go with the flow" motto, I hugged her back with the same intensity. When we were done, she took a step back to look at me.

"You look thin, dear. Are you eating enough?"

"I'm eating just fine, Mom," I said.

"I made your favorite—macaroni and cheese."

"Yes! Oh my God, homemade macaroni and cheese! Love it!"

My mother frowned. "Don't use the Lord's name in vain, Sky." She walked over to Grace. "And who is this lovely lady here?"

"This is Grace Webster. I told you she was coming."

"So nice to meet you, dear."

My mom took Grace's hand into both of hers and gave it a small squeeze before letting go.

"Likewise, Mrs. Valentine," Grace said.

"Your hair is awfully short, dear. If I didn't get a good look at you, I would've mistaken you for a young man. Aren't you cold with your hair so short?"

"Mom!"

Grace laughed. "Yes, Mrs. Valentine, it is short, but I like it this way and I'm not cold at all. In fact, it's actually warmer here than it is in New York."

"Yes, I suppose that's true," my mom said. "I hope you're a better eater than Sky. I'm making a nice feast for us tonight."

"I will eat as much as I can. And thank you so much for cooking and allowing me to stay in your home."

"My pleasure," my mom said. She turned back to me. "Go downstairs and say hello to your father. He's been waiting for you."

"Okay, come on Grace."

We walked to the little door that was adjacent to the kitchen. I opened it and we began our descent downstairs to the basement. I stopped halfway and turned back toward Grace. She looked at me puzzled. I took one step back, pulled her head down, and kissed her hard and quickly. She smiled then mouthed, "Cut it out" to me. I laughed as we continued on our way.

The basement actually seemed bigger and nicer than I remembered. Someone had gotten rid of the drab blue color that was on the walls and painted them white, put in new light fixtures, and mounted a large TV high on the wall across from the couch.

Dad was watching the annual Thanksgiving Day Parade and Mickey Mouse's large head floated across the screen.

"Daddy," I said as I walked up behind him and threw my arms around his shoulders. He felt thinner. I kissed him on the cheek.

"My baby," he said, a big smile on his handsome face. "Come on around here and sit by your old man."

He patted the space beside him on the couch. I walked around, taking Grace with me. I plopped down next to him. Grace stood for a minute then took a seat in the recliner across from us. She sat perched on the edge.

"Oh, I'm sorry. Who do we have here?" Dad asked.

"This is Grace Webster. Mom did tell you I was bringing a guest, right?"

"I suppose, but sometimes I don't hear everything your mother says. Hello, Ms. Webster. Nice to meet you."

My father leaned forward in an effort to get up and shake Grace's hand, but he was having difficulty.

"Please don't get up," Grace said. She popped off her perch, walked over to where my father sat, and shook his hand.

"Nice to meet you too sir. How are you feeling these days?" Grace asked and let go of his hand.

"Old," my father said, then laughed.

"Oh, Daddy." I squeezed his shoulder. "Are you following the doctor's orders and doing all of the things you're supposed to do?"

My father fanned his hand around in the air in an effort to push all that had happened to him aside.

"Yeah, yeah. Your mother has got me on some sort of diet and she's always pushing some pill my way. I tell ya, I've never taken so many pills in my life."

"Well, you gave us all a scare. You have to take care of yourself," I said.

"Hmm, Ms. Webster, have you ever seen such a fuss? I'm sixty years old. I thank the Lord that he brought me along this far, but when he says it's time for me to go, I'm ready."

"Well, let's hope he don't come calling on you no time soon," I said.

"Enough about me. How are you two young ladies doing? Flight here good?"

"Yes," Grace and I said at the same time.

"Good, good."

We heard my mother's voice at the top of the stairs.

"James, tell Sky I need her to run to the store for me. I thought I had enough breadcrumbs, but I don't."

"She done heard you already, Etta. What's Henry doing?" my father yelled back.

"He went home. Had to help June with something."

"It's fine, Dad," I said. "Sure, Mom. I'm coming," I yelled. The basement door closed. I gave my father another peck on the cheek and stood to leave.

"We'll be back. Remember, I'm here for four days so there's plenty of time for us to sit and chat."

"Okay, baby. I'm a sit here and finish watching the rest of this here parade."

My father settled back down into the couch as Grace and I headed back upstairs.

"Sorry to send you back out so soon, dear," my mom said as soon as we entered the kitchen.

"Not a problem, Mom. I wanted to go see Odeta anyway."

"Oh, that's good. She's been asking about you. Here's some money and here are the keys to the car."

"Breadcrumbs, right?"

I had taken the car keys out of my mother's hand and Grace and I were headed toward the door.

"Yes, plain. See if they have any without added salt for your father."

"Will do," I called back over my shoulder.

Henry's car was gone which allowed access to the garage from the driveway. I bent down to pull at the handle and the garage door slid up with ease. My dad's car practically filled the space. Grace and I squeezed along the sides. I pushed the unlock button and all four locks popped up like tiny jack-in-the-boxes. We opened the doors as far as we could and squeezed inside.

"I didn't know you knew how to drive," Grace said as I put the key in the ignition.

"I don't, but if you kiss me I might be able to wing it," I teased.

Grace glanced around to see if anyone was looking, then she leaned toward me. I grabbed her head and forced my tongue into her mouth. I was feeling very horny. That coupled with the prospect of getting caught added to the tantalizing feeling of danger.

"We will definitely get busted if you keep on doing that," Grace said, looking over her shoulder once again.

"Relax. No one's around. This is not New York where random folks just happen by. No one really walks around here."

I backed the car out of the garage, made a left turn, and proceeded down the street.

"First stop—Odeta's," I said.

"And Odeta is?"

"Childhood friend who helped me move to New York under major protest," I said.

Grace's face lit up with a sly smile.

"Did you and Odeta do any fooling around?"

"Oh, God, no. Odeta is as straight as an arrow."

"So, she doesn't know that you're gay either."

"No, she doesn't."

The light ahead turned red. Clouds were forming in the sky and the trees were bending and bowing down a bit further than they were earlier in the day. I put my foot on the brake as we approached the stoplight.

"I'm sorry, babe. I know you're way past this stage in your journey, please just bear with me."

I reached over and put my hand on her thigh. She held it.

"Actually, I'm happy to be here as your witness. I mean, I'm scared for you, but I'm glad I can serve as some form of support."

"Thank you. I appreciate that."

"I think your mom is going to be the one who takes it the hardest. I see her as the one who will definitely give you some flack. Your dad, on the other hand, seems more easygoing."

"Yeah, he is, but he usually gets railroaded by my mom into thinking a certain way about things, so…the whole situation is iffy."

"Oh, so he wears the pants, but she wears the hat," Grace said.

"Exactly. Head Chief Officer Etta Valentine." I laughed.

"That reminds me, what's up with the names—Etta and James, Henry and June? Completely unfathomable. Totally crazy! I take it you're supposed to end up with someone named Lark?" We laughed.

"I know, like what are the odds?" I said.

"Odds are someone named Lark would definitely be female, so you're just following your destiny."

"Seems that way to me," I said as we pulled into Odeta's driveway.

CHAPTER THIRTY-FIVE

Odeta lived in the same house that she grew up in. Her mother had remarried and moved to Virginia right before I moved to New York, and she left the house to Odeta. I noticed Odeta had painted the outside of the house lavender and had installed new, white shutters beside each window. Now the house had a cottage-like feel.

There was no fence surrounding the property, so Grace and I were able to cut through the grass, which was patchy in spots, and make our way up the front steps.

The front door was open, but the screen door was locked. I knocked on the screen door's wooden frame, which was painted white to match the shutters, a few times. No response. I knocked again, harder.

"Who that is?" Odeta said. "I say, who that knocking on my door so hard? Oh, I'm coming. I'm coming."

Through the netting of the screen door, I could see her working her way down the small flight of stairs that separated the top of the house from the bottom. Grace stood beside me, but the doorway was not very wide so she could not see Odeta until she approached the screen.

Odeta did not open the door right away. Instead, she stood peering out at me, no discernible expression on her face. But when she stapled her fist to her hip I knew she meant business.

"Well, well, well. What do we have here? And what you banging down my door for Miss I-moved-to-New York-and-I-can't-write-or-call-nobody? Made your way back home, huh?"

"Odeta, I don't recall tearing up any envelopes with your name on them nor do I recall hearing your voice on my answering machine, so I guess we both have some explaining to do."

Odeta laughed heartily as she unlocked the screen door.

"Get on in here, girl!" she cried.

Odeta grabbed me in a big bear hug and pulled me inside. The scent of her perfume was overpowering. I coughed and pushed her away gently so as not to be rude.

"Well, let me lookatcha," Odeta said. Then she proceeded to scrutinize me with her sharp eyes.

"You ain't changed a bit. Hair's a tad bit longer, bones poking through your collar more than they were before, but other than that, you look the same. Hmm, well, your skin's not as vibrant as it used to be. Probably all a that dirt and grime you livin' in. Ha. Ha!"

Odeta clapped her hands together, laughing and feeling good about her own joke. Then she straightened up fast and looked at Grace like she didn't notice her until that very second.

"And who do we have here? Is this another one that done lost her way? Don't be hiding behind, Sky. Speak up, what your name is?" Odeta demanded.

Grace stuck out her hand. "Hi, I'm Grace Webster. Nice to meet you."

Odeta shook Grace's hand with a limp wrist and gave her the same once-over she gave me.

"Grace is from New York, born and bred," I commented eagerly. "She's my guest for the next coupla days, so you be nice. Thought I'd give her the limited version of North Carolina while I'm here."

"Limited, huh? Well, it's a pleasure to meet you, Grace," Odeta said. "Come on into the kitchen y'all and get something to drink."

The kitchen was small, but relatively bright. Sunlight, filtered by several layers of encroaching clouds, fell across a round glass table that had a large bowl of brightly colored fruit at its center. Four chairs, transparent and very modern looking, with straight, hard backs were pushed far under the table so that each chair back made contact with the table's rounded glass edge.

"Nice setup," I said as I pulled out a chair and sat down. Grace followed suit.

"Yeah, Mama bought the table and chairs before she left. It's not to my liking, but it's useful, so it works. Plus, everybody who comes to visit seems to like it so…"

Odeta pulled a large pitcher out of the refrigerator and set it down next to the bowl of fruit. Then she grabbed three glasses from the cupboard and proceeded to pour.

"I know you ain't drinking none of this in New York City. Am I right? When's the last time you had yourself a nice cold glass of delicious sweet tea?" Odeta asked.

"Probably around the end of summer," I said, taking a big gulp.

"How that hit ya, Grace? Good ain't it?" Odeta asked.

"Mm, very," Grace said, a wide smile across her face.

"Y'all hungry? What y'all want to eat? I got some leftover rice and peas with some collards that I made yesterday. Got some pork shoulder that Mrs. Johnson from down the way gave me two days ago. I could warm all a that up. Y'all got to be hungry. Are you hungry?"

"I'm good," I said. "I'll just have some of these grapes from this here bowl, if you don't mind."

"That ain't no *real food*, but knock yourself out," Odeta said. "How about you, Grace? Can I offer you something? No need acting polite if you're starving. There's plenty here to share."

"No, no thank you. This tea is doing the job."

"Y'all too polite. Since when you start being all polite, Sky? Long as I known you, you always hungry." Odeta huffed.

"Gotta save some room for Thanksgiving dinner later. Mama's cooking. You coming?" I asked.

With each word uttered, I felt my tongue loosen and slip back in time into the old vernacular, into the easy flowing dialect of the South.

"You know I am. But first I gotta stop by Cookie's. She and the kids expecting me."

"How is Cookie? And the kids?" I asked. Then I told Grace: "Cookie is Odeta's older sister."

"She all right. Still fooling around with that lazy-ass, no-good, daddy of her children even though he got another woman and child over in Charlotte."

"Crazy," I said not wanting to delve deeper into the drama that was Cookie.

"Damn sure is," Odeta said.

She pulled out a chair, sat down, and took a long swig of tea from her glass.

"Girl, your hair is short, short! Betcha it's nice that you ain't gotta fuss around with it much, huh? Don't your head get cold though? You cut it that way yourself?"

Grace ran her hand over her head with, what seemed to be, a bit of hesitance, uncertainty. Her hair, or lack thereof, had become the main topic of the day thus far. I'd forgotten about the importance of hair and all of the baggage that came with it in the African American communities of the South. In New York, black women wore their hair in various styles, but in North Carolina, anything non-traditional or anything that wasn't long, flowing, and European-inspired, stuck out. I recalled my plethora of hairstyles—the high top, the Grace Jones, a short-lived mohawk, and then, finally, dreadlocks. I remembered when I first got them. Odeta pulled at them and touched each one with only the very tips of her fingers as she circled my head with a look of distaste and disapproval on her face. People yelled, "Hey, Whoopi Goldberg!" at me wherever I went. It pissed me off and sometimes rattled me, but for the most part I ignored them. Now, almost five years later, here was Grace basically getting the same treatment.

"No, Odeta. She cut it that way by accident. What kind of a question is that?"

"I'm just asking a simple question, Sky. No need in gettin' hostile." Odeta sucked her teeth. "Look here, so tell me about New York. How you like it there? How's teaching them little crumb snatchers? Where y'all two meet?"

I drained my glass, set it back down on the table and then looked at my watch.

"It's getting late. You need to get to Cookie's, and we need to go to the store for my mom, but we'll talk later. I'll fill you in," I said and stood.

"All right then," Odeta said.

She didn't seem happy, but I wasn't about to divulge my whole New York experience over a glass of sweet tea. She walked us to the door.

"I'm a try to finish up with Cookie and the kids quick so we can catch up," Odeta said, holding the screen door open for us to exit.

"No need to rush," I said from the top step. "I'll be here for a few days. We don't have to do everything tonight."

"Okay, well, I'll see. Nice meeting you, Grace. I'll see both of you later on tonight."

"Yes, nice meeting you too. Thank you for the tea. It was delicious," Grace said.

"Girl, you just too polite. I love it!"

"Bye, Odeta," I said with a tone of finality.

It felt to me like she was mocking Grace. The, oh-so-polite Northerner. Ha-ha. Since when was being polite a crime or something to make fun of?

We cut across the grass and got into the car. As we pulled away, Odeta waved and I honked the horn twice as in, "Fuck you!"

"Okay, why are you being so bitchy?" Grace asked when we turned the corner.

"Me?"

"Yes, you."

"You didn't think Odeta was being bitchy with her stupid ass comments about your hair?"

"Maybe she was just curious. Seems everyone is."

"Yeah, and it's beginning to annoy me. What are we living in the 1950s or something? Get with the program people!" I yelled with frustration at the windshield.

"Sky, calm down. I'm used to comments and questions about my hair. People say stuff all the time. Some of it good. Some, not so good, but I don't pay people any mind. I like my hair this way and that's what matters. My hair is an expression of who I am, and I like who I am, so no worries."

I parked the car in the store parking lot and let out a big sigh.

"You're so brave and patient, that's why I love you," I said.

Grace smiled. I leaned over and kissed her firmly on her soft lips. We pulled away and gazed into each other's eyes. As we turned, ready to exit the car, I saw Delbert staring at us through the windshield.

"I knew it! From the moment I spotted you both in matching bathrobes, I knew," Delbert blurted the minute I emerged from the car.

He pointed a rigid finger in my direction, accompanied by a smug look on his face as if he'd won some major contest because only he'd known the correct response. Grace had closed her car door and stood beside it with her arms folded across her chest in what appeared to be frustration or some sort of defense. I slammed my car door, walked closer to Delbert, and stood my ground.

"Wow, you knew! Big deal! If you're looking for a prize, there isn't one. But I do have some advice—mind your own business and stay out of mine!"

Delbert smiled and then he laughed. A little at first, then a big hearty guffaw like an imbecile. I shook my head as I walked past him. Grace and I had gotten as far as the automated doors when we heard Delbert yell.

"Boy, I can't wait until your folks get wind of this!"

"Mind your business, Delbert!" I yelled back.

"The truth is my business," he replied coolly.

I was about to charge back toward him, but Grace grabbed me by the elbow.

"Ignore him. He wants you to get all worked up. Just ignore him and let's go."

Grace led me inside Piggly Wiggly where even the arctic blast from the droning air conditioner was unable to lower the temperature of the blood that boiled inside of me.

CHAPTER THIRTY-SIX

"Now that's a turkey!" my dad said when I moved the turkey from the top of the stove, where it was cooling, to its honored place at the center of the dining room table.

Mom had her good wedding china that was still flawlessly intact after thirty-five years of marriage stacked on the counter waiting to be placed on the table.

I sucked up turkey juice with the baster and squirted it across the bird's ample breasts. Then I found the placemats and put seven orange and brown ones on the table, alternating the colors to create a pattern. Afterward, I placed one piece of fine china on each placemat.

I was hoping that Odeta would ultimately get stuck at her sister Cookie's house and the extra place setting wouldn't be needed. Actually, it was hard for me to recall a Thanksgiving dinner at our house without Odeta. When we were younger, she'd have biscuits and gravy at her house then head on over to our house for the rest of her Thanksgiving meal. She said her mama threw down when it came to making biscuits and gravy, but that was the highlight of her culinary skills. Everything else she attempted to bake, fry, broil, boil, or steam turned out to be terrible.

"Henry will be joining us, but he told me earlier that June left this morning to spend the holiday with her family in Georgia," Mom said as she walked back into the room.

"Oh," I said. "And Henry didn't want to go with her?"

"Sky, your father just got out of the hospital. Why would Henry want to go traipsing all the way to Georgia when his family is here?"

"Okay," I said. I threw my hands up in surrender. I didn't want to make a scene. I needed everyone to remain in good spirits—especially my mother. My thinking was, if she felt jovial, then maybe hearing that Grace and I were lovers wouldn't be such a blow. It was wishful thinking at its best, but it was the only hope I had.

"Grace, your family isn't missing you?" my mom asked.

Her face looked all innocent, but the negative spaces surrounding each word weighed them down.

"No, my family doesn't celebrate Thanksgiving," Grace replied.

Here we go, I thought. Another strike against her. I was about to grab the napkins to add to the table, so I'd have an outlet for all of the nervous energy I felt, but my mom reached for them before I did.

"Oh!" my mother exclaimed with a look on her face that suggested she was highly insulted by this act of negligence. "Why not?"

My mother had stopped fussing with the napkins and turned to stare at Grace, her hands folded high above her breasts.

The word "stuffing" ran like a stream from one side of my brain to the other and back again. My mother was not a big woman, but she was overstuffed with proprieties and morals.

"During our teenage years, after having read several books about the holiday, my sister and I, along with my mom and dad, decided that we didn't want to partake in a feast that celebrated the genocide of the indigenous people who once were the great stewards of this land," Grace said.

"Great stewards, huh?" my mother replied—eyes wide and her eyebrows lifted. "Interesting. So..." My father cut her off.

"To each his own, Etta, right?" my dad said as he made his way to the table. He took the plate my mother had picked up to remove from the table and placed it back down to where it had been before. Just then the phone rang.

"Got it," I said. I gave Grace a "This is not going well" look as I made my exit toward the living room to answer the phone.

It was Henry. "I'm a take a nap. I'll be over later on. Probably after dessert."

"Copping out on us, huh? Mom was so looking forward to your company and there's some big breasts here waiting for you to carve them."

"I'll let Dad do the honors. I just need a little rest. June had me up all night with her packing."

"I'll let the big boss know," I said and hung up the phone.

When I walked back into the kitchen to deliver the news, Grace was parceling out the dinnerware and lining up the cutlery. I figured she must have found a way to redeem herself because no one was ever allowed to finger my mother's fine china and dinnerware.

"Henry said he needs some rest, so he'll be here after dessert," I announced to the kitchen and its occupants.

My mother stopped cranking the tiny wheel of the can opener that went around the top of the cranberry sauce can and let out a deep sigh.

"Looks like there's even fewer of us now," my mother said.

"Hey, more for us!" I exclaimed. My mother smiled.

"You always could see the bright side of things, dear," she said, then continued cranking open the can of cranberry sauce that no one ever ate.

Finally, the table was set, the food was beautiful and bountiful all cradled in bowls and pans of various sizes, and we were all seated—Mom and Dad at the table's heads, Grace and I flanking the sides. Everyone held hands and bowed their heads as my father led us in prayer. Grace had informed me that as a rule, her family wasn't very religious. Her mom and dad left the decision regarding spiritual beliefs to her and her sister. They believed that Hope and Grace would form their own opinions and would practice whatever they saw fit, so I was glad she didn't protest the prayer or let on that this was also not in her tradition.

"Thank you for keeping us safe, Lord, and giving me another chance at life. Thank you for my lovely wife of many years who continues to love me and look after me. Thank you for bringing my daughter back to me to help celebrate this day, oh Lord. Thank you for family, oh Lord, as it is the most important thing."

"Amen!" my mother proclaimed then reiterated, "Thank you, Jesus, for family! And for being here for one another in tough times. In your name we pray. Amen."

"Amen," we all said and dropped hands.

"Get some of that macaroni and cheese, Sky, and make sure you give Grace some. We need to fatten her up a bit," my mother said. "She's long and lean like I used to be. Remember that, James?"

"Sure do, Etta," my dad replied.

I was putting the first spoonful of mac and cheese on my dad's plate when the doorbell rang.

"I'll get it," my mother said. She pushed her chair back while eyeing what I was doing. "Your father cannot have macaroni and cheese. Please remove it from his plate," she said as she left the kitchen.

"Sorry, Daddy," I said. I scraped the mac and cheese onto my plate. "Maybe next year."

"Yeah, maybe," he said, running his fork through his rice and peas. His face looked sad.

I looked at Grace across the turkey's distended belly. It was strange to have her here, in my mother's kitchen, sitting and eating dinner with the family. I'm sure she felt a bit weird too, but she was going with the flow like a real trooper. I felt extremely grateful to have her in my life. She saw me looking at her and made a questioning face. I smiled, looked over at my dad and saw that his head was down, focused on his plate. I looked back at Grace and silently kissed the air between us. Her eyes widened and she pushed her face out a bit to indicate that I should stop my risky behavior. I laughed, but then she froze. The expression on her face changed as she looked past me. I turned around to see my mother standing in the doorway of the kitchen with Delbert at her elbow.

"Look who I found on our front porch," my mother sang.

CHAPTER THIRTY-SEVEN

Both of the empty place settings were beside me, so that's where Delbert sat, spreading his elbows and legs out wide to make contact with mine. He asked me to pass him one dish after another and as he reached for the food, his hand would linger on mine.

"So, Grace is it?" Delbert asked. My mom had just introduced them and here he was acting like he'd never seen Grace before.

"Yes, it is," Grace said. I could tell by the look on her face and the tightness of her voice that she was trying to control an overwhelming feeling of annoyance.

"Grace, tell us, how did you and Sky meet?"

He held his knife and fork like some sort of culinary professional, stabbing at the turkey breast with extreme precision and cutting it into tiny pieces before devouring it. One of the many things I used to hate to see him do—eat!

"I believe it was at Ola's party. Am I correct, Sky?" Grace asked like she wasn't quite sure, but I knew better. We'd talked about our initial meeting many times when we were cuddled up together. We always discussed how, in retrospect, lucky we were to have met at all.

"Yes, that's correct," I said.

I put my fork down and gulped down some of the ginger beer Mom had made. The ginger burned my nose and produced a shock of heat that traveled down to my chest.

"Ola, huh? How is she? She's made a bit of a name for herself as an artist, hasn't she? I toured her gallery on my last trip to New York," Delbert said, then looked at Grace and me as if he was unleashing some great secret. I just rolled my eyes.

"I didn't know Ola was doing so well," my mother said. "That's good to hear. She had such a rough time of it growing up with no father and all."

"Well, she's doing great now," Delbert said. "But, you know those artist types. Always looking for ways to act out or try to buck the system," he said to my mother.

"Talk plain, Delbert. What's Ola been up to? Something illegal? I was never crazy about that girl," my mother said as she threw a thin bone onto the napkin in front of her plate.

"I'm sorry, Mrs. Valentine. Actually, this may not be appropriate dinner conversation," Delbert said.

"Well now you've really piqued my interest! Hasn't he, James?"

"Yes, dear," my father said as he stabbed at an overcooked carrot, his head still in his plate.

"If it's inappropriate, then maybe we should leave it at that. I'm sure there are more interesting things to discuss, like Daddy's health. How are you doing, Daddy?" I asked.

I reached over and clasped his arm above the wrist. He lifted his head a bit and looked at me with sad, watery eyes. In that moment, I realized my father was actually old.

"I'm fine, baby. Thanks for asking."

"I set up an appointment with that much sought-after cardiologist for you, Mr. Valentine," Delbert said.

"Why, thank you so much, Delbert." My mother beamed at him. He beamed back. Then he picked up his glass of water.

"So, you ladies don't mind that Ola is a lesbian? I mean, she hasn't tried to drag the two of you into that lifestyle, has she?"

Delbert put on a concerned face as he looked at Grace then at me, but I saw a sly smile give way when my mother slammed her hands on the table beside her plate.

"What in God's name did you just say? Ola is a what?" my mother yelled and pushed her seat away from the table a bit.

"I said she's a les..."

"Stop! Do not repeat that word at my Thanksgiving table!"

My mother slumped back in her chair and clutched her chest as if her heart was about to give way. I glared at Delbert then addressed my mother.

"Mom, calm down. There's no need to get yourself all worked up. So, what if Ola likes women. That's her business."

I stressed the last part and directed the words at Delbert, using a greater force in my voice. He raised his eyebrows and put his hands up in surrender with a "Don't shoot the messenger" face attached. I glared some more.

"No need to get all worked up?" my mother said. "Indeed, there is. That child has positioned herself against God with her...her...nastiness. That's what happens when one is raised in a household without a father and without Christ!"

My mother's voice was filled with emotion and her usual rigid, self-righteousness.

"What happened to 'God is love?'" I asked. "If God is love then love is God."

"Do not pervert the scripture, Sky." My mother leveled a cutting look at me. "You know very well the love that is being put forth in the scriptures is the love between a man and a woman."

"Do I? Do we? That is not stated but assumed. It just says that God is love." I threw my napkin down, pushed my chair back with an angry scrape against the floor, and turned to leave the kitchen.

"Delbert, get up! We need to talk!" I commanded.

I heard Delbert excuse himself from the table. His voice sounded light, playful. He was enjoying the havoc he'd come to pander.

I walked through the living room and out the front door with Delbert on my heels.

The temperature had dropped from earlier in the day. The air was frigid and dry and smelled sort of metallic, like rain was gunning down the mountains. Yellow and white lights glowed in the neighbors' kitchens and living rooms and I imagined them eating their dry, flaky turkeys with giblet stuffing. Content, big smiles on their faces as they actually spent quality time with their families.

"What the hell do you think you're doing?" I growled at Delbert when he stepped outside and closed the front door behind him.

"Me? What? I'm not doing anything. Just catching your folks up on current events," Delbert said.

"Delbert, don't be an ass your whole life," I said.

"An ass, huh?"

He shoved his hands into his pockets, widened his stance, and leaned toward me.

"Fuck you, Sky! You'll see how much…how *big* of an ass I can be when I spill the beans about you and your little girlfriend in there!" he yelled.

"Keep your voice down," I said.

"Why? Afraid Mommy and Daddy won't like that their little girl is a carpet muncher?"

"All of this because you got jilted at the altar? Wow! Shit happens, Delbert. Buck up and move on already."

Suddenly his body seemed to soften. He removed his hands from his pants pockets and put them gently on my shoulders. "I can't move on, Sky. I still love you so much. It's crazy, I know, but I do. You're my one and only."

"Really? How do you know? You haven't given anyone else a chance. Stop obsessing over me, please."

"Sleep with me one last time. Then, maybe, I'll be able to move on."

I scoffed. "Oh my God, you *cannot* be serious. That will *never* happen," I said.

"Well, then, you leave me no choice," Delbert said.

He turned, pushed open the front door, and marched toward the kitchen, his body rigid with determination and sabotage.

This time, it was me at his heels. Scenario after scenario streamed through my mind as I searched for the best option to put into play. The best way to assuage my mother's disdain for women like myself, women who found love and solace in the arms and between the legs of another woman.

Delbert got to his chair and stood behind it. As he placed his hands on the back of the chair he cleared his throat. Grace, my mom, and my dad stopped mid-chew and looked at Delbert.

"Mrs. Valentine, Mr. Valentine, uh I'm sorry but…I must inform you…"

"I'm gay!" I blurted out. "I'm a lesbian. Grace and I are lovers," I said.

My mother dropped her fork and fell from her chair.

CHAPTER THIRTY-EIGHT

Grace and I rushed to gather my mother from the floor. My father shot up from his seat, but he was no longer nimble enough to save my mother before she'd tumbled to the ground.

"See what you did, Delbert!" I yelled at him.

"Me? I was only going to say that I couldn't stay. I need to leave. Thank your mother for me. I'll let myself out."

Delbert left Grace and me to balance my mother's petite frame upright on the kitchen chair. She recovered quickly and pulled her arms out of our reach.

"Let go of me!" she shouted.

"Careful Mom. You don't want to fall again," I said.

My hands were outstretched, palms flat out like five-fingered barricades. Grace sat on her haunches ready for any wayward movement.

My father finally made it around the table. He stood behind my mother's chair and held her shoulders in his large hands.

"Calm down, Etta," he said.

"Don't tell me to calm down!" my mother shouted up at him as she tugged at one of his hands trying to remove it from where it gripped her bony shoulder. But my father held fast.

"Sky, how could you?" she said. She'd given up on the tug-of-war with my dad. "First you humiliate me by running out on your wedding, and now this! Please, tell me it's not true."

My mother's eyes were moist and pleading. I thought about placating her, telling her she was right it was not true and that I was still that innocent little girl who'd slept under her roof once upon a time. I wanted to make her happy. I wanted her to continue loving me, but then I looked at Grace who was looking at me. Grace with the soft lips and hooded eyes that I loved looking into. Grace with the warm arms that wrapped around me at night and made me feel safe. Grace whose kisses sent me stumbling amongst the stars. I thought about these things and my choice was clear. I knew I'd choose Grace.

I stood up beside my mother's chair and looked down at her. She looked so small. It was as if over the years her self-righteousness had beaten her down. I wondered, briefly, who she'd been before she committed herself to this path. What had she gained and what had she given up?

"It's true, Mom. I'm in love with Grace. We are lovers. She makes me happy."

My mother's face drew up into an ugly scowl. "Get out!" she yelled, index finger pointed in the direction of the living room and the front door.

"Don't you want me to be happy?" I asked.

"I want you out of my house!" she yelled again.

"What happened to a mother's unconditional love? What happened to family being most important? I need to live *my life*, Mom. Not some ready-made life you've manufactured for me!"

Surprisingly, my mother sprang to her feet sharp and quick like an unhinged jack-in-the-box.

"GET OUT!"

This time she yelled at the top of her lungs, her face red and flushed with anger.

"You'd better go, honey," my father said calmly. "Maybe we can talk this thing through later." He gripped the back of my mother's chair with both hands and lowered his chin to his chest.

Grace rose to her feet and, together, we headed to the living room to gather our coats and suitcases. As we began our exit, my mother yelled at me from the kitchen.

"Sky, you have hurt me enough with your choices. Don't you step foot in my house again!"

I pulled the door shut. I closed it tight against her ignorance, hoping that it would remain inside with her and that it would not spill out and onto the rest of the world, but I knew it was already too late.

CHAPTER THIRTY-NINE

"Where y'all going?" Henry asked as he slammed his car door and made his way over to the porch where we sat waiting for him to give us a lift. Mrs. Robinson next door was nice enough to let me use her phone to call him.

"Odeta's," I said. Grace and I got to our feet and grabbed our bags. I had phoned Odeta right after I called Henry. She didn't pick up, but I left a message on her answering machine.

"What happened? Why y'all leaving?" Henry asked while taking the bags from our hands.

"I'll tell you in the car. Just, let's go," I said.

Henry shook his head. "Okay," he said.

We all got in, buckled up, and Henry pulled away from the house, made a right turn, then looked at me.

"So, you gon tell me what happened or am I gonna have to guess?"

I looked at him, then I turned my head and looked out my window. I wasn't sure as to the words I should use. I wasn't sure if I should just get to the gist of it or beat around the bush some.

And what would happen when I told him? Would he kick us out
of the car like Mom kicked us out of the house? Would I lose my
whole family tonight because I'd fallen in love with a woman?
Henry could be a shit of a brother, but he was still my brother,
my family.

"Miss Grace, maybe you'd care to shed some light on the
situation," Henry said, his neck craned back so he could look at
Grace directly.

"I…I really think this is something Sky needs to handle,"
Grace said. I felt the reassuring touch of her hand as she placed
it on my shoulder.

"Okay, then, baby girl, you need to tell me something cuz
y'all making me miss my Thanksgiving dinner."

"You missed that hours ago, Henry. Can't blame us for that,"
I said.

"Yeah, well, I coulda been eatin' by now, except I'm here
driving you. Now you gonna tell me what went down or not?"

We had reached Odeta's house, but Henry didn't pull all the
way into the driveway. I was glad to see the lights on upstairs.
I was hopeful that it was a sign Odeta had returned from her
sister's house already. She'd mentioned that it might take her
quite a while to get back.

I rubbed my eyes and forehead with both of my hands, then
ran them along my neck. My muscles were bunched up tight
and I felt the tension as it slipped down toward my shoulders.

"I'm gay," I said.

"Sky, you're talking into your chin. I ain't heard a word you
said."

"I said, I'm gay, all right!" I yelled. "Heard me now?"

Henry looked at me. He just sat there and looked at me for
what seemed like the longest time, then he turned to Grace.

"You gay too?" he asked.

"Yes," Grace said.

"Well, I'll be damn," Henry said. He didn't say anything
else, just turned and stared out the front window.

I turned slowly in my seat and faced him. I glanced at Grace
and saw that she was watching him too. I eased backward. I

stopped when my back was pressed hard up against my door. My hand was on the lock release, ready to press the button and fall out backward, if need be, to make a quick getaway. Henry leaned forward. My body tightened, my finger taut, tempted, and at the ready to press the lock release. Henry let out a big sigh. He rested his forehead on the thick shaggy nap of his sheepskin steering wheel cover. Grace sat upright, snug against the back of her seat and I pressed farther back against my door. Uncertain of the enormity of Henry's wrath, we resolved, telepathically it seemed, to allow a bigger path for his rage.

With his head still supported by the steering wheel, Henry turned and looked at me.

"I'm leaving June," he said.

"What?" I asked.

"Yup. I'm leaving her. Found me a gal over in Fayetteville. That's how come June ain't here for Thanksgiving. She went on over to her momma's house in Georgia."

Henry sat up, stretched his arms out, and gripped the steering wheel's fluffy mass again.

I released some of the breath I'd been holding. I lifted my hand and leaned over to touch Henry's shoulder in empathy, but because I was still uncertain as to what his confession meant in connection to the news I'd just told him, I placed my hand in my lap instead.

"Oh, Henry. I'm so sorry to hear that," I said.

"I'm not!" Henry exclaimed.

I drew back, surprised.

"I'm tired of June and her nonsense. Never listens to me. Always trying to boss me around. Everything's too hard with that woman! If we need to work so hard just to enjoy being around each other, then, maybe, we didn't belong together," he said. "Now, Miss Fayetteville, she sweet. Don't run me ragged. Don't give me no hard time. She lets *me* be a man. She ain't trying to wear the pants in the relationship. Not like June! I need some respect and June don't show me none. I've had it. Enough is enough."

Sweat peppered the top of Henry's forehead. Steam began to climb the windows like wild ivy and Henry suddenly seemed like a little boy to me.

"Well, I'm…I'm happy you found someone who makes you happy and who respects you. Being respected and compatible are important in a relationship. Uh, have you told Mom? I know she really likes June."

Henry rubbed his forehead with his hands. "No, haven't told the folks yet. I was home practicing, thinking about what I'm gonna say to Momma. She likes June a whole heck of a lot."

"Yes, she does," I said.

"I think I'll just go on back home after this. Let Momma stew on your…uh…your ordeal."

"Gee, thanks, Henry," I said.

Henry unlocked the doors and climbed out of the car.

"Come on round here now and get these bags. Odeta know you coming, right?"

"I left her a message," I said.

Henry opened the trunk and deposited our bags on the ground, a few feet away from the car.

"I'll sit here, make sure y'all get in," Henry said like he was our chaperone.

I led Grace up the path to the front door. Odeta responded on the second bing-bong of her doorbell.

"Girl, what is all the fuss about now?" she asked while pushing the screen door open.

As Grace and I picked up our bags, Odeta spotted Henry.

"Nightcap, Henry?" she yelled.

"Rain check," Henry yelled back. "And Sky…" he said.

I turned around. "Yes, Henry?"

"I'm…I'm here, if you need me."

I smiled and put up my hand to say goodbye. Henry tooted his car horn twice, then sped away.

CHAPTER FORTY

"Thanks for letting us stay, Odeta," I said.

"Yes, thank you so much," Grace added. She blew on the cup of green tea Odeta had given her a few moments before, sipped it and then placed the bright orange teacup back on its yellow saucer.

I fiddled around with the Lorna Doones that were huddled together on the delicate plate before me. Odeta, smelling like rum mixed with cotton candy, sat down heavily in her chair. Immediately, she asked a bunch of questions and demanded answers, but I hemmed and hawed, too drained and numb and not wanting to out myself yet another time that night.

"Odeta, I'm sorry, you're right. You deserve some answers, but I just can't get into it right now. I'm drained. Tomorrow I will answer anything you want, but right now, I'd…we'd like to just get some rest. We've had a long day."

I yawned and stretched to emphasize my point. Grace watched me yawn and then she yawned too.

"All right, tomorrow then," Odeta said, but she sat there. The slight scowl on her face matched my mood.

"So, what, you plan on having us sleep here, at the table, or are you gonna show us to our room?" I asked.

I knew I was on the verge of unleashing my frustration onto Odeta, but I couldn't help it. I just didn't want to deal with any more aggravation or pestering from anyone.

Odeta gave me a look, put her teacup down on its saucer, then used the edge of the kitchen table to hoist herself up.

"Right this way, your Highness," she said and bowed. I rolled my eyes.

We made our way up the narrow staircase with our bags in hand.

"I only got the one extra bedroom so y'all gonna have to share. Unless one of you wanna sleep on the couch downstairs?" Odeta asked.

"I think we'd both like the comfort of a bed tonight," I said. I turned to Grace. "What do you think?"

"Bed. Definitely a bed," she said. She even looked a bit weary.

"Okay, well y'all in luck. Queen-size bed in here. Beats a twin, huh? Most folks don't think about other folks' comfort when they plan their guest rooms. I did." Odeta seemed very proud of herself, but I was too tired.

"Excellent," I said and pushed past Odeta as I entered the room.

"I'm a go on down to my bedroom now, 'cause I'm 'bout to forget my manners. Here I am doing *you* a favor and you're getting all funky with *me*?"

Odeta moved a tightly closed fist to her hip and widened her stance. I recalled that same stance from childhood. She had stood in that same manner just moments before she'd beat the crap out of Damon Bradley.

"She's just tired and needs to sort through some things," Grace said, offering a small olive branch.

Odeta looked at Grace, then at me, then back at Grace. She let out a large sigh.

"Night," she said and ambled back down the narrow staircase.

Finally in bed after brushing our teeth and putting on our pajamas, I sunk into one of the overstuffed pillows Odeta had propped up on the bed. It was as soft as what clouds promised to be. Only the pillow did not disappoint.

"The lavender plants are a nice touch," Grace said.

Grace slid her feet under the bedsheets and rubbed her cold feet on my warm ones.

"Maybe you should sleep with some socks on," I recommended.

"Socks are no fun," Grace said. She turned on her side and faced me. I was on my back staring at the ceiling.

"Helluva day," she continued. "Wanna talk about it?"

"No," I said and closed my eyes, but they popped open again.

"Fucking Delbert!" I shouted, but not loud enough for Odeta to hear.

"What an asshole!" said Grace.

"And my mother! Throwing us out! Really? It's the eighties not the forties or the fifties! She needs to get with the times!"

"Maybe she'll change her mind after she gets over her initial shock," Grace offered.

"Who cares? I don't anymore. I'm tired of trying to fit the preconceived notion of what she thinks I should be! You hear that, Mom? I'm tired of it!"

Grace put her arm over my stomach and cuddled closer to me. "Oh, baby, I'm so sorry about the way things turned out," she said.

She kissed me once on the cheek and then again beside my ear. I felt her looking at me. I batted my eyes, feeling a wave of heat at the base of my neck. Then a wall of flames blossomed and matured into an outright fire. I held back the tears for as long as I could, but something inside me rumbled and they burst forth from my eyes like clear, salty lava that revealed my inner turmoil.

Grace wiped my tears and pulled my head into her bony shoulder which, at that moment, was more home to me than home would ever be again. I held on tight and bawled.

When Grace and I made it downstairs the next morning,

the air was ripe with the smells of pancakes, eggs, toast, bacon, sausage, and coffee.

Odeta was reaching up toward a shelf in the kitchen cabinet and pulling down a large, brown, wide-hipped, female-shaped bottle of pancake syrup.

"Y'all finally up, huh? Thought you two were gonna sleep all day," Odeta said.

I looked at her incredulously. "Odeta, it's only ten o'clock," I said.

"Only? I see you done picked up some of them lazy New York habits. Around here, we get up with the sun, not after it."

"Oh, please. Sit down! You sound just like your mother." I laughed.

Odeta laughed too. "Don't I though? I'm telling you, as I get older, I'm slowly turning into her. It's a damn shame too. Come on now, sit, eat."

We all pulled out kitchen chairs for ourselves, plopped down on them, and proceeded to fill our plates.

"Sorry I couldn't make it back in time to have Thanksgiving dinner with your momma and daddy. My nieces and nephews would not let me leave."

"No worries," I said and sipped at my orange juice.

Odeta looked at me waiting to hear more, but I wasn't ready yet.

"So, how's your daddy doing? I heard he was sick. I haven't had the chance to visit." She clearly decided to take the back way to get the information she really wanted.

"Daddy's getting better," I said. "He just looks so old and helpless to me now."

I put on a sad smile. I had to chase away the memory of his watery eyes and bowed head so that I didn't start crying again, but a tear escaped anyway. I wiped it away quickly. Then, as a diversion, I got up to get more juice from the fridge.

"More juice, Grace?" I asked.

"No thanks."

I put the pitcher back in the fridge, sat back down, and began buttering a new piece of toast.

"Why y'all so quiet? Somebody die? Sky, you ain't never been this quiet," Odeta said. "When you fixin' on telling me what happened?" she added.

I put the butter knife down and held my piece of toast in both hands. Grace looked at me over her glass of water, then she looked at Odeta. I sucked in a big breath and let it out slowly.

"My mom kicked us out of the house last night. That's why I asked if we could stay here," I said.

Odeta frowned. "She kicked you out! Mrs. Valentine, your mom, kicked you out? Why?"

"Because I told her that I am gay," I said and looked at Odeta's face for a reaction.

Odeta squinted her eyes and furrowed her brow a bit.

"You're gay? Since when? This is the first time I'm hearing about it and I've known you your whole life."

Odeta grabbed two more strips of bacon and plunked them down onto her plate as if they were two greasy exclamation points she needed to emphasize her words.

"Well, I don't tell you everything, Odeta," I said.

Odeta was sopping up tiny pieces of scrambled egg with the corner of her toast when she suddenly stopped.

"What? What does that mean, you don't tell me everything? What do you mean by that, Sky? Are you trying to say I'm a blabbermouth or something?"

Odeta had left the egg and toast at the corner of her plate. She wiped her hands and mouth, rested her elbows on the edge of the table, folded her hands under her chin, and stared at me.

"What are you trying to say, Sky? 'Cause we done been through some things together and I've kept all a our shenanigans to myself."

"Don't get all riled up. I'm just saying that there are some things I've kept to myself. People stop wanting to hang around you, stop wanting to be your friend. Hell, even stop wanting to be your mother when they learn that you're gay. They even kick you out of the house, I've learned."

"Well, I'm not your mama. I'm your friend. Your best friend, I thought. Or maybe I wasn't really your best friend all along and you neglected to tell me that too!"

Odeta pushed her chair back forcefully and its slender legs screamed out in protest against the movement, Odeta's weight, and the floor. Odeta picked up her fork, knife, and plate from the kitchen table and slung them into the sink.

"Wow, Odeta, really? So now you're making this whole situation about you, huh? Typical," I said and shook my head.

Odeta turned and pushed up the oddly shaped silver handle of the faucet. The water gushed down for an instant, but Odeta cut it off, turned, and pointed to Grace.

"She's your lover?" Odeta asked.

"Yes, she is," I said. My voice defiant and edged even after the big gulp I took before speaking.

"You two fuck in my guest bedroom last night?" Odeta looked sharply at me.

"What! Oh my God, the audacity! And if we did? What?" I asked. I threw down my fork and stood up, ready to pounce. Enough was enough.

Grace jumped up. "Ladies, ladies. Let's be civil, shall we? I'm sure we can talk and conduct ourselves in a civilized manner. Yes?"

Grace addressed both Odeta and me. Odeta rolled her eyes at me, turned back toward the sink, and turned the water back on. I rolled my eyes back at her, sat back down, and picked at the rest of my pancakes. Grace seemed leery at first, but, eventually, she sat down too.

Odeta slammed and scrubbed at the pots in the sink. The water seemed to attack the porcelain bowls as it ran out of the faucet with rage—angry and loud. The food I'd just eaten hardened and turned to boulders in my belly.

"I don't tell you everything either," Odeta said, her back to us still.

I scoffed. "Oh, so now you've kept secrets because you just found out that I've kept secrets. Convenient and so original, Odeta. Anyway, I've never expected you to tell me everything. I don't think *anybody* tells *anybody* everything. If they say they do, then they are lying."

No one said anything after I spouted my philosophy about the state of human relations. We all just sat with our thoughts.

The white noise sound of running water filled the air, but it could not wash away the tension.

Odeta turned off the faucet, but remained at the sink, her hands gripping the sink's edge. A breeze blew in from the kitchen window that was cracked open a bit and the curvy calls of sparrows snuck in too.

I looked at Odeta's back. Saw that tension had made columns of her arms and neck. Saw how she was probably fighting the urge to cuss me out while controlling her emotions. I felt bad about the flare-up between us. I thought I should apologize. After all, she *was* my friend. She'd let me into her home without hesitation and so far, she hadn't thrown me out after having learned about me being gay.

"Odeta I…" I'd started to apologize but she cut me off.

"I'm seeing Delbert. Actually, we're engaged. We plan to be married by spring of next year," Odeta said.

CHAPTER FORTY-ONE

Odeta remained at the sink, her back to us. She seemed to be giving us, me, room to examine and digest her words before she sought to speak again.

"Un-fucking-believable!" I said.

Odeta hunched up her shoulders as if making a shield to deflect my early morning profanity. Like her body was unaccustomed to being around such a vile combination of morphemes so soon after daybreak.

I shook my head incredulously and looked over at Grace for some sort of confirmation for my outburst, but she just put the piece of toast she'd been eating on her plate and slapped her hands free of crumbs. I shook my head again and stared at Odeta's back until I imagined seeing a celebratory smirk on her dumb face.

"Un-fucking-believable. You just couldn't wait, could you?" I asked.

Odeta spun around. Her body hard and arched.

"What do you care? You're doing Little Ms. Gracious over there!" Odeta yelled and pointed at Grace.

Grace's eyes widened as if to say, *Hey, don't drag me into this mess!* Too late. She was accomplice and jury.

"Grace just came into the picture. You, however, have been on Delbert's jock for quite some time! Some friend. Now, I know why you couldn't wait to head back here after driving with me to New York!"

"I couldn't wait to come back here because this is my home. And if my memory serves me correctly, I recall you basically pleading with me to take up with Delbert before we even left for New York! You were all 'He's not what I'm looking for.' Now, I know what you were looking for." Odeta huffed and glanced at Grace.

"I was looking for the freedom to be who I am without folks judging me and thinking I'm a freak. That's what I was looking for," I said.

"Well, I guess you found it. Hope you're happy. I know I am. Like I told you before, Delbert is a good man. Good men are rare around here so I'm happy he's in my life. One woman's trash is another woman's treasure. You do well to remember that Sky."

I shook my head and scoffed. "Treasure, huh? Don't be blinded by the dollar signs, Odeta. Your 'treasure' propositioned me last night. Asked…no begged me to sleep with him. Said *I* was his one, his soulmate. Is that the kind of 'treasure' you're looking for?"

Odeta's mouth dropped open and her fists balled by her sides.

"Fuck you, Sky! You're such a liar! Your mama's right, it's time for you to leave! You done overstayed your welcome!"

Odeta pushed off from the edge of the sink and marched past me out of the kitchen.

"Fine!" I yelled after her. "We're leaving!"

"Good!" Odeta yelled back. "Get to steppin'!"

I shook my head in disbelief again.

"I can't believe her! She acts like she's fifty-five years old and has to bag a man because any minute now her breasts will start to sag," I said to Grace.

"Stop selling yourself short!" I yelled out the room at Odeta.

Grace stared at me. "You failed to mention to me last night that Delbert asked you to have sex with him. Why's that?"

I picked up my glass of orange juice and drained it.

"Because it was irrelevant that's why. And whose side are you on anyway?"

Grace looked at me for a long time without responding. I looked at her, then looked away. I watched the edge of the kitchen curtain lift and fall and lift and fall in the breeze. When I glanced back at Grace she was looking down at her empty plate.

"Your side. I'm on your side," Grace said, then looked up at me.

"I'm sorry I dragged you into a Donahue episode," I said and put my hand on top of hers.

"This whole thing would definitely make a great episode."

Grace smiled. I smiled too, briefly, then I put my glass down, and held my head in my hands.

"She's right. I did practically throw Delbert in her lap, but I didn't think she would really pursue him. It just seems...wrong."

"I think it's great. Now, he can focus all of his attention on her and leave you, us, alone. That's what you want, right?" Grace asked as she got up and started gathering our plates, discarding our scraps, and setting the dirty dishes in the sink.

"Yeah, but he's a snake and a bastard. Odeta deserves better."

"Maybe, but it's not your problem anymore. Your problem is changing our airplane tickets so we can catch an earlier flight back to New York. Unless you have some more friends with guest bedrooms," Grace asked.

I looked at her with my lips twisted.

"Funny," I said. Grace smiled and I did too. Then I got serious again.

"Maybe I should stop by my mom's house again before we leave. Try to talk to her or at least so I can give my dad a hug," I said, but the sentences were really questions. Hopes floating on air. I wanted Grace to help me give them direction. Wanted her to help me anchor them.

"It's up to you," she said.

CHAPTER FORTY-TWO

"Hey, you. What's going on?" Grace asked while closing and locking the front door.

"Nothing," I said, pressing frantically at the game's control buttons. Things weren't going well since we'd returned to New York from North Carolina. I felt angry and resentful and for some reason everything Grace did seemed to annoy me.

With furtive glances, I saw Grace remove her boots and backpack at the door, then she threw her coat, scarf, and gloves on the empty chair by the closet.

I thought about how, if, and when we did live together, she'd have to stop throwing her stuff all over the place. It bugged me because I didn't want my place to end up looking like hers with piles of things strewn everywhere.

Grace sat at the end of the couch near my feet and gently rubbed them. This bugged me too. Normally, I thoroughly enjoyed Grace's foot rubs, but not today.

"You do plan on hanging those things up, right?" I'd asked as I continued to play Tetris on my new Game Boy. I took my eyes off the screen for a second to see her face. Her brow was furrowed.

"What things?"

I stopped playing, inhaled deeply, let out an exasperated sigh, and then pointed to the chair.

"Those things! I just finished straightening up in here."

"And how was I supposed to know that?" Grace asked.

"Duh! Look around," I replied.

Grace let go of my feet, sat back on the couch, and folded her arms across her chest.

"Okay, what's going on? I know you're still upset about North Carolina, but why the funky attitude with me?"

"No attitude. I'm just tired of cleaning up after you," I said. I went back to playing my game, ignoring the incredulous look on Grace's face.

"Wait, what? Cleaning up after me? Wow, that's rich. I'm just going to go upstairs and take a shower. You need to sit there and think about what you're saying."

Grace sprung off the couch and ascended the stairs with a heavy tread.

Think about what *you're* doing! I thought to myself. I don't go to your place and throw shit around!

"Yeah!" the little devil on my shoulder whispered. "And what's this crap about you not being ready to move in with her? Sounds like a dis to me!"

"Yeah," I said softly to myself as I felt anger coagulate and take shape inside of me.

I put the Game Boy down beside me. It made one last blip before its face went dark. I went to the back door and opened it; cold air rushed at me all sharp-edged and steely. It cleared my head of the fog and fumes that entangled it, but the shadow of sadness remained. I felt unwanted on so many levels. I started wondering if it was all some sort of sordid conspiracy, some plot set against me by someone I'd slighted, ignored, or hurt. But maybe it was just life. My life. My sucky life!

CHAPTER FORTY-THREE

I had phoned my mother several times since getting back to New York, but upon hearing my voice on the line, she'd hung up each time. When I called right back, she let her answering machine pick up. I'd left message after message, but she never returned my calls. Henry advised me to give her some time, some space, but I felt orphaned, uprooted. I decided to throw myself into my work and my friends. I was determined to foster new connections in order to create some form, some outline of family.

"You gonna eat that last piece of tempura or you just gonna let it hang out there on your plate?"

I was hanging out with my friend Sammy Rodriguez from work. He was the only male teacher at the school, and he was gay. We were at Dallas BBQ, which was becoming our favorite spot in the West Village, drowning our sorrows in giant, pastel-colored margaritas.

"You can have it," I said and pushed the plate toward Sammy.

Sammy picked up the large piece of broccoli tempura I had ordered, double dunked it in soy sauce, and gobbled it down.

Then he dabbed at the corners of his mouth with the edge of his paper napkin and surveyed the table as if looking for other stray morsels to conquer and consume.

"I have to stop eating like this," Sammy said. His eyes had finally met mine.

"Ever since Troy left me nearly a month ago, I've been eating like a pig, chile. Just nonstop stuffing. Probably put on ten pounds by now!"

Sammy pressed his hands to his stomach and sucked in his not-yet-existent gut.

"But then again, I'm sure the boys still love this."

Sammy ran his hands down his sides then threw them up in the air while he made his best "I'm a model" face. I laughed. "And if they don't, fuck 'em!" Sammy said.

He raised his glass and I raised mine to complete and validate his toast.

"So, you gonna hang out at the pier with me after this?" Sammy asked while he checked out the other guys in the restaurant.

"So you can ditch me while you go run off with some random guy? No thanks," I said.

I sucked down the last bit of my margarita and it went straight to my head. I shut my eyes tight against the brain freeze.

"Don't hate, hussy! Girls just wanna have fun," Sammy said.

I opened my eyes. The squat waiter was standing beside our table, pad in his hand, pencil in the air ready to scribble.

"Something else? Or can I take this stuff away for you?" he asked.

"You can take it away, Papi," Sammy said while applying gloss to his lips with his pinkie finger and giving the waiter a seductive look.

"Have you no shame?" I asked after the waiter walked away.

"What? He was cute," Sammy said and glanced again at the waiter's retreating back. "Cute ass too."

"Anyway, I was thinking about going to Nanny's. Or maybe I'll just go home. I still need to prepare my science lesson for tomorrow," I said.

"Chile, take your ass to Nanny's and have some fun. You teach kindergarten. Blow up a damn balloon and call it science. Them kids don't know!"

"You are crazy," I said.

"Life's too short," Sammy said. He removed his makeup bag from his satchel. "Excuse me, gotta go freshen up."

The waiter returned to the table with our bill. I paid it and started gathering my things while I waited for Sammy to return. I looked around the restaurant at all of the smiling faces and wondered how many of them had lost their families. Was the woman with the buzz cut and blue tie who had just pecked the woman beside her on the lips thrown out of her house too? Were the gay guys practicing their Vogue dance moves at the table near the door chucked to the streets by their fathers? Why were we so easy to discard? So easy to harden one's heart against? Difference, they've said, was to be celebrated, but that's not true. Not here. Not now. To be different in America, and anywhere else, really, was to be targeted for annihilation. History shows us that and yet, people think being gay or lesbian is some "lifestyle" that we have "chosen." I've come to believe that for most of us, at least when we'd first come to recognize who we were, we fought against it. It was something we wanted to push aside. I had tried for many years to wear the "hetero mask" and every day it had gnawed at me. I was being eaten alive, dying slowly, one cell, one atom at a time.

I watched Sammy head toward our table. The slight sashay in his hips, the finger he rolled seductively over his lips as he smeared on more lip gloss and he looked about the room hoping, I'm sure, that he was being watched. I thought about the courage it took for him to reveal himself to just this tiny sliver of the world within this room. I thought about all the people, including his family, who wanted to cut him down—cut *us* down—and I wanted to wail at the bravery and pain of it all.

CHAPTER FORTY-FOUR

Christmas was about two weeks away and as I nursed my beer on the hard barstool at Nanny's and stared at the red, blue, and green bulbs that decorated the edge of the mirror that stared back at me from behind the bar, I thought about my parents again. They still hadn't phoned, but it didn't hurt as much as it did before, or, at least, that was my "on my way to healing" mantra. I said it every day when I woke up and every night before I headed to bed and anytime I had a breach of confidence in between. I thought about my childhood Christmases and how my mom and I always got my dad a new shirt and tie and how we always picked out something special for Odeta. What would this year bring? Would they miss me, miss our tradition? Would they call by then? Even Odeta hadn't phoned which really surprised me. I didn't think she'd throw away our friendship, which was more like a sisterhood, so easily. I thought we'd meant more to each other. Which brought my thinking around to Grace and how the other night while I was sitting on the couch, feet curled under me, head rested on the couch's arm playing my new Nintendo Game Boy, she'd let herself in. We'd exchanged keys to each other's apartments as a show of continued commitment and a step forward in our relationship. We'd discussed moving in together when we returned from North Carolina, but Grace felt that I, "we," weren't "quite there yet" as she'd put it. I agreed at the time, but I felt a bit disenchanted. A bit upset.

My head was further down in my beer than I'd realized. The journey upward to see who had tapped me on the shoulder seemed far and the music from the jukebox was suddenly blaring.

"Sky Valentine, is that you?"

I turned around to see a woman standing beside me. Her face was gorgeous, eyes big and bright, and she had a full, luscious smile. For a moment, I just stared and then my brain clicked, and the distant memories slid into place...Zenobia, my first love!

"Oh my God, Zee! Is it really you?"

I leapt off the barstool and into Zenobia's open arms. She hugged me hard and I held her close as I smiled from ear to ear. Her perfume smelled sensual and the soft curl of her hair brushed slightly against my cheek.

"Let me look at you," I said and took Zenobia's hand in mine as she twirled around for me to admire her fully.

"You look fantastic!"

"Thank you. Thank you. You're looking great as well."

"Come, sit, have a drink with me. Tell me what's been going on in your life."

I pulled another barstool closer to my own and patted the top of it. Zenobia sat down.

"What's your pleasure?" I asked, sounding like some dumbass pirate. Zenobia laughed.

"I'll have vodka and orange juice," Zee said. I called the bartender over. "One vodka and orange juice and one kamikaze, please."

"I was drinking beer, but I want to have a real drink with you," I said looking at Zee, trying to take her all in. "Your hair is longer. I love the bangs."

"Thanks. Yes, I cut it recently, but it's growing again." She ran her hands over her bangs and through her thick black bob.

"I see you have locs now. They look good on you," Zee said.
"Thanks," I said with a huge idiotic smile on my face.
"Finally decided to let my hair grow too."

I felt shy and nervous, the same way I used to feel around
Zenobia, but I knew I needed to power through it.

"So, what have you been up to? Where do you live now? Do
you come to Nanny's often?" I blurted out. I wanted to know
everything at once.

Zenobia chuckled and swept a stray strand of hair behind
her ear.

"I live in San Francisco now. It reminds me a lot of where we
went to school in Rhode Island. I'm just in town for two, maybe
three weeks visiting family and friends for the holidays."

While Zee talked, I checked out her bare forearms. They
were smooth and sun-kissed a coppery brown. Her lips looked
soft and ripe and she had maintained the same slim, but curvy
build that she'd had in college.

"What do you do in San Francisco?" I asked.
"Computer programming."
"Oh, yes, math whiz. I forgot," I said with a smile.
"Uh, more like genius," Zee said with a straight face, then
busted out laughing.

"Okay now," I said and laughed along with her.
"What about you? What do you do?" Zee asked.
"I teach kindergarten," I said.
"Wow! That's cool. I never figured you for a teacher."
"Really? I did major in education."
"Yes, I recall, but I thought you'd end up doing something
more creative for some reason. I thought because you loved to
write and travel that those things added up to you becoming a
journalist."

The bartender put the drinks down on the bar in front of
us. I threw a ten-dollar bill on the bar to cover the cost, then I
raised my glass in the air.

"A toast," I suggested. Zee smiled and raised her glass as well.
I thought for a moment then exclaimed, "To fond memories and
new beginnings." I knew I was being presumptuous, but I told
myself it was because I was so excited.

"So, yes, true, about what you said about me becoming a journalist, but teaching forces me to be very creative and I feel like I'm making an impact on the future," I said after I placed my drink back down on the bar.

"Big responsibility," Zee said.

"I think my shoulders are wide enough," I replied with a bit of bravado as I took another swig of my drink.

"So, are you currently involved?" I asked as I looked over the edge of my glass at Zenobia, wanting to hear her response, but not wanting to hear it at the same time.

"No, not seeing anyone right now. And you?"

"Yes, but not sure how it's going," I said, which was true.

"Uh-oh, trouble in paradise, huh?" Zee commented.

I let out a big sigh. "The forecast is stormy."

Zee nodded her head, a sympathetic look on her face. Then she reached over and rubbed my knee. It was as if she'd pressed a surge button. Sparks flew and continued to multiply.

"You'll be okay," she said. "I should get back to my friends, but take down my number. I'd like to get together again."

"Me too!" I said, sounding much too eager. "I'd like that a lot. We could, uh, catch up on old times."

"And maybe create some new ones," Zee said with a sly smile. At least, I perceived it to be sly, but maybe it was just wishful thinking.

"Yes, that would be nice too," I said.

Zenobia wrote down her number on a soft napkin, placed it in my hand, and gently cradled both the napkin and my hand in her own.

"Don't lose it," she said. Her sexy brown eyes flashed bedroom and the feel of her hand on mine sent butterflies straight to my groin.

I gulped, trying to tame my horniness, my desire for her.

"I won't," I said and watched the beauty of her backside as she walked across the room toward her friends.

The next day, I called Ola and told her about how Grace seemed to be putting the brakes on things. Ola informed me about the Christmas party she planned to have on Saturday.

"You and Grace should definitely come. I think you gals just need to have some fun. Your trip to North Carolina was a lot. You two just need a shake-your-booty break." Ola laughed.

"Yeah, I guess so. North Carolina was a lot," I said. "Oh, and guess what? I ran into my first love yesterday at Nanny's!"

"What! Wait, you were at Nanny's and you didn't invite me?"

"I was out with my coworker, Sammy. He went to the pier and I went to Nanny's for a quick drink after we ate and there she was looking fine as ever!"

"Uh-huh. This is the college roommate you told me about. The one you were head-over-heels for?" Ola asked.

"She's the one! It was nice seeing her again. We didn't talk long because I had to get home and she was with her friends, but still."

"Did you get her digits?" Ola asked.

"Sure did!" I laughed.

"Okay, player, player!" Ola yelled. "You should invite her to my party so I can finally meet Ms. Thing."

"Mm, I'm not sure about that. Don't think that's a good idea. I'd like to hang with her alone first, so we can really talk and catch up," I said.

"Suit yourself. Anyway, girl, I'm working on a new painting. I may debut it at the party if I finish it in time."

"Hope you do. Looking forward to seeing it," I said.

"Talk later," Ola said, then hung up.

I was surprised Grace took to the idea of attending Ola's party so readily. I thought she was going to hem and haw and be resistant to the idea of going with me.

"A party sounds good right about now," Grace said over the phone. She was eating something and still managed to convey some excitement about the party between bites.

"What did you make for dinner? Or did you order in again?" I asked.

After our last squabble, Grace hadn't been coming over or spending the night at my place as much. At first I was upset, but then I started feeling sort of sad about the whole situation.

"Didn't feel like cooking, so I ordered a sandwich and a salad," Grace said.

"You could have come over. I would've whipped up something nice or we could've made something together like old times," I said.

"Yeah, but I have to go out of town tomorrow for a gig, so I need to prepare," Grace said. "Anyway, I'll meet up with you at Ola's on Saturday."

"What is the problem?" I asked. I wanted us to talk; get to the root of the issue instead of dancing around it.

"No problem. I just need to pack, so I'll see you Saturday," Grace said.

Of course, she was lying about there not being a problem as was evident in her curt tone and avoidance of a real conversation.

"Hey, sure thing," I said, completely annoyed as I hung up the phone.

I glanced at the key holder plaque that hung near the front door. It exclaimed "love" in big red letters. Two keys, one to Grace's place and one to mine, dangled from two separate hooks, sad and alone.

CHAPTER FORTY-FIVE

It was an hour before Ola's big bash and I was having a hard time deciding what to wear. Ten possible outfits were thrown across my bed and a pile of possible shoes to match littered the floor. It reminded me of the night I'd first met Grace. Only Grace would not be there. Said she picked up some extra interpreter assignments and ran into an interpreter buddy who lived in Maryland and they were going to hang out. Whatever. It just helped prove my point about me being the only one who was trying to fix our relationship because, to me, it felt like Grace had already given up.

When I told Ola that Grace wasn't coming, she insisted I call Zenobia and invite her. At first, I was a bit apprehensive, but then I thought it would be nice to invite her to a party—dance, eat, drink, have some fun. Nothing too serious, just fun.

I'd gone to Harlem earlier in the day to get my hair re-twisted and styled, so it was perfectly coiffed. I just needed to come up with a sexy, but not too sexy, outfit. I wanted to wear something that said, "sexy and cool" not "sexy and desperate." I decided to call Sammy.

"Hey, it's Sky. I'm going to a party tonight, what should I wear?"

Before Sammy responded, he coughed a few times. Phlegm-filled coughs that rattled his chest and briefly affected his breathing.

"Are you okay?" I asked.

"Yeah, just a little winter cold," Sammy said. His voice was weak, raspy, not filled with the vigor I'd come to expect from Sammy.

"Well, I hope you went shopping 'cause you sure can't wear what I've seen you wear to work," Sammy said, then coughed some more.

There was the tinge of the Sammy that I knew. I laughed.

"I do have other attire," I said.

"Girl, how long were you in Rhode Island? Attire! What kind of party is it?"

"Christmas bash, but I invited my first girlfriend whom I haven't seen in a long time."

Sammy cleared his throat. "Where's Grace?" he asked.

"In Maryland hanging with some friend."

"Better not let Hope see you with the first love. You know her—Grace's watchdog!"

"And what makes you think Hope will be there?" I asked.

"Hello, lesbians—small community. Black lesbians—even smaller."

"Well, I doubt Hope will be there since Grace won't be, so all is good," I said.

I held the phone receiver in one hand while I moved shirts and pants around on my bed to see what might work together.

"Christmas party, huh? Don't do the red and green thing, that's lame. Go classic. Fresh Jordache jeans, crisp white shirt, long sleeves, and a pointed collar preferred. Stylish black boots and a fly black leather jacket or a fly maxi black wool coat. It is cold out there."

"Okay. Okay. I can do that," I said after taking inventory of my clothes.

"Disaster averted!" Sammy said and coughed some more.

"Yes, and you need to eat some soup, drink some green tea with honey, soak in a hot tub, and get lots of rest so you can get rid of that cold and feel better," I told Sammy.

"Will do, mamacita. Enjoy!" Sammy said and hung up the phone.

I got dressed and headed out.

CHAPTER FORTY-SIX

Ola's party was a big blowout as usual. People packed into her apartment and spilled into the hallway like overcooked pasta in a boiling pot. I pushed my way through the crowd and into the living room, saying hello to the ladies I'd become acquainted with since moving to New York.

I spotted Ola standing beside a huge canvas mounted on the wall. Easter egg-colored swirls with deep black accents hammered in between jumped out at me. She had a large goblet in her hand, presumably filled with chardonnay, since Ola loved chardonnay, and she'd changed her hair. Now, it looked straight as a steel nail with bright red highlights all along the edges and it fell past her shoulders. The goblet jerked dangerously back and forth, threatening to splash its contents onto some poor soul's fly outfit as Ola gesticulated excitedly about something. Most likely her new creation. She saw me, waved, and continued entertaining her captive audience. I waved back, then scanned the room for Zenobia.

I saw her across the room, seated on the edge of the windowsill along with a bunch of other ladies, but she seemed apart, separate from them. I liked that idea, since I had hoped she'd show up on her own, sans the entourage a lot of the ladies traveled with. She was sipping from a glass as her eyes roamed the room then landed on me. She smiled and her face and eyes lit up, which made me smile and I felt just as bright. I slithered through the crowd, moving toward Zee.

I kissed her on the cheek and leaned toward her ear.

"I'm glad you came," I said as a wisp or two of Zee's hair touched and tickled my nose. I brushed it aside.

Zenobia yelled into my ear, "Lovely to see you too."

The music was loud as it leapt out of the immense speakers. Add to it the intense buzz of talk and uproarious outbursts of laughter, and it was almost impossible to hear anything.

"You look great," I yelled.

She smiled and nodded at the comment, but I could tell she had no clue as to what I'd said. I grabbed her hand, made a "Come with me" gesture with my index finger, and then pulled her onto her feet and through the crowd. I wanted to dance and drink and party with Zenobia, but mainly, I wanted to talk to her, become reacquainted. That would not be possible if we remained in the thick of things.

I dragged Zenobia out of Ola's apartment and found a quiet, cubby-like corner of the hallway for us to talk.

"Sorry for yanking you out of there, but it was way too loud," I said.

Zenobia smiled. She lifted her right foot, planted the sole of her shoe on the wall across from me, then leaned her body against it. She seemed completely relaxed.

"Taking the lead. I like that," Zenobia said with a sort of smirk on her face. I smiled too.

"So, like I said before when we were uh…in there," I pointed in the direction of Ola's apartment. "You look great. Love the red dress. It really complements your uh…complexion."

Zee smiled. "I remember you telling me the same thing several years ago. It's why I wore this dress. Wanted to see if you really meant what you'd said," Zenobia replied.

"Oh, I meant it. And you better believe I remember this dress. You had it on the first time we met. You were standing by

Ruth's desk leaning over it to look out of her window. I walked into the room to ask her something, but I totally forgot what it was when I laid eyes on you."

"I remember that look. It was very sexy. Sort of like the look you're giving me now." Zenobia licked her bottom lip seductively. She had been a very skillful flirt when we met back in college. It was one of the reasons we became roommates; her flirting made me curious. Now, she seemed to be a master.

I shuffled from one foot to the other, released a nervous laugh, and stared down at the floor for a moment deciding how to proceed. When I looked up, Zenobia's eyes were still on me. I looked back down at the floor again, then back at Zenobia.

"Um, today I was thinking about the past—our past—and I really want to apologize for the abrupt way I left and how things ended and everything," I said.

Zenobia stared at me. She looked puzzled, but it was difficult for me to tell what she was thinking since I hadn't been around her in so long.

"Thanks. I was kind of hurt by how things played out," she said. "It felt like one minute we were good and then the next, we weren't."

"I'm sorry. I was still figuring things out, trying to come to terms with everything. And I thought…well, I really don't know what I thought. I just knew I needed to think things through."

"I had hoped we would've done that together, but…" Zee shrugged her shoulder, blinked, and took a deep breath. She placed her foot on the floor and stood up straight. Her chest was up, and her shoulders were back like she had made a decision about something.

"Anyway, the past is the past. We were both figuring things out and coming to terms with ourselves. I let go of the anger I had toward you years ago—with the help of some therapy." Zenobia smiled quickly, then her face settled back into itself.

"Okay, now I really feel bad," I said.

Zenobia held on to my shoulders. "Sky, don't feel bad. We were young and each other's firsts. I'm just glad my first experience with a woman was with you."

"Really?" I asked.

"Yes," Zee said.

"Why?" I asked.

"Because you showed me what being in love *really* felt like. I loved you with my whole heart. I was devastated when we broke up; I cried for weeks. I'd never felt that deeply for another person before and, so far, I haven't felt that way again."

"Really?"

"Really. I was hurt, but the love I felt for you just wouldn't leave. Seeing you the other day in that bar made me realize how much I still care for you. I feel like…I feel like my heart is always open to you. Like no matter how bad things get, I'd still be able to love you unconditionally," Zenobia said.

I was tremendously touched by her words. I stared into her dark brown eyes and she stared back into mine. A magnetic field formed between us; the attraction between her lips and mine grew exponentially. Zenobia leaned toward me. I leaned toward her. The heat between us charged and sparked until finally our lips were pressed together. The soft sweetness of her lips made me moan as images of our past lovemaking flooded my brain. As our tongues intertwined, a powerful need to taste all of her pulsed through me. We kissed with a passion and longing I hadn't felt in quite some time and it felt so, so good. *She* felt so, so good! I didn't want to stop kissing her, but we were morphing into the "get a room" stage of things, and I remembered we were not in the privacy of my apartment, but in the hallway. I drank in Zenobia one final time before slowly breaking away. I opened my eyes first and then Zenobia opened hers. I felt our longing as it hung between us, a smoldering bubble of sexual desire that we did not want to break but had to. I ran my fingers through her hair and kissed her on the cheek.

"Let's go dance," I said.

Zenobia laughed. "Okay," she said, but before we moved I gave her a quick peck on the lips and took her hand in mine. We turned toward the party. The loud music jumped off our backs and onto our faces. We readied our bodies and prepared to push our way back toward the dance floor. We took two steps forward.

"What the hell is this?" Grace yelled as she took the last step onto the top of the landing. Hope at her side, her eyes like pointed javelins aimed directly at Zee and me.

CHAPTER FORTY-SEVEN

"Grace," I said. My voice trembled with surprise and shock. Quickly, I dropped Zee's hand. "What are you doing here?"

"She could ask you the same question! Who the hell is this and why were you kissing her?" Hope asked. Friggin' Hope! She always had her nose poked into Grace's affairs.

"Uh, I think this is between Grace and me. There's no need for you to involve yourself, Hope. Grace is a big girl," I said.

Hope rolled her eyes, put her hands on her hips, and was about to blast me with some unkind words, but Grace put her hand out to stop her.

"And this 'big girl' wants to know, who the hell is this and why were you kissing her?"

I glanced at Zenobia. There was a look of surprise and a small shadow of hurt in her eyes when she looked at me. She held the fingertips of the hand I'd dropped in haste in her other hand as if she were trying to hold onto my touch, trying to recall it in some way.

"Stop ogling her and answer me, Sky!" Grace yelled.

"Yeah, stop ogling," Hope chimed in.

The same could be said of the crowd. People had seemed to lose interest in their personal conversations and had started to stare and whisper at the four of us.

"Maybe I should let you deal with this, Sky. I'm going to get a drink," Zenobia said. "Maybe I'll see you later."

"Don't count on it!" Grace yelled at Zenobia as she walked past her.

"Okay, yes, later," I called after Zenobia. I wanted to let her know that I would not kowtow to Grace so easily.

"Really?" Grace asked. "Really? This is what you do when you think I won't be around?"

"You are so busted!" Hope chimed in.

I rolled my eyes at Hope. "Look, can you and I talk away from the crowd and the peanut gallery?" I asked Grace, clearly directing the latter part of my request at Hope.

"We can talk downstairs," Grace said and motioned, with an open hand, for me to precede her down the steps.

I glanced into Ola's apartment before descending the stairs. In the short hallway that led to the living room, I spied Ola and Zenobia talking. Zenobia was pointing in my general direction. I guessed she was filling Ola in on what had happened. Maybe Ola would come to my rescue.

When Grace and I made it to the lobby, it was quieter with only a couple of folks hanging around, their lips locked around their cigarettes. The lobby door had been propped open with a few stray cans so as to let the smoke out and let the frigid December air in. I'd left my black wool coat upstairs on Ola's bed, so I was freezing. I hugged myself tight and rubbed my arms vigorously to create a bit of heat. Grace still had on her coat and it didn't look like she planned to offer it up.

"Let's go stand over there, away from the draft."

Grace pointed to a tiny, dimly lit alcove under the stairs and away from the door. In this space, the cold air was not as direct as before, but I was still cold.

"Can we get this over with?" I asked while I rubbed my arms.

"Sure thing, just tell me what the hell is going on? Who's the chick you had your tongue rammed into?"

"There was no tongue ramming," I said.

"Yeah, well, your lips were all over hers. How do you explain that?"

"Explain? You want me to explain *myself*? What about you, Grace? Explain why you've been such an asshole lately—not talking to me, not coming over to my place, not wanting to hang out with me, not wanting us to move in together. Explain that!"

"So that's what this is about? I become a bit distant and you what, cheat on me?"

"I wasn't cheating! I just kissed her. Anyway, what do you care? You seem to be gone from this relationship already, so what does it matter what I do or don't do?"

"Gone? Hardly. I've been somewhat in my head about us, that's true, but gone, no. But this is how you handle it? Why didn't you try talking to me?"

I couldn't believe she said that. I scoffed.

"Try talking to you? Grace, I've done everything in my power to engage in a conversation with you about us since we came back from North Carolina and you've shut me down over and over again. You've been distant and terse since we came back. What am I supposed to do?" I said. "But, hey, no worries. I finally got the message."

"You were distant too, Sky, but I've been distant, as you say, because you lied to me."

"About what?"

"You never told me that Delbert asked you to sleep with him one last time. Why didn't you tell me about that, Sky? Is it because you considered his offer?"

"What the hell are you talking about? I told you what he said."

"No, you told Odeta over breakfast to get back at her when she told you that she was involved with Delbert. If she'd never said anything about her and Delbert, I may never have found out about his little request. And, if you hate him as much as you claim, why throw that particular dig in Odeta's face? Answer that."

"There was nothing particular about it. I just repeated to her what Delbert had said to me. I was trying to be a good friend and warn her about that asshole. That's why I told her. Nothing else. No ulterior motive."

"Yeah, right, not sure I believe that. You seem to care a little too much about their relationship and the amount of 'assholes' you spout when referring to Delbert seems a bit too much. Thou doth protest."

"Believe what you want, Grace. I can't believe this is your so-called reason for being distant. The short answers. The not wanting to move in or hang out even! All because of some stupid proposition and the amount of assholes I say? Wow." I shook my head.

"I consider your big reveal to Odeta a lie of omission. Something you would not have told me if the topic never presented itself. It made me wonder what else you're hiding."

"Well, if you think I'm lying to you all the time then maybe we shouldn't be together. I want to be with someone who trusts me. Someone who knows how to communicate effectively. Not someone who is weighing every word I say for honesty and second-guessing everything that comes out of my mouth. And not someone who can only interpret what other people say but fails to produce words of her own!"

"Oh, and so I guess you think Little Miss Hot Lips is going to love you unconditionally, huh?"

"Maybe she will. She says she's still in love with me. Says she loves me deeply. Hmm, don't think I omitted anything. Wouldn't want to do that! Now, if you'll excuse me, I'm going back upstairs."

I moved to walk around Grace. I was almost clear of her when she snatched my forearm in a tight grip.

"What do you mean she's 'still in love' with you? You two have history?"

I pulled my arm out of Grace's grip. "Yes, we do. And now it looks like we just might be able to continue from where we left off. Thanks for the opportunity," I said and stormed up the stairs.

CHAPTER FORTY-EIGHT

I woke to a horrific stream of sunlight flooding the one eye that I was able to muster open. My head felt like a piano, it was so heavy. I tried lifting it but couldn't, so I flopped back down onto the bed. Even the pillows hurt.

"Mm, good morning," a voice said beside me.

I thought for a moment, trying to recall the events of the previous night. That is not Grace's voice, I thought to myself. I took another moment to gather my thoughts. With my eyes shut against the torturous brightness of the day, and with my voice scratchy and my words slow, I asked, "Zee, that you?"

"In the flesh," Zee giggled.

I rubbed my head and my eyes. "What day is it?"

"Sunday, silly."

"Okay, good. I've only lost a couple of hours somewhere along the way. How the hell did we get here?"

"Your friend Ola called a cab and told the driver the address. I paid the man against your wishes and, voilà, here we are."

Zenobia pulled the comforter up and over to her side of the bed.

"You know that's redundant," I said as I planted my arm across my eyes like a blindfold.

"What?" Zenobia asked.

"Saying 'voilà' and 'here we are,' since voilà essentially means, 'Here we are' or 'There you are' or 'There it is.' Oh, never mind," I replied in a whisper. "Damn. I don't remember any of what you described. Did we stay long at the party?"

"Long enough for you to throw back a bunch of drinks and raise hell with your ex."

I lifted my arm and dragged one eye open again.

"Did you say *ex*?"

"Yes, silly, you two had a major argument. At first, when you came back upstairs, everything was fine, but after several drinks… Anyway, you both got all up in each other's faces and then you slapped her, and she slapped you back. Ola and I swooped in and broke the two of you up. You shouted at your now ex. What's her name? Grace? You shouted that it was totally over and then I took you downstairs to wait for the cab. You were extremely agitated, to say the least, but you calmed down during the ride here."

I draped my arm back over my eyes, shook my head slightly, and swallowed.

"Oh my God. I am so sorry I put you through that," I said.

"It's okay. I'm just glad I was there to take care of you."

"Jeez, I totally made a spectacle of myself and probably ruined Ola's party. Not good. So not good," I groaned.

"It can happen to the best of us. Especially after too much booze," Zenobia said.

A thought struck me. I reached under the comforter and felt for my clothing or some pajamas. There were none.

"Uh, where are my clothes?" I turned and looked at Zenobia, who was looking right back at me smiling.

"You tore them off like they were burning your skin!" She laughed.

I furrowed my brow questioningly. "Did we?"

"We kissed once and hugged once and then spooned. You fell asleep like five seconds after that, so, no, we did not."

I covered my face with my hands. "Oh my God! I'm a mad woman!" I yelled into my hands.

"No, you're cute and you're funny and you're sexy, and... you're a bad drunk."

Zenobia pulled my hands from my face.

"Everything is fine now, Sky. Don't beat yourself up. Shit happens, right?" She leaned in and kissed me softly on the mouth.

"In fact," Zenobia said in a husky whisper, "I know of some shit that I would love to happen right now."

Zenobia kissed me again, but harder this time. My desire for her pulled at me, but I felt like I was in no shape to satisfy it, her, or me.

"Whoa, tigress," I said, shifting my body a bit to get more leverage and control. "Take a breath and calm down."

"Calm is boring," Zenobia said. "I'd rather frolic in the field of excitement."

"I'm so not ready to frolic," I said. I eased away from Zenobia.

"Really? I thought maybe you'd want to consummate your emancipation from your overbearing ex-girlfriend."

I was on my back again. Eyes closed, chin to the ceiling. Zenobia talked and caressed my stomach, rubbing a continuous maze of circles over and over again into my skin like a mother would do for a child whose stomach was upset. It soothed me, but it also made me think of Grace and how I used to make the same exact movements on her stomach when we'd lain together, here, in this very same bed. Her body taut and lean like an arrow, breasts molded so perfectly on her chest they reminded me of a breastplate or coat of arms with large, rounded nipple shields. There was a heraldic subliminal motto of "Touch me" that sang in my head every time I saw her breasts.

"So, are you ready to engage in a little emancipation celebration?" Zenobia inquired.

"I don't really feel free," I said and turned onto my side.

CHAPTER FORTY-NINE

The first snow of the season fell silently onto grass, cars, and trees, Wednesday morning. It made the world around me look like a giant powdered donut. Ordinarily, I would have loved the beauty of the snow, but today, it made me think of family and how home, with the passage of time, seemed to be slipping away. I reasoned with myself that a Christmas tree was exactly the thing I needed to preserve that old feeling of a family-filled holiday, so I tugged the small, fake, silver Christmas tree that I bought at Alexander's out of the cardboard box it was lodged in and began putting it together limb by limb.

At home, in North Carolina, we'd always had a real Christmas tree. My dad would go out and bring home a tree that bent downward from the ceiling and we'd have to get the old, rusted saw from the garage and lop off the top of the tree. As a result, the angels and stars we placed at the top of the trees leaned crookedly to one side as if they were rum and eggnog filled, but we loved it: the blinking red and green lights, the shimmery shine of tinsel as we threw it onto the green tree limbs, the scent of pine that ran up to greet us every time we opened the front door. Mom would play Stevie Wonder and Gladys Knight and The Pips Christmas albums, and we'd sing along as we baked cookies for Santa. I missed all of that. My only consolation was that I didn't have to work because of the impending snowstorm. I wanted to see mountains of snow! I wanted to see snow piled up to the tops of the trees because we'd never gotten much snow in North Carolina. I also had an urge to be snowed in, to isolate myself from the drama that had seeped into my life and the drama that laid just outside my door, like the racially motivated incident that occurred at Howard Beach, where black teenager Michael Griffith was killed by a mob of white teenagers. It seemed like something negative was always brewing; shutting myself off from the rest of the world to nestle in memories of home seemed like the best thing to do.

Zenobia had called me early in the morning to ask about coming to my place later in the day. Dinner and a movie, she'd said on the answering machine. I'd told her to swing by, but now I wasn't sure I wanted the company.

Grace hadn't called me at all since Ola's party, but I really didn't expect to hear from her yet because she liked to stew in negative emotions for as long as she possibly could. Truthfully, on one level, I welcomed the quiet, the peacefulness of solitude. But on a deeper level, I missed her dearly.

I pulled two silver, cylinder-shaped glass bulbs out of the box of Christmas ornaments that I bought last week and set them on the couch. I was looking for the hooks to attach to the bulbs when the phone rang.

"Hello?"

"Girl, it is so nice to get a day off work I don't know what to do with myself!"

"Sammy, you're crazy!"

I had a huge smile on my face as I pictured Sammy pacing the floor of his apartment while going stir-crazy.

"You have cabin fever already?"

"Definitely in the throes of it! I done washed every dish in the damn place. Took out the garbage, made a large pot of vegetable soup from scratch, and vacuumed the whole damn place. I mean, the place ain't that big, but damn!"

"Well, hey, you can swing by my place and tidy up if you want. Bring some of your homemade soup with you and I'll supply the drinks."

"And get trapped outside when the big snow hits? I'll pass. But I'll be thinking about you as I finish up this pitcher of mimosas that I'm whipping up right now. Mm, so good."

Sammy slurped loudly from his drink, but it was interrupted by an elongated avalanche of coughs that sounded as if they originated deep within Sammy's chest.

"You still coughing, huh? Are you okay?" I was concerned.

"Still fighting this cold, girl. Can't seem to shake it, but I'm gonna be all right."

"I hope so. Anyway, sit down and get some lesson plans done, you lush. Be productive!"

"Oh, I'm working on something much more important."

"Great, what?"

"My buzz!"

I scoffed. "You and your buzz are going to be looking for employment soon if you keep up with your shenanigans."

"Yeah, yeah. Cluck, cluck, mother hen. Bye."

I wanted to ask if he'd gone to the doctor to see about that cough, but Sammy extinguished our conversation like a used cigarette. I was worried. He had missed several days of work recently and when I last saw him in the teacher's lounge, he looked thinner. But he'd already hung up, so I went back to decorating my Christmas tree.

I was attaching the hooks to the tops of the bulbs when the phone rang again. I dropped everything onto the couch and ran, with a big smile on my face, to answer the phone.

"Too many mimosas, huh? Forgot you called me already?" I laughed into the phone thinking it was Sammy calling back to comment on his abrupt departure.

"Johnny Walker Black is more my style," the voice said. "Guess you forgot about that too, huh Sky?"

Delbert!

CHAPTER FIFTY

Why, oh why, wouldn't this man leave me alone? I hesitated for a moment, thought about slamming the phone down in Delbert's ear, but I thought maybe my mom had asked him to check on me or to relay a message that she was sorry and wanted us to reconcile or even just sent him to nose around in my damn business.

"Did my mother tell you to call me? I know you two are probably still in cahoots."

"No, she did not, although she does mention you often followed by a curse word or two," Delbert paused, and I thought I heard him snicker. "But, no Sky, I'm not calling you as a favor to your mother."

"Then why are you calling? You should've totally lost my number by now. I mean, come on already!" A question came to mind. "Does Odeta know you're calling me?"

"No, she does not."

"Figures. Just what I warned her about."

I shook my head in disgust as I walked to the kitchen, tripping over the extra-long phone cord, to get myself a glass of water.

I pulled a tall, clear glass down from the cabinet and placed it on the kitchen counter. Then I turned to the fridge to grab the pitcher of cold water I'd placed inside a couple of hours before.

"Odeta is pregnant, Sky."

I almost dropped the heavy pitcher on my toes.

"What?"

"Odeta is pregnant. Our child is due to arrive this spring."

I stood beside the kitchen counter frozen, so shocked by the news that I was having trouble processing and pouring my water at the same time. I just kept trying to visualize Odeta pregnant. Odeta giving birth. Odeta cradling a child.

"Wow, that was fast," I said.

"Yes, we're both very excited. Anyway, I called because I plan to procure a very upscale event space to have a baby shower for Odeta. Possibly the Hilton, and…well…even though there's been some bad blood between you and…well…everyone really, I know Odeta wouldn't want you to miss it."

"So, this is an invite?"

"Yes, indeed it is."

"So Odeta doesn't know you're inviting me?"

"Well, no, but the whole shebang is a surprise, so what's one more?"

"Mm-hmm," I said.

I'd finally filled my glass with water and was sipping it down when it knocked up against my teeth. I braced myself for the cold, numbing sensation as I listened to Delbert and tried to figure out if there was some ulterior motive in play.

"Please be an adult. Let bygones be bygones and come celebrate the birth of my child," he said.

Did he just say *his* child? I thought to myself. Not *our* child.

"I'll think about it," I said.

"Good. I'll mail you an invite. Goodbye."

"Uh, don't you want to jot down my address?" I asked.

"I know where you live, Sky. Remember?" Delbert chuckled and hung up the phone.

"Bastard!" I yelled as I hung up. I could almost see the smug smile on Delbert's face with his last comment. "Fuck him and his lame shower!"

Zenobia showed up around six o'clock that evening looking like a lost snow bunny. Snow had piled up around the flipped edges of the curls that hung outside her hat, creating a fluffy snow cliff that encircled her head. Her nose was deep red like a blazing fire iron and her eyes were wet with tears from the cold.

"Get in here you," I said as I pushed open the screen door as much as I could. Snow had piled up on the steps making it difficult to open the door all the way. Zenobia squeezed through.

"My God! You live in West Bubblefuck!"

Zenobia clapped the snow off her gloves and stamped it off her boots and onto the small rug I'd placed by the front door while I pulled off her hat, destroying the rock face of the snow cliff that had taken shape on her curls.

"Yeah, it's kind of far."

"You are literally at the end of the line. I didn't realize it the other day since I was sort of sauced and riding in a cab. Couldn't find a cab today, so I had to take public transportation. That sucked, big-time."

I handed Zenobia some tissues for her nose and one of my thick terrycloth bathrobes—the one Grace used to wear—and I directed her to my cozy couch.

"Take a load off. Snuggle up in that blanket if you want while I make us some hot chocolate."

"Oh my God, hot chocolate sounds fantastic right now. Will there be tiny marshmallows and whipped cream on top?"

"Do you want tiny marshmallows and whipped cream on top?"

"Yes, please!"

"Sorry, ain't got none."

Zenobia sucked her teeth and we both laughed.

"Just joshing. Tiny marshmallows and whipped cream it is."

"Thank you, my dear."

"My pleasure," I said as I made my way to the kitchen.

It was nice having someone to talk to, make food for, and share myself with. I didn't realize how lonely I'd been the last few days without Grace. The absence of my family had been constant; losing Grace was an added layer to deal with.

"I'm glad you're here," I yelled out to Zenobia over the noise of the water running in the kitchen sink. "I wasn't sure you'd make it."

"I wasn't sure either, but I made it through. I wanted to spend some time with you."

I placed Zenobia's cup of hot chocolate in front of her on a bright red, Santa-shaped coaster that was sitting on the coffee table. I placed my cup on a bright yellow, reindeer-shaped coaster. I was glad I had finally remembered to buy coasters, but now I thought I'd have to buy more when Christmas was done because Santa coasters in July was just lame.

We sat side by side and watched as the steam rose from our mugs like spirits. I'd thought about adding a shot of vodka or brandy to our cups, but decided against it although I thought Zee could have used it.

I looked her in the eyes and held her still cold hands. "I want to spend time with you too," I said.

Zenobia leaned in and kissed me softly on the lips. Her lips were cool, but they felt nice. I slipped under the blanket and we snuggled and laughed at the cold as we sipped our hot chocolate and held hands.

"So, are you planning to go home to North Carolina for Christmas?" Zee asked.

I hadn't told her about my excursion back home and all the bad stuff that went along with it and I didn't really want to get into it.

"No, I'm just going to stay in New York and check out the Christmas happenings around the city like Rockefeller Center, oh, and the Christmas train exhibit at the Bronx Botanical

Gardens. I may take a trip with my students to see that. I think it'll be fun."

"Yeah, sounds great."

"What about you? Are you planning to go back to San Francisco before or after Christmas?"

"I was planning on heading back on Christmas Eve to be there by Christmas Day, but now that we've reconnected, I'm not sure if I still want to do that."

Zenobia looked up at me with a coy grin on her face. I was flattered so I smiled back, but I felt a tiny twinge of apprehension run through me.

CHAPTER FIFTY-ONE

Zenobia stayed the night and, against my better judgment, we engaged in some very satisfying sexual activity. But I felt a bit wary that I was leading her on. She was my first love and we'd always have that, but that was years ago. I'd moved past that—or at least I wanted to think I had. Maybe I was jumping the gun. Maybe Zee had someone special back in San Francisco. We hadn't really talked much about her life and the people in it yet. Maybe she'd decided to take this opportunity to engage in a fling since the situation—me, myself, and I—had presented itself. Maybe, maybe, maybe.

I woke before Zenobia. Her head was buried in the crook of my left arm, which had gone numb as I laid there in the dark wondering. I eased her head onto her pillow without waking her, then I slipped out of bed. It was five a.m. The room was dark and cold. I looked out of my bedroom window and saw that it was the same outside—dark and cold. Snow still drifted down like ice encrusted dandelion seeds offering everyone massive amounts of free wishes. Snow drifts, beautifully powdered blockades, formed against screen doors, car doors, and trees. I thought about how something so small and inconsequential as a snowflake could become so very significant, formidable even, when those tiny flakes stuck together. I thought about how we all needed to take more cues from nature.

I went downstairs and turned on the television, hoping to see an announcement saying school would be closed for another day. I turned the volume down low and sat at the very edge of the couch with my fingers crossed.

"Well, if you happened to get out of bed already, there was no need. You can put your pjs back on and head back to bed because schools have been shut down for another day! Yes, folks, it's true. New York City public schools have been shut down for another day," the meteorologist said. "We've got more on the way about this snowstorm, so stayed tuned."

I turned off the television and did a quiet yet elaborate happy dance. Afterward, I laid down on the couch, pulled the oversized, terry cloth blanket up over me, making sure to cocoon my toes, and stared at the ceiling with a big smile on my face. I loved teaching my students, but any break from it I could get, I took.

I fell back to sleep on my orange couch, staring at the ceiling with a stupid grin on my face, the blanket tucked tightly under my chin. I dreamed that Grace and I were on an old country road. The land was heavily guarded by an abundance of mature trees whose fluffy white seeds, resembling parachutes, blew in droves across the sky. Grace stood in front of me near a boxy row of neatly trimmed hedges, but then, suddenly, she took off running. I ran fast and hard to catch her, but she was always a stretched palm's length out of reach. When I woke up, Zee was sitting on the edge of the coffee table staring down at me. I looked at her for about two seconds, then I yelped and sprung into a seated position, frightened.

"Very funny," Zenobia said with her lips twisted to show she was not amused.

"Sorry. I wasn't trying to be funny or anything. I was just startled. Why are you sitting there watching me sleep?"

I turned and pulled the blanket around me while I stretched my legs out across the coffee table. Zenobia took my shifting as a sign to take up residence beside me on the couch.

"You looked so cute, so innocent, all curled up and asleep with your little blankie." Zee laughed.

I smiled, draped my arm over her shoulder, and then dove right into the questions on my mind.

"So, are you seeing anyone in San Francisco?"

Zenobia turned her head and looked at me with her eyebrows dark and furrowed. "Where is this coming from?"

"Well, we haven't really discussed much about your life there. I just want to know what's going on."

Zenobia took my arm off her shoulder and held my hand in her lap instead.

"Oh, okay, I see. Uh, so, right now, I'm not seeing anyone. I did just break up with someone though."

"Ouch. Sorry to hear that. How long had you two been together?"

"Two years, off and on."

"Sounds like it was sort of serious."

"Yeah, I guess. I'm going to be honest. It's been hard for me…in relationships, I mean. I've consciously and, often times, unconsciously, compared everyone to you and to what we had."

"Really?" I was flattered, but then puzzled. "But we were only together for, what, six months?"

"Yes, but in those six months, I knew you were *the one* for me. We just clicked. Don't you think? Didn't you feel the connection?" Zenobia looked up at me.

"Um, yeah, we totally clicked," I said.

I didn't know how to tell her that although she was great, and I really enjoyed her company, she was not 'the one' for me. I couldn't really explain why because from the outside, Zenobia was definitely the whole package—looks, brains, body—but there was something missing for me that I couldn't, for the life of me, put my finger on.

"Ever since college, when we got together and became intimate, I knew you were the one for me. I was so pissed when my mom pulled me from our school and stuck me in that super strict Catholic college when she found out about us, but—"

"Wait. That's why you left?"

"Yeah! Didn't you get my note? I gave it to that nosy girl, Sharon, to give to you."

"Nope, never got a note. I just thought you were done experimenting and moved off campus somewhere to live your life. Remember, things were not all peaches and roses with us at that time," I said. "But all this time I'd blamed myself, thinking I was the reason for your sudden disappearance when all of this time it was your mom who took you out of school. Wow. Why didn't you mention this before? You had me apologizing, thinking I'd done something wrong."

"Yeah, well, my mom told me that she wasn't spending her hard-earned money for me to become a bulldagger. And, anyway, you *did* do something wrong. Don't you remember why we weren't good at that time?   You slept with that cute girl, Alex."

Zenobia dropped my hand.

"Yeah, right, uh, anyway," I said. "What friends are you visiting in New York? I mean, it's wild that we both ended up in the Bronx at the same time."

"My friend Brenda lives here," she said. "And your subject change was a bit too quick."

"Yeah, okay," I said to Zenobia, but her head was down and she'd begun wringing her hands. I sensed she wanted to say more, so I remained quiet, allowing her the space she needed.

"Actually, and this may sound crazy, but, uh, actually, I came to the Bronx to find you."

Zenobia looked up at me with big puppy dog eyes. I, on the other hand, felt my face crumple into confusion, my eyes questioning.

"How did you know I was here?" I asked.

"Friends of friends of friends," Zenobia said almost flippantly.

I turned around on the couch to get a better look at Zee.

"What do you mean, 'friends of friends of friends?' What friends? When? Where? Have you been stalking me? Are you a stalker?" I asked, alarm bells ringing in the back of my head.

Zenobia laughed. "Stalker? No! Just following my heart. Not ready to give up on love is all. I needed to find you, spend time with you, make sure all of the feelings that I felt for you before were still in place, and they are. I mean, you feel them too, right?"

Zenobia looked at me with such intensity. Her eyes were bright and wet with anticipation and longing coupled with a shiny shot of crazy that I'd never noticed before. I threw off the blanket and headed back to bed like the weatherman suggested. This was all way too much to contemplate at the moment.

CHAPTER FIFTY-TWO

I stood on a bridge looking down into turbulent water. A warm breeze blew over me and I looked up to see Tracy Chapman standing beside me singing the soundtrack of my life. She was taller than I'd imagined and even though she sang of heartbreak and lies, there was a shred of a smile on her face, her dimples so deep I dove in.

I awakened with a start, my breath cold and sharp in my chest. I looked toward the window. It was opened just a bit, but the curtains sprinted back and forth toward the ceiling like birds repeatedly startled into flight. I shivered and pulled the comforter up to my neck. The room was dark. Tiny clouds of breath appeared then disappeared in front of my mouth. The ceiling flashed green, then red, then green again, and the incessant whine of "Silent Night" that played on a steady loop from the Christmas display in the neighbor's backyard sidestepped the curtains and tiptoed into my bedroom.

Zenobia liked the room cold. I didn't understand why because every night she'd bury her whole body deep beneath the comforter with only the top of her head to be seen. I sighed as I thought about ripping off the covers to expose her to the cold temperature she claimed to love. Why was I always the one out of bed in the middle of the night shaking and shivering my way across the floor, battling frostbite in my skimpy nightgown to shut the window against the cold?

Christmas was one day away. Zenobia had been crashing at my place for two weeks and the novelty of her had definitely worn off. I missed my space, my autonomy, the ability to roll over twice in my bed without being blocked by another body. I also missed being in love! I *liked* Zenobia. She was smart and, oftentimes, funny, but she had definitely creeped me out when she told me about the stalking. She hated when I called it that, but sometimes a spade is a spade. It also bugged me that she refused to take ownership of her actions. On the other hand, as pathetic as it was, I was extremely flattered. Here was someone who was so smitten with me that she'd searched for me and didn't give up until she'd found me. She'd kept tabs on my life in hopes to become a part of it. She knew what she wanted, and she'd set out after it. I admired her zeal, her tenacity, her love for me. But as I stared at the blinking ceiling and processed and sifted through our relationship, I was troubled by the parallels I saw between Delbert's behavior and Zenobia's, and the patterns in my life that kept repeating. But I was pleased that I was finally able to spot the repetitiveness.

Grace had been on my mind more than ever lately. Hope had given me dirty looks every time she'd seen me in the hallway last week. When she'd finally spoken to me, she claimed that I'd broken Grace's heart with my "infidelity." Such drama! I reminded Hope that Grace was the one who had thrown a huge wrench in our relationship due to her poor communication skills and told her to tell Grace that anytime she wanted to practice communicating effectively, I would be willing to see her or take her call. Hope just rolled her eyes. Now, the vastness of the ceiling allowed me to see the situation from a variety of angles. I concluded that both Grace and I had been pigheaded and prideful, but I wasn't ready to reach out to Grace just yet.

There was Zenobia to consider, and after all these years apart, she and her desire for me were like pieces of candy that I'd had a long time ago and needed to taste again. I couldn't say no but saying yes had taken me far away from what I felt in my heart.

I gripped the comforter in both hands and did an aggressive turn toward the right, hoping that I had snatched enough covers off Zenobia to awaken her.

"Hey!" Zenobia croaked sleepily.

I smiled to myself. It worked!

I tried to sound like I'd just awakened myself when I responded. I made my voice into a dreamy, lackadaisical whisper.

"Since you're up, can you close the window, please?" I asked.

Zenobia huffed. The mattress shifted under her weight as she got up.

"Oh my God, it's freaking freezing!"

I heard her footsteps fall fast on the floor as she made her way to the window, slammed it shut, and then ran back to bed. As some form of punishment, or as some form of passive-aggressiveness to match that of my own, as soon as Zenobia made her way back under the blankets, she embraced me from head to toe, burning the night's coldness into my warm flesh.

"Ugh!" I screamed as I tried to jump from her grasp. "What the hell, Zee? I'm trying to sleep!"

"Are you really?"

"Yes, I am."

"You're no fun. I thought we could warm each other up."

"Uh, I'm already warm or at least I was."

"Someone's grumpy. What's wrong, had a bad dream? I can fix that for you."

I removed Zee's hands from my breasts.

"Just go back to sleep, Zee. I'm not in the mood."

Zenobia pulled her hands from out of my clasp. "Fine! I'll leave you alone." Then she turned onto her left side. The comforter pulled tight with her departure.

The next time I awakened, the smell of cinnamon and soy bacon peppered the air. I yawned and stretched like a languid lioness—back arched, toes curled under—then dragged myself to an upright position. My stomach purred like a kitten. I caressed it gently and noticed that there seemed to be a small mound of fat forming around the muscles. Zenobia had been whipping up elaborate breakfasts and dinners for us almost every day since we'd been shacked up. The meals were nutritious and tasty and taking their toll.

"Gonna miss that cooking when she's gone," I muttered to myself while I sucked in my stomach and bent over to look for my slippers under the bed.

"There's no need for you to miss anything," Zee said from the bedroom doorway.

My head rose sharply. I hadn't seen her standing there. There was a moment of awkward silence, then I cleared my throat and asked, "Food ready?"

Zenobia looked at me hard and then she gazed down at the floor before she responded. "Ready when you are."

"Great, be down in a sec," I replied. It felt like we might need boxing gloves instead of forks at breakfast.

"Did I ever tell you the story about how I ended up in San Francisco?" Zenobia asked me as soon as I'd entered the dining room.

The table brimmed with the bounty of breakfast—eggs, soy bacon, blueberry waffles (the frozen kind, but they still smelled fantastic!), sliced strawberries that surrounded the bluest blueberries I'd ever seen, freshly buttered toast, and tall frosted glasses of what looked to be orange juice.

"You've told me many things since you've been here, but that, my dear, was not one of them," I responded.

I picked up my juice glass as I sat opposite Zenobia. I gulped the juice down like I'd just completed a marathon. It was actually orange mango juice—my favorite.

"I followed a woman to San Francisco a couple of years ago. I was madly in love with her and she said that she was madly in love with me too."

"Wait, wait, wait. I thought I was the love of your life. Now, I see that ultimately you were able to forget about me for a bit

while you pursued her. A break from stalking, that's good."
Zenobia rolled her eyes.

"Anyway, it was only my second lesbian relationship after us. She reminded me of you—smart, beautiful, funny, exciting, sexy. We did a lot of crazy things together. She showed me all around Frisco, introduced me to all her friends, got me an apartment, hooked me up with some up-and-coming computer companies, and then she said goodbye. Just like that. Out of the blue. Just up and left me. She said she'd always planned to move to Morocco if the opportunity presented itself and, apparently, it presented itself just two months after my arrival. I was devastated for about a year."

"Wow! Why didn't you go with her to Morocco?"

"She didn't ask."

"Wow," I said again as I munched on a piece of toast. "That sucks."

"Yeah, but I survived and I'm grateful for everything she did for me which, ultimately, was showing me that I could stand on my own two feet. That was the best thing she did for me. I stayed in San Francisco and stuck it out. It's a beautiful city. Way prettier than New York. Have you been?"

"No, but I've heard it's picture perfect."

Zenobia smiled and looked down at her blueberry waffle thoughtfully as she cut into it.

"Maybe you should get out of New York and come with me to San Francisco." Zee raised her eyes and looked at me.

I swallowed a piece of soy bacon, smiled, and wagged my finger at her.

"Sounds like you're trying to create a pattern," I said. I popped the rest of the soy bacon strip into my mouth and gulped down some more juice. "Anyway, I just got here. I have a job, this place, and…uh…did I mention my job?"

Zenobia laughed. "Sky, those are just things. You could get another job, find another place. Maybe even better ones than you have here."

"Maybe. Maybe not. But *maybe* isn't firm enough of a word for me to pull up stakes again and move across country. Besides, I have a connection to this place."

"A connection named, Grace? I think that connection died like two weeks ago. She hasn't called you, hasn't reached out to you in any way. Yeah, I'd say it's a done deal. Time to move on. Learn to be your own person."

"But if I'm going to San Francisco with you, how is that me being my own person? You'd just end up dumping my ass just like you got dumped."

I hadn't meant to sound cruel, but, really, Zenobia knew little about the connection that Grace and I had so I didn't appreciate her belittling it.

Zenobia frowned. "I wasn't 'dumped,'" she said. "Anyway, I'm just trying to say that I think you and I make a great team. We always have. We should embark on a new journey together. March forth into the future together. It just makes so much sense."

"Sometimes doing the thing that does not make sense is actually the right thing to do. Everyone thought it would've made sense for me to marry Delbert, but it wouldn't have. Your mother thought it made sense to take you out of one college and place you in a more religious one, but you're still who you are, right? I'm just saying that…"

"You're just saying that you're still in love with Grace and, essentially, I've been wasting my time," Zenobia said.

I looked down at my plate. Zenobia pushed her chair back and stood.

"I won't be washing the dishes," she said as she left the room.

CHAPTER FIFTY-THREE

I got what I'd wanted: space. I was now free to roll across my bed, end-to-end, without obstruction.

Soon after our conversation, Zenobia hastily gathered her things, stuffed them all into her bright pink duffel bag, rolled her eyes and shook her head at me as she walked down the path in front of my apartment. She hopped into a cab she'd called while I was in the shower, then slammed the cab's door before it made a U-turn and sped away.

I was sitting on my couch, sipping hot chocolate and staring into space, when I thought I heard the screen door creak. I thought about getting up to make sure it was closed properly, but just then the phone rang. I sighed, thinking it was probably Zenobia ready to reel off a fair number of expletives at me for not being as committed to "us" as she was. I was tempted to not answer the call, but then I thought it would be better to deal with her immediately and get it over with so on the fourth ring, I answered the phone.

Wearily I murmured, "Hello."

"Merry Christmas, bitch! Thanks for coming to my baby shower!"

"Excuse me, who is this?"

"Oh, now you don't even remember me, huh? Sky, I can't believe you let our petty little argument get in the way of you coming down here for *one day* to help me celebrate the coming of my child! I know you got beef with Delbert, but the baby shower was about me and my baby, not him! I thought we was sistahs."

Odeta. I stretched the phone cord to the couch and sat down. On the coffee table in front of me—amongst other envelopes that needed to be opened—was the bright blue envelope that contained the baby shower invitation. How could I tell Odeta that I hadn't even looked at her invitation?

"Odeta, I'm sorry," I sputtered.

"Yeah, your ass is sorry all right!"

"I've just…I've been going through some things lately that have kept me occupied."

"Too occupied to come share in my joy? You didn't even call to say congratulations, didn't sent a gift, a card, nothing! After all these years, Sky? Wow."

"Honestly, since Delbert called and invited me and not you, I wasn't sure you really wanted to see me."

"I wrote you a long apology letter, Sky. It was tucked inside the envelope with the baby shower invita…Oh my goodness. You never even opened the damn invitation, did you? Did you?"

"I was…I was…" was all I could manage.

Odeta's voice turned icy. "Today you have shown me who you truly are, Sky Valentine!"

The phone went dead. I sat there with it pressed to my ear, feeling my heart grow heavy with regret and with words I should have said. I was so focused on not giving in to Delbert and his schemes that I'd lost sight of Odeta and her dreams. She'd finally gotten the man, the child, the family she had wanted, and I'd missed celebrating that with her because I never even opened the invitation. I felt like an asshole dunked in stupidity. I was thinking of a slew of things I could do to make it up to her when my mind spooled backward through the angry words Odeta said until it landed on the words "Merry Christmas." I had forgotten it was Christmas Day.

I hung up the phone, rolled myself into a tight ball on the couch, pulled the blanket that was on the back of the couch over my head, and sulked.

This was one sucky Christmas! I heard the screen door squeaking on its hinges again, so I jumped up and marched over to the front door ready to release some anger by slamming the screen door shut to stop the racket. But when I opened the storm door, a large colorful bouquet of flowers and a huge heart-shaped box sat on the ground in front of me. I looked around, but I didn't see anyone. I was tempted to throw on my coat and take a walk down the path toward the mailboxes to see if someone was staked out over that way, but decided against it—too cold.

I picked up the heart-shaped box—which I assumed was chocolates—tucked it under my arm then picked up the dazzling bouquet and brought both into the house and sat them on the coffee table. I went back and locked the screen door, shut the storm door, and then sat on the couch and stared at my bundle of wrapped happiness. I could smell the chocolates through the cellophane and imagined thick layers of gooey sweetness wrapped delicately in frilled white sheaths like little girl's ankles wrapped in the turned down, crisp, frilly white lace of Easter socks. I saw an envelope shaped like a tear drop and knew immediately that this surprise was from Zee and that she'd be back to stalking me within a month's time.

"And, so it begins again, huh Zee?" I said to myself while shoving some flower petals up toward my nose. I didn't want to like these gifts, didn't want to need them, but I did. They were, most likely, the only gifts I'd receive today. I'd sent presents to my parents and Henry weeks ago. They were my family after all and I'd wanted them to know that no matter what, they were always in my heart and on my mind. But after I smelled these beautiful irises and imagined picking and eating my way through the chocolates, I felt crummy that I'd never even thought about getting Zee a gift. Well, I'd thought about it, but I dismissed the thought because I didn't want her hanging around. Getting her a nice gift would have sent a mixed signal, but now, I felt bad.

I removed the envelope that was stuck between two red roses. The envelope's front was empty, so I turned it over, ripped the tiny triangle away from the rest of the envelope, and took out the card. It was covered with X's and O's. Zee used to put X's and O's on the little notes she'd left for me on my pillow and on my desk and in my knapsack when we were together during our college days. I shook my head at her nostalgia and her desperation. Not even gone for one day and already sending flowers and chocolates. I felt terrible about Zee and my heart tugged a little bit for her. Maybe I had been too hasty. Maybe I had thrown away a good thing. Maybe San Francisco was the place to lose one's heart. I opened the card and read.

Dear Sky,
I miss you more than I'd imagined I would.
I have been a fool. Please forgive me.
Call me. I'm ready to talk.
Love you, Grace

CHAPTER FIFTY-FOUR

I smiled from ear to ear after reading the card Grace sent me. Grace! Not crazy stalking Zenobia. Grace! I smelled some white and yellow flowers I didn't know the names of and ripped open the heart-shaped box of chocolates. I fingered a dark brown nugget described on the back of the box as a piece of dark chocolate with an almond inside, my favorite. I ate one and imagined Grace saying to me what she had written in her card, and I grinned like a fool once again. But I decided, after swallowing, that I wasn't gonna rush to the phone to call Grace just yet. I wanted her to stew for a bit. Wanted her to hopefully feel some of the longing that I'd felt while she was away. Wanted her heart to ache for me like mine ached for her. Wanted her to feel some of the anguish and pain of love and loving someone. I guess, really, I just wanted her to care, to really care about me. She always told me that I was "the whole package," but she couldn't seem to let go of my past or the fact that it didn't mirror hers as closely as she wanted it to.

I threw the rest of the chocolates in the garbage and plopped back down on the couch. The one I ate was delicious, but I needed to lose the extra pounds I'd gained while shacking up with Zenobia.

"Yeah, let her stew," I said to myself. Then the phone rang.

"Hey! Couldn't let the day pass without saying Merry Christmas to my long-lost sister."

"Henry! Oh, it's nice to hear your voice!"

"What's going on over there, baby sis, you ain't never sounded this happy to hear from me!"

"That's not true."

"Sho nuff is. Seriously, you all right?"

Briefly, I thought about unloading my troubles onto Henry's lap and shoulders, but then just as quickly I decided against it. I didn't want to ruin his Christmas, so I just stuffed my misery back down into that little pocket located in the corner of my chest.

"I'm fine, Henry. How are you? How's the new love of your life?"

"We're still kickin' it, so I guess that means things are good," Henry replied and laughed. He was trying to play it off, but I felt the happiness in his voice. He hadn't sounded this happy in years.

"Good. I'm glad for you. Don't go messing it up now," I said.

"Nah, not gonna do that. How about you? You still seeing... uh...that uh...girl? What's her name again?"

"Grace. Her name is Grace. Yeah, we cool," I said.

I wasn't going to get into the details of my love life with Henry. Especially since he couldn't even recall my lover's name. But at least he'd asked. Baby steps, I thought.

"So, how are Mom and Dad? Are you hanging with them today?" I didn't want to say it but then I did, "Do they talk or ask about me?"

"They're good. They're good. Dad's doing much better since Mom watches over him like a hawk now, poor guy. But he's doing great. And Mom is Mom. You know how she is. Still mad at me for breaking it off with June, but she'll get over it. Shit, I did!" Henry laughed, but it wasn't a hearty, real laugh and I realized that my mother had managed to hurt him too. She was like a tornado wiping out love that didn't fall within the rigid parameters that she'd set as she roamed the land.

"Dad asked about you when I spoke to him the other day. Said to tell you hello when I talked to you."

"Tell him I said hi and that I miss him."

"Will do, baby sis. Will do. Okay, well, let me get on outta this here house and go buy this list of groceries Anais done gave me like a half hour ago. I love you. It was good talking to ya. Don't be a stranger neither."

"Nice talking to you too, Henry. No strangers here. Enjoy today and thanks so much for calling."

"Bye now."

"Bye."

CHAPTER FIFTY-FIVE

Two days went by before I reached out to Grace. I had been contemplating several things—what to say to her, how to act when I saw her (didn't want to seem desperate), if we should hash things out over the phone or do it face-to-face, and most importantly, if we did meet face-to-face, what to wear because I wanted her to drool when she saw me.

The "see me and drool" option won, so I'd left a brief message on Grace's answering machine Friday morning saying that we should get together at her place Friday evening to talk things through and to possibly go dancing afterward. I hadn't been dancing in a while and I loved dancing with Grace.

Early Friday evening, I put on the sexiest outfit I could wear considering it had snowed quite a bit Friday morning, and set out to meet up with Grace.

The cab ride to her place was arduous. The driver had cursed plenty and hit his horn often as he'd fought to maneuver around stalled cars and snow mountains that stood solidly in the middle of streets as people shoveled off the avalanche of snow dumped onto their cars by the sanitation department.

I sat back in my seat and watched the Bronx landscape jog past me as we trotted through it. Empty lots that were once filled with multicolored wildflowers like black-eyed Susans, dainty pink butterfly bushes, and tall, bushy-headed, yellow Indian grass were now barren prisons of black, yellow, and gray-colored snow.

The sky had begun to darken, and the trees stood bare and gnarled against the sky. Someone had covered every inch of their home with yellow, green, and blue Christmas lights, along with plastic reindeers whose red noses were brightly lit. There was also a fat, brown Santa whose cheeks glowed dimly since his face had been painted over.

We drove past the school where I worked. The building looked squat and gray like the night. An old, faded mural depicting children reading, writing, and running had been painted across the front of the building, while a black, pointed, steel fence, that looked fairly new, ran around its perimeter. Despite the fence, some kids had managed to get into the schoolyard and snowballs littered the sky and the spaces between them.

As I absorbed the scene, I thought about how different this landscape was from North Carolina. Snow was something I'd hardly ever seen as a child growing up in Durham. We got maybe an inch or two every now and then, but nothing major. Except for that time in 1973 when I was seven years old. I remembered it clearly because it was the day after my birthday, and I'd gotten the purple bicycle I'd asked for. Odeta and I had planned to take turns riding my new bike the next day, but when I awakened, there was about a foot of snow on the ground. Odeta was pissed, but a few snowballs ricocheting off her arms and legs had gotten her out of her funk and shifted her focus to catching me. Odeta. After our last conversation I wrote her an apology letter since she refused to take my calls. She hasn't written me back or called, but I suspected, or at least hoped, she would eventually get around to it.

The driver parked the cab directly in front of Grace's apartment building. I paid him, then climbed out of the car and over a mound of snow that was a frozen divider between the car and the sidewalk. I had on my cute, black leather boots with the kitten heels and I quickly learned that these boots were not a great choice; I almost slipped and fell on a patch of black ice, but I regained my footing and saved myself from a moment of embarrassment.

Outside Grace's apartment door, before I knocked, I felt my locs to make sure they were in place, straightened out my clothes, and thought about ways in which the conversation might flow or turn. I was nervous. I chuckled to myself at the thought of being nervous, but I knew the feeling to be true.

Grace opened the door right after the first ding of her doorbell. My heart jumped around crazily at first then it morphed into steady, rapid beating like the beat of the conga drum I'd heard on the cab's radio on the way over.

Grace smiled widely when she laid eyes on me and I responded with a huge silly smile of my own.

"Hey you. Come on in here. So good to see you."

"Good to see you too," I said as I entered Grace's apartment.

Things hadn't changed much from my last visit. More books, maybe. Maybe another poster or two on the walls, but nothing major. The space was still cramped and tight. Grace had her radio on. The volume was slightly higher than a whisper, but I recognized Anita Baker's voice as she belted out her new song, "Been So Long," and I thought, *Yes, it definitely has been.*

"Coat," Grace said from behind me.

"Yes," I replied.

I unbuttoned my long, black, wool coat and slipped my arms out of it as Grace held on to the coat and gathered it into her arms.

"You look…ravishing," Grace said as she eyed me from head to toe while she folded my coat and put it over the back of a chair, all with an appreciative smile on her face. When she was done, she took a seat directly across from me.

I looked at her and asked, "So, how are you?"

Graced raised her hand and gently stroked the side of my face then my hair.

"Now, I'm good," she said.

I wanted to leap into her lap and kiss her sweet face, but I kept my composure.

"Thank you for reaching out," I said. "And for the beautiful bouquet and the delicious chocolates."

I felt awkward, as if it had been years and years since we'd separated and all intimacy was, now, somehow lost. Like there was too much space between us, too much time, too many words hanging and dead.

I stood and walked over to where Grace was seated. I kneeled in front of her.

"I missed you so much," I croaked. "You were right. I was so busy ranting and raving and pointing fingers at you and saying you lacked the ability to communicate effectively, but when I sat and examined our relationship, I saw that I wasn't communicating effectively either, and it left you feeling cautious about us. About me. I promise, if you give us another chance, I will do better at making you feel more secure with what we have. No more information left behind or left out of conversations for you to wonder about. I promise to tell you everything, Grace. Everything. I want us to work because I know there's no one else for me," I sobbed.

My eyes were wet with tears and my throat felt thick and coated. I hadn't planned on crying or on breaking down, but I couldn't help it. I was tired of bottling up the love I'd felt for this woman. I knew I deeply and truly loved Grace. She was my soulmate and I felt like no matter what happened between us, no matter how far apart we might wander from each other, she would always hold a place in my heart. I carried her and the love I had for her around with me. She was a part of me.

Grace pulled me into her arms and cradled me. "I know, baby. I know," Grace murmured into the top of my head. She stroked my hair and rubbed by back while I sobbed into her chest.

"I'm always going to choose you Grace Webster. No matter what happens or the amount of time that passes. I'm always going to choose you."

A GLANCE

Epilogue

I was true to my word. I told Grace everything and my honesty helped us make it through some tough times, much to Hope's chagrin.

Sammy was a diva until the end. Neither of us realized that he had been battling HIV, as it was a new ailment at the time. Unfortunately, it reached out and took many lives within the LGBTQIA+ communities over the years. I miss him dearly.

Ms. Parker went on to become principal of my school then she moved further up the education ladder and became superintendent of schools. Hope still dreams about being under her tutelage.

Odeta finally reached out to me and, during summer break, I traveled back to North Carolina to see Odeta's bouncing baby boy—Delbert Jr.. Delbert was so enamored by his son, that his obsession with me ceased and he focused all of his energy on his son. Hallelujah!

I also visited with Henry during summer break. He married his new love, Anais. And he finally verbalized his support for me, saying that he just wanted me to be happy like he was.

I got to visit with my father too. I met him at my favorite restaurant in Durham—Backyard BBQ Pit. We talked and laughed, and my dad had two forkfuls of macaroni and cheese. I enjoyed seeing him again, but my heart ached because my mother still refused to talk to me. Maybe, somewhere down the line, she will find it in her heart to choose me.

—Sky Valentine

Pandora's Box aka The Duchess, The Duchess II, The Grove was once a lesbian bar that catered to the Black and Latina lesbian population. It was one of the few spaces Black and Latina lesbians had that was predominately for them. It was a place to get together with community within the community of the West Village/Christopher Street/Sheridan Square area in New York City.

Bella Books, Inc.

Women. Books. Even Better Together.

P.O. Box 10543
Tallahassee, FL 32302

Phone: 800-729-4992
www.bellabooks.com

Books Available From Bold Strokes Books

Turnbull House by Jess Faraday. London 1891. Reformed criminal Ira Adler has a new, respectable life—but will an old flame and the promise of riches tempt him back to London's dark side...and his own? (978-1-60282-987-9)

Stronger Than This by David-Matthews Barnes. A gay man and a lesbian form a beautiful friendship out of grief when their soul mates are tragically killed. (978-1-60282-988-6)

In Between by Jane Hoppen. At the age of 14, Sophie Schmidt discovers that she was born an intersexual baby and sets off on a journey to find her place in a world that denies her true existence. (978-1-60282-968-8)

The Odd Fellows by Guillermo Luna. Joaquin Moreno and Mark Crowden open a bed-and-breakfast in Mexico but soon must confront an evil force with only friendship, love, and truth as their weapons. (978-1-60282-969-5)

The Seventh Pleiade by Andrew J. Peters. When Atlantis is besieged by violent storms, tremors, and a barbarian army, it will be up to a young gay prince to find a way for the kingdom's survival. (978-1-60282-960-2)

Cutie Pie Must Die by R.W. Clinger. Sexy detectives, a muscled quarterback, and the queerest murders...when murder is most cute. (978-1-60282-961-9)

Going Down for the Count by Cage Thunder. Desperately needing money, Gary Harper answers an ad that leads him into the underground world of gay professional wrestling—which leads him on a journey of self-discovery and romance. (978-1-60282-962-6)

Light by 'Nathan Burgoine. Openly gay (and secretly psychokinetic) Kieran Quinn is forced into action when self-styled prophet Wyatt Jackson arrives during Pride Week and things take a violent turn. (978-1-60282-953-4)

Baton Rouge Bingo by Greg Herren. The murder of an animal rights activist involves Scotty and the boys in a decades-old mystery revolving around Huey Long's murder and a missing fortune. (978-1-60282-954-1)

Anything for a Dollar, edited by Todd Gregory. Bodies for hire, bodies for sale—enter the steaming hot world of men who make a living from their bodies—whether they star in porn, model, strip, or hustle—or all of the above. (978-1-60282-955-8)

Mind Fields by Dylan Madrid. When college student Adam Parsh accepts a tutoring position, he finds himself the object of the dangerous desires of one of the most powerful men in the world—his married employer. (978-1-60282-945-9)

Greg Honey by Russ Gregory. Detective Greg Honey is steering his way through new love, business failure, and bruises when all his cases indicate trouble brewing for his wealthy family. (978-1-60282-946-6)

Lake Thirteen by Greg Herren. A visit to an old cemetery seems like fun to a group of five teenagers, who soon learn that sometimes it's best to leave old ghosts alone. (978-1-60282-894-0)

Deadly Cult by Joel Gomez-Dossi. One nation under MY God, or you die. (978-1-60282-895-7)

The Case of the Rising Star: A Derrick Steele Mystery by Zavo. Derrick Steele's next case involves blackmail, revenge, and a new romance as Derrick races to save a young movie star from a dangerous killer. Meanwhile, will a new threat from within destroy him, along with the entire Steele family? (978-1-60282-888-9)

Big Bad Wolf by Logan Zachary. After a wolf attack, Paavo Wolfe begins to suspect one of the victims is turning into a werewolf. Things become hairy as his ex-partner helps him find the killer. Can Paavo solve the mystery before he runs into the Big Bad Wolf? (978-1-60282-890-2)

The Moon's Deep Circle by David Holly. Tip Trencher wants to find out what happened to his long-lost brothers, but what he finds is a sizzling circle of gay sex and pagan ritual. (978-1-60282-870-4)

The Plain of Bitter Honey by Alan Chin. Trapped within the bleak prospect of a society in chaos, twin brothers Aaron and Hayden Swann discover inner strength in the face of tragedy and search for atonement after betraying the one you most love. (978-1-60282-883-4)

Tricks of the Trade: Magical Gay Erotica, edited by Jerry L. Wheeler. Today's hottest erotica writers take you inside the sultry, seductive world of magicians and their tricks—professional and otherwise. (978-1-60282-781-3)

Straight Boy Roommate by Kevin Troughton. Tom isn't expecting much from his first term at University, but a chance encounter with straight boy Dan catapults him into an extraordinary, wild weekend of sex and self-discovery, which turns his life upside down, and leads him into his first love affair. (978-1-60282-782-0)

In His Secret Life by Mel Bossa. The only man Allan wants is the one he can't have. (978-1-60282-875-9)

Promises in Every Star, edited by Todd Gregory. Acclaimed gay erotica author Todd Gregory's definitive collection of short stories, including both classic and new works. (978-1-60282-787-5)

Raising Hell: Demonic Gay Erotica, edited by Todd Gregory. Hot stories of gay erotica featuring demons. (978-1-60282-768-4)

Pursued by Joel Gomez-Dossi. Openly gay college student Jamie Bradford becomes romantically involved with two men at the same time, and his hell begins when one of his boyfriends becomes intent on killing him. (978-1-60282-769-1)

Timothy by Greg Herren. *Timothy* is a romantic suspense thriller from award-winning mystery writer Greg Herren set in the fabulous Hamptons. (978-1-60282-760-8)

In Stone by Jeremy Jordan King. A young New Yorker is rescued from a hate crime by a mysterious someone who turns out to be more of a something. (978-1-60282-761-5)

Combustion by Daniel W. Kelly. Bearish detective Deck Waxer comes to the city of Kremfort Cove to investigate why the hottest men in town are bursting into flames in broad daylight. (978-1-60282-763-9)

Strange Bedfellows by Rob Byrnes. Partners in life and crime, Grant Lambert and Chase LaMarca are hired to make a politician's compromising photo disappear, but what should be an easy job quickly spins out of control. (978-1-60282-746-2)

The Jesus Injection by Eric Andrews-Katz. Murderous statues, demented drag queens, political bombings, ex-gay ministries, espionage, and romance are all in a day's work for a top secret agent. But the gloves are off when Agent Buck 98 comes up against the Jesus Injection. (978-1-60282-762-2)

Night Shadows: Queer Horror edited by Greg Herren and J.M. Redmann. *Night Shadows* features delightfully wicked stories by some of the biggest names in queer publishing. (978-1-60282-751-6)

Secret Societies by William Holden. An outcast hustler, his unlikely "mother," his faithless lovers, and his religious persecutors—all in 1726. (978-1-60282-752-3)

The Jetsetters by David-Matthew Barnes. As rock band the Jetsetters skyrockets from obscurity to superstardom, Justin Holt, a lonely barista, and Diego Delgado, the band's guitarist, fight with everything they have to stay together, despite the chaos and fame. (978-1-60282-745-5)

The Dirty Diner: Gay Erotica on the Menu, edited by Jerry L. Wheeler. Gay erotica set in restaurants, featuring food, sex, and men—could you really ask for anything more? (978-1-60282-677-9)

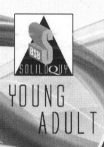